COME
AGAiN

Also by Robert Webb

How Not to Be a Boy

COME AGAIN

ROBERT WEBB

CANONGATE

First published in Great Britain in 2020 by Canongate Books Ltd,
14 High Street, Edinburgh EH1 1TE

canongate.co.uk

1

British Library Cataloguing-in-Publication Data
A catalogue record for this book is available on
request from the British Library

ISBN 978 1 78689 012 2
Export ISBN 978 1 78689 013 9

Typeset in Sabon by Palimpsest Book Production Ltd,
Falkirk, Stirlingshire

Printed and bound in Great Britain by Clays Ltd, Elcograf S.p.A.

For Mum

Awake, dear heart, awake! thou hast slept well;
Awake!

Prospero, from The Tempest

Part One

COME UNDONE

Chapter 1

S he woke with her mouth forming a single word. 'You.'
This was how they always ended, her dreams of Luke.
The details varied but they would always be alone together
in his room back in college. Two people still in their teens,
asking their first questions, sharing their first jokes. Kate
noticed the freckle on a knee showing through his ripped
jeans; his ready smile; the way he tilted his head when he
listened. The twenty-eight-year conversation was a few hours
old – the first night of their first week. This was the beginning.

She sat in the little armchair in the corner of his student
room, Kurt Cobain watching her with an intelligent smirk
from the Nirvana poster on the wall opposite. Below Kurt,
sitting on his bed and leaning against the wall, was Luke
– similarly slim but darker, unbleached, and with a face that
had seen less trouble. He was jiggling his foot off the edge
of the bed. Kate had just given him something to jiggle about.

'I mean, I wouldn't have to take *all* my clothes off, right?'

Kate adjusted the A4 pad on her lap and carried on
sharpening her pencil. 'No, of course not. Just slip your
shirt off if you like. The trouble is, I'm not good enough
to draw clothes. That pyjama top would present quite a
challenge.' She looked up from the pencil and met his
mock-insulted gaze.

'It's not a pyjama top,' he said, slightly pouting, 'it's a grandad shirt.'

'Ah yes, of course,' Kate smiled, 'the blue and grey stripey cotton thing with four open buttons at the top that definitely doesn't look like you're wearing pyjamas.'

Luke pinched the top of the shirt to one side and frowned at it. 'Yes, it's possible,' he nodded like a barrister. 'It's possible that there's a resemblance with—' Abruptly, he glanced up at her. 'Hang on, where did you get that pencil sharpener from? This is my room, isn't it?'

Kate stopped turning the pencil and took a breath.

No, not yet. Let's not wake up yet.

The intrusion of logic threatened to end the dream too soon – she felt the beginning of a rise towards consciousness but resisted it by talking. She wanted to stay right here, in this room, in this moment. She wanted to stay here forever.

'Oh, it's my pencil sharpener. I carry it around everywhere in case I run into a boy I want to seduce.'

Luke stopped jiggling his foot. 'I'm being seduced, am I?'

'Certainly. Why do you think I told you to strip? You don't think I can actually draw, do you?'

Luke looked around his room with a mixture of surprise and excitement. 'To be honest, yes I did think you would at least make a token effort.'

Kate put the drawing materials to one side and moved over to sit beside him on the bed. 'And what was going to happen after I'd made a token effort?' She ran a hand slowly over the shoulder of his shirt, her fingers tracing the v-shape of the top buttons down to where they met the sprinkling of chest hair. She knew this body like no other: nineteen-year-old Luke, Luke in his twenties, Luke in his thirties . . . and then, halfway through his forties . . .

He gave her the quizzical smile that always signalled the end of the dream. He said, 'What's the matter?'

She searched his face helplessly. 'You died.'

He took her hand and gently said, 'I know, my love. I know. But you have to wake up.'

'Can't. Don't want to. Can't.'

'You can, sweetheart. Rise.'

'Go to the doctor! You're still young! The tumour's tiny now, they can take it out, you can—'

'Kate, my love,' he said, 'it's too late.'

Luke looked down at their hands. She followed his gaze: down to their wedding rings and then back up into the eyes of her middle-aged husband. He said, 'You're going to be all right, Kate. Come on – you know things. You're the Girl from the Future.'

She gently took her hand away and whispered, 'I'm not going to be anything like all right.'

'Get some help.'

'No,' she said with certainty. 'No one can help me. And I've had enough of the future.'

His shirt was clutched in her fists.

'You,' she breathed.

Kate brought it up to her face but of course it had lost his smell long ago. Now it was tie-dyed with mascara and crinkled with dried snot.

Needs a wash. Can't be bothered. Maybe tomorrow. No, not tomorrow. Today's the day.

Memory stick. Where is it? Keys downstairs.

Wonder who'll find me? Maybe the mice I hear at night. Don't go for the liver, guys. You'll get smashed out of your tiny minds on the liver. I wouldn't want you to start making bad choices.

Kate slowly bundled the shirt under her pillow and began to think about the effort it would take to get out of bed. Too numb for tears now and long past words – the only person she wanted to discuss Luke's death with was Luke. She gazed at the window opposite, through the curtains she hadn't drawn – a single cloud in the blue March sky. A puffy cumulus, like a freeze-framed explosion.

Sometimes, over these last nine months, she would manage to get back to sleep. She would sleep until she gave herself a headache. This morning, for better or worse, she already had a headache from last night's Pinot binge. In these first few seconds of consciousness the fingertips of a monster hangover were beginning to find a grip around her brain. She would have to get up. A more organised widow bent on self-destruction would surely keep some ibuprofen nearby.

'Rise', *he says. Easy for you to say, Lukey.*

Kate sat up and stared at her battered and reddened hands against the white duvet as they closed into fists.

She dared herself not to look over to the empty side of the bed. Maybe if she just avoided the standing insult of his absence and just got on with her day then by the time she got back from the bathroom he would be there, sleeping safely. She looked over anyway. Just the normal tally of beer and wine bottles.

The bed clinked as her feet found the floor.

Socks.

At least she'd taken her shoes off.

'Best foot forward, Katie.'

It was something her dad used to say. Onwards then, downstairs in search of Nurofen. The headache was the one pain that she could do something about.

Memory stick. Must make sure the memory stick is safe. No, need a piss first. God, this day is relentless.

She grimaced at the bathroom mirror. At least she didn't have to see herself undressed this morning because she was still wearing the clothes she had passed out in. Baggy jeans, black long-sleeved top covered by a black loose-knit jumper, faded with time. She entertained the vague memory of what this five-foot-three body used to be capable of – this winner of medals and trophies. She saw her dark eyebrows raised at the thought, neither proud nor bitter. Sport belonged to a different lifetime.

What they don't tell you at Widow School, she had come to understand, was the way you age. You meet and fall in love with someone when you're eighteen, and the two of you are still together when you're one day older, and then another day older . . . until all the days of twenty-eight years have gone by. So there's a part of you that sees yourself through their eyes – a part of you that is still eighteen. And when they die, when that connection is lost, you start to see what other people see instead. Kate gazed at this middle-aged woman, almost a stranger. A cruel sort of time-travel but in her mind it seemed just. Luke was gone and he had taken her innocence with him. Fair enough. What did Kate Marsden need of innocence?

She inspected the diaspora of the make-up that she applied five days ago. Why the hell was she wearing make-up, anyway? She remembered with a shudder. Her mother had made one of her regal visits and Kate thought she ought to make some kind of effort. The eyeliner had spread south, as if to find a new life away from the war zone. Her hair was a tangle of neglect. With attention, it could be coaxed into a wavy stream of dark brown, falling just short of her shoulders. Now it sat defiantly on the top of her head like a mad hat. She thought of looking for a hairbrush but the idea nearly sent her back to bed.

No, check the memory stick. In the kitchen. Oh yeah, that piss.

It was a three-bedroom terraced house in Clapham. Too

big for a couple with no children but reasonable given Kate's age and salary. Or her former salary. She had been fired yesterday afternoon.

'Charles,' she said as she sat on the loo. Tentatively she encouraged her colon.

Come on then, Charles.

She waited for the usual all-or-nothing verdict: the shitquake or the turdfast. Nothing, then. What was this – day four? It was hardly surprising. It wasn't like she had eaten anything. She was about to haul up her knickers and jeans but decided they were such a disgrace that she just took them off and left them on the floor. There was no point putting them in a laundry basket since the distinction between 'special places for dirty clothes' and 'the rest of the house' had evaporated. The effort of reaching down to get the fabric past her heels almost made her throw up so she stood and leaned on the sink to get her breath back.

She washed her hands with what was left of the coal-tar soap she had found in the bathroom cabinet a few days after the funeral. Not a favourite of hers but Luke had used it occasionally when the nights drew in and he got a flare-up of eczema. The thin bar reluctantly foamed. She spent a long time rinsing under the cold tap, mesmerised by the splashing water. 'Who asked you to dance, then?' she asked with a tenderness that surprised her. She looked up to find the scary-looking woman again. Her cobalt eyes still flickered with life, having somehow missed the memo that everything else was closing down. She kept her own eye-contact as she found the tap and strangled the flow. From this angle she looked fully dressed but she didn't care anyway: she snorted a mirthless laugh at the idea that personal modesty could ever be an issue in a house as implacably empty as this. The jumper came down past her hips and she expected no company.

Kate took back Luke's soap gently in one hand and gripped the edge of the sink with the other. She closed her eyes and recalled yesterday's confrontation with Charles. Well, what had she expected? The guy was a criminal. In his office, she had managed to conjure a version of her old self: the bold and self-possessed person she was before the sky fell in. A tribute act which had taken a heavy toll on what was left of her energy. Today she felt like Yoda, agedly picking up his walking stick after ten minutes of leaping around and twizzling his lightsaber like a demented frog.

She had expected a fight. She hadn't expected threats of terrible vengeance.

Kate met her own eyes again, refusing to blink.

Charles – the attendant lord to the Russian gangster. And how did he begin?

'Thanks for coming to see me, Kate, and may I say for the record that I'm sorry about Luke et cetera.'

Chapter 2

Kate pushed her hands into the pockets of her baggy jeans. Her eyes flicked to the window behind Charles and focused on the rooftops of West London. She said, 'That's very good of you, Charles et cetera.'

Her job was to rewrite history. That's not how she described it to Luke when she first took the job and it wasn't how Charles Hunt described it now as he swivelled in his chair and considered exactly how to fire her.

He nodded gravely for slightly too long. It was as if Charles had studied doctors in TV medical dramas and had decided this is the thing you do with your head when you want to signal compassion. He had an angular, pale face with permanently flushed cheeks and a side-parting of thinning blond hair which needed no maintenance, although he swept a hand across it frequently. His private office was a large room with homely touches – an antique sofa his mother had given him, a toast rack he affected to use for incoming mail. He liked to give his clients the impression that his work was a hobby. Kate faced him across an impressive mahogany desk, the one he used to say was a gift from Harvey Weinstein but which he now claimed he had personally whittled from the bark of the *Mary Rose*.

She watched him working out what to say next. Was it

her imagination or was her chair two inches lower than usual? Or was his higher? She'd never noticed before. Nine months ago, Charles had given her a fortnight off and then had called to say . . . what had he said? She had been drowsy with lack of sleep and a permanent hangover.

A voicemail: 'Kate, I'm really sorry as usual about Luke et cetera, but we could really do with you back here ASAP. Obviously you're a woman and therefore natch need a bit longer than normal. I get that. Take as long as you need . . . I mean, the sooner the better if you ask me because with my mother – I mean, Christ, widows just collapse, don't they? Like windows. Click on the top-left cross of an Excel sheet and the whole thing goes [croaking sound]. No offence. Anyway, take as long as you need. You're a woman. I get that.'

In the office Kate smiled pleasantly and waited. She knew what was coming: the idiot had put 'Sack Kate' in the e-calendar he thought she couldn't access. It was a pity she hadn't got in there first and resigned. Where was her moment with her co-workers gazing on as she strode out of the office with an Aretha Franklin soundtrack and a big smirk on her face?

She wasn't going to get that and she had reason to believe that she didn't deserve it. But at least she had something else to take away with her. She crossed her legs and her right hand fingered the memory stick attached to her bunch of keys.

Charles had founded Belgravia Technologia with nothing more than his own merit, flair, hard work and £394,000 from his father, a former defence minister in a Conservative cabinet. Kate had met Charles in the same first term she had met Luke – as students at the University of York. But over the years she had heard him start to describe that place to clients as 'New York'. In his mind, the simple addition of 'New' was a harmless embellishment and Kate was sure that the man himself had come to believe it. His company was an early and leading exponent of ORM – Online Reputation Management. Kate was the IT manager but Charles owed her work much more than the title suggested and considerably more than the salary he paid her. She designed and edited the website; she had built and optimised the impregnable firewall; she created and continually upgraded the software architecture that kept the whole thing running smoothly. And, of course, she told the rest of the staff how to turn their computers off and on again.

In 1992, Kate had laced her boots and set out to arrive early for her first Computer Science lecture. If someone had told her she was about to devote most of her working life to revising the online histories of powerful men, she would have laughed. Well, life is long and full of surprises. And what is this 'internet' anyway? But if you'd told her she'd be doing it in the employ of Charles Hunt, the amusement would have turned to incredulity.

Charles was a walking punchline. Bart Simpson had a Charles Hunt duvet. Charles DeMontford Alphonso Hunt, the remarkably wealthy, fully oblivious, invincibly complacent prat. Charles who had attended Matthew Chatsworth College, a boarding school devoted to the advancement of the less gifted boys of the English upper-middle class. Kate could almost feel sorry for Charles if he were not such a committed and promiscuous liar. He could scarcely part his lips without spilling forth an unstoppable stream of instantly disprovable bullshit. His Jaguar was a Bentley. His surname meant 'royal' in Latin. In the Cadet Corps at school he had driven a tank. In fact, he had done so with such proficiency that he had been 'seconded by the Territorial Army to Northern Ireland' (where he had killed a man). He had an

IQ of 176. The Richard Attenborough character in *The Great Escape* was based on his great-uncle. His father was a Tory cabinet minister (that was actually true) but had previously been, at various times, a renowned fencing instructor, Martin Luther King's speechwriter and the Ambassador from the Court of St James to North Korea. His mother, by contrast, had merely invented the card-game bridge. Hers was an achievement affectionately admitted by Charles to be 'actually pretty impressive when you think about it'.

BelTech had all started innocently enough. *Because Everyone Deserves a Second Chance* was a principle Kate could sign up to, despite the wanky italics above the reception desk. A nurse unfairly accused of negligence here; a Rotarian who lost his head and punched a traffic warden there – imperfect humans who needed the historical mud to stop sticking to their search results. Unfairly accused or guilty as charged, they needed to move on. In either case, Kate had managed to convince herself that she was just a techie who went around fixing photocopiers. But in her more honest moments she knew that her entanglement was far knottier than that. As the digital security expert and key-holder of every password in the building, Kate had access to any file received by Charles. She had, from time to time, taken an unsanctioned peek at what the company was up to. Restless and greedy, Charles had recently begun to exploit his father's contacts in the delightful world of arms procurement. Kate told herself that she was there to keep him honest. The fact that she knew perfectly well that Charles was the least honest person she'd ever met was a nuance to be set against the other thing she knew about Charles: he was a chump and a nitwit. Guys like Charles, she thought, were never the problem.

*

'Kate, as you know, I didn't always see eye to eye with Luke and his amusing ideals or whatnot. But you liked him, which must count for something, and he was obviously a perfectly all right guy.'

Kate nodded sympathetically. 'Wow, Charles. If I'd thought you felt that strongly about him, I'd have asked you to deliver the eulogy.'

'Well, as you know I missed the funeral because I was advising Prince Andrew on a certain matter. You wrote a card to say that you understood.'

'I certainly understood.'

'In fact I scanned it and I have the copy right here . . .' Charles opened a drawer and started to look for the piece of paper Kate knew he had just invented.

'Charles, don't worry. I remember the card.'

Charles slammed the drawer shut. 'Good.'

She watched as he tried to remember the speech that he'd rehearsed. There had been times, in the early years, when she could walk into his office without knocking and interrupt Charles Hunt in his only creative moment: acting out his part of the telephone call he was about to make. The unnaturally deep voice for clients, the cajoling bonhomie, the CBeebies-level empathy, the name-drops audible from orbit.

She picked casually at an imaginary piece of spinach between her lower teeth. He was going to have to be nice. Very nice. He needed her to find the Nestor Petrov file but still hadn't worked out how to ask for it.

Charles said, 'Your colleagues insist that the quality of your work has remained unaffected by the Luke situation, so I've tried to turn a blind eye to your timekeeping. Sometimes you don't come in till after four o'clock.'

Kate said, 'Right, yes. Just to check – the "Luke situation" being that my partner of twenty-eight years recently dropped dead while unloading the dishwasher? That situation?'

'Bingo. And then obviously there's the matter of your dishevelled appearance.'

For the first time in nine months, Kate nearly laughed. She'd caught a glimpse of herself in the bathroom mirror that lunchtime. She looked like Suzi Quatro after two months on a desert island being chased by dogs. She said neutrally, 'I really don't know what you're talking about.'

'But that's not the issue.' Charles produced a plain Manila folder from his drawer and left it on the desk, significantly unopened. He looked at her as if he had just landed a royal flush.

Christ, he's going to do this like he's in a Bond movie. Not yet. Keep it together.

Kate took her nail out of her teeth and peered at the folder. 'What have you got there, Charles? Not your latest rejection letter from the MCC, I hope.' Charles didn't even like cricket but she knew it bugged him that there was at least one club in England that considered him beyond the pale.

'A-ha, no, something even more depressing, I'm afraid. It's the message you sent to Mr Petrov.'

She kept her voice steady. 'So many Petrovs. The tax evader?'

'You know which one.'

'Oh! The paedophile. I thought I did quite a good job there.'

'You're a techie. It's not your job to talk to clients. And where did you get his contact details?'

'Hmm. Lucky guess?'

Charles kept a lid on his rising temper. Kate could see that he'd worked out that she'd been spying on him for years but could scarcely admit it to himself, never mind say it out loud. He opened the folder and took out a single page of A4, handling it as if wearing surgical gloves, then placed it before him and launched into his speech.

'As you know, the allegations have been made by women interested only in money and publicity. Mr Petrov came to us in good faith and, as always, I set out a comprehensive ORM strategy. His charitable works would be emphasised. Personal testimonies of his good character would become prominent through all platforms. His website would be remodelled and links to it would increase by five hundred per cent via the usual methods. Original copy would be produced in both Russian and English, focusing on Mr Petrov's impeccable business record and exemplary family life. All allegations of sexual conduct with minors would be cleared from at least the first three pages of any search engine enquiry, except where the integrity of his accusers was called into question. The moral character of these women would be brought into legitimate disrepute. Unfortunate information about the personal lives and questionable mental health of those journalists pursuing the story would be disseminated through the usual channels. Mr Petrov would be given a clean sheet, or as close as is possible. That's what he paid us to do.'

Kate re-crossed her legs and cocked her head to one side. 'Did we not do that, then?'

Charles picked up the sheet of paper and read. '"Dear Mr Petrov, I only work here but I've had a few thoughts. You clearly belong in prison. I can't guarantee that's where you'll end up but if you do, I hope you get bum-fucked by burly Cossacks on a daily basis. My considered reputational advice is as follows: try not to be such an appalling shit in future. Love, Kate. Kiss. Kiss. Kiss."'

Kate looked out of the window and frowned. 'I agree it lacks a certain lightness of touch.'

'Mr Petrov is extremely unhappy.'

'Not enough kisses?'

'Kate, don't be so—'

'I know the bum-fucking thing is a bit homophobic but I thought he wouldn't mind, what with his thrillingly right-wing views on the subject. If you like, I could—'

'Kate!' Charles slammed his hand down on the desk. She waited for him to regain his composure, which wouldn't take long because he was already rubbing his reddening palm on his trousers. In a second flurry of violence he tried to toss the page at her but it flapped across his sleeve and landed in front of him again, face down. He looked beyond her, calming down and visibly recalling a line that he had practised. 'You know, it surprises me that a woman of your intelligence would do something so very stupid.'

Kate nodded. 'That's funny, because it surprises me that a man of your intelligence doesn't live in a skip.'

'Uh-huh,' said Charles, smiling thinly and swivelling his chair again. Somehow he regarded Kate as his intellectual equal and put this kind of thing down to 'banter'. She could say literally anything to him and he would contrive to take it as a compliment. For years, this had suited them both very well.

Kate took a breath and waited for his next move. At the same time, she remembered how her hand had trembled as she stole the Petrov file.

Last week, as was her habit, Kate had idly hacked Charles's inbox and scrolled through his correspondence. But then something in her attitude had changed. She'd felt a numb, out-of-body understanding that her life was about to end. What was she doing here? What had she ever been doing here?

There was something new. There was one particular man in the emails – a London-based billionaire. She recognised his celebrity: Nestor Petrov was a Premier League football club owner and a regular fixture on comedy panel shows where his fiftysomething good looks and hokey eccentricities had endeared him to millions. Or at least to a couple of TV producers and the board of a struggling football club.

The more she read, the more curious she became. By its nature, BelTech relied on discretion but the two men were having a veritable secrecy jizz-off.

Petrov: 'the deeply sensitive matter we discussed in person', 'the heinously missing file', 'the urgent need to rectify this delicate aberration'.

As for Charles, Kate had to concentrate to get past his usual feat of making his own English sound like it had gone through Google Translate: 'our deepest regret vis-à-vis that the matter remains hitherto unresolved', 'our most talented people operating 24/7 to alleviate the discomfiture', 'the file will be located with premium haste'.

What file?

Kate opened Petrov's first contact – his original submission to BelTech.

His lawyers complained that he had been recently accused of historical sexual harassment and assault in the early 1990s when he first moved to London. He wanted a skin-job and a make-over. He wanted to be on the right side of fake news by employing Charles to create it.

There wasn't much in her stomach but Kate very nearly threw up. Hiding in the dungeon of her grief, she hadn't turned on the news for months. But now she read the reports and testimonies of the women accusing Petrov. She believed them. She was no judge or jury but she was entitled to a private opinion: this man was a menace. He needed to be arrested, not protected. That Charles could countenance working for such a person was a new low. But there was more.

From what she could make out, Petrov or someone

working for him, had accidently shared a highly compromising file with BelTech which Charles had promptly lost. She understood his panic. She had built the company's bespoke file-sharing system and no one else knew where to start looking if something went wrong. A deeply unwise way to operate a security system but Charles had taken little interest and Kate simply didn't trust anyone else with her turf. It took her roughly ninety seconds to figure out what had happened and locate the encrypted file while glancing nervously over her shoulder.

It looked like a standard AVI file, lasting four minutes and forty-two seconds. That day, Kate waited until everyone else in the office had gone home before playing the video.

Four minutes and forty-two seconds later, Kate Marsden was staring at her monitor in a state of shock. Her discovery had implications that could topple some of the few civilised governments left on the planet. And Charles was up to his neck in it. She was furious with herself that she had slept through her years at BelTech, all the while kidding herself that she was innocent.

She dreamed of Luke every night and the moment of waking had become unbearable. She had made her plans. But first, she would atone for her part in this rolling shitwagon. An apology for the dozy waste of her extraordinary gifts. She owed the world a parting shot or, more accurately, a parting kiss.

Petrov was coming down, she'd decided. And Charles with him.

Kate waited for Charles to address the more urgent source of his agitation. He eyed her warily and picked up her Petrov email again. "'PS, I loved the video you sent Charles. Highly creative. Although I have different feelings about semolina.'" He looked at her for an explanation and attempted to inject a casual jokiness into his tone. 'What the hell's that about?'

The attempt at levity was embarrassing but Kate joined in, chuckling lightly. 'Oh, that! Yes, that was an absolute scream. I was just tidying up the server and came across a funny video Mr Petrov had sent.'

Charles had gone very still. He said through scarcely parted lips, 'Funny . . . video?'

'Very.'

'Of what?'

'Nothing important. I was just having a bit of a clear-out and I *think* I deleted it. Can't remember.'

'You deleted it.'

'*Think* so.' Kate suddenly feigned alarm. 'Oh Charles, don't tell me you hadn't seen it! Oh, I feel awful. You really missed a treat.'

Kate sat back and watched with fascination as Charles tried to process the new information. He literally didn't know what to do next. At length, he just carried on with what he was going to do in the first place. He gestured to the Petrov email: 'Well, I'm afraid I'm going to have to take this as a resignation letter.'

Kate's fist tightened over the memory stick. 'I understand.'

Charles looked at her carefully. 'I'm not minded to give you much in the way of severance pay, but I suppose . . .' Kate saw this was the opening gambit in a protracted haggle. She had no intention of being bribed into returning the file.

'No,' she said sharply, 'I don't want anything beyond what you owe me up to this moment.'

'Really? I mean . . . yes, I see. Well, that's . . .'

'And what you owe me is this.' She produced her own piece of paper. A handwritten list, folded neatly into quarters. She reached across and left it in front of him.

Charles unfolded the page. He mumbled out loud as he

read in confusion. 'Camden Women's Refuge, 50K; Index on Censorship, 50K; CALM, 50K; Save the Children, 50K . . .' He looked at Kate with genuine fear. 'What the fuck is this?'

'You're going to give two million pounds to charity. Specifically, 50K to the forty charities listed.'

Charles gaped at her and blinked rapidly. 'Have you completely lost your mind?'

'I think that's quite likely, yes.'

'And why the hell would I do that?'

'Oh, I know that one. You'll go along with it because if you don't I'll spill the beans about some of the things we've been doing around here. And then you and Mr Petrov will go to prison.'

Charles gave a strangulated laugh. Kate smiled back at him sweetly. He rose from his desk and started pacing back and forth. 'No one will believe you.'

'I've seen evidence.'

'Evidence isn't what it used to be.'

'Agreed. And that's down to people like us. Time for a change, Charles.'

'You wouldn't dare.'

'Really? Let's find out.' Kate got her phone out and pressed a contact.

'Who are you calling?'

Kate held the phone to her ear. '*The Guardian*.'

'Stop . . . doing that.'

'Oh, hello. Features desk, please. Sorry? Oh yes, well, she'd be great but it doesn't have to be her.'

'Stop! Okay, just fucking stop!'

Kate cancelled the call. Charles realised he was fiddling with his shirt sleeves in agitation and put his hands in his pockets. Then he took them out again and picked up Kate's list, shaking his head in disbelief. He tossed it aside, turned to the window and then back again to face her. Kate popped a piece of chewing gum in her mouth, enjoying the show.

'This is outrageous. I mean, for a start, why me?' he whined. 'If you love these people so much, why don't *you* give them two fucking million?'

'I haven't got two million. But I have left my house to Shelter. I've made my will and everything's in order.'

Charles stared at her, the gravity of the threat finally beginning to dawn on him. If there was one thing more dangerous than Kate Marsden it was Kate Marsden with nothing to lose.

'Okay, you can have your job back.'

'Don't want it,' Kate said, chewing. 'It's a shit job.'

'Well, what do you want then!?'

'I've told you. You'll use the secret account – I'll be watching the transfers. You've got till this time tomorrow.'

Charles rapidly swept his parting. 'Look. Come on. Hey, there. Look.'

Kate just chewed at him.

'Remember the old saying? Everyone deserves a second chance? That's what ORM is, right? We all make mistakes and it ends up on the internet and people need help to de-emphasise that. Hmm? That's all a reputable Online Reputation Management company is.'

'Cool. Except we haven't been reputable for years, have we, Charles? Kind of ironic when you think about it.'

'Oh, come on. You were there at the start, Kate. Remember that nurse we helped? Accused of misconduct? She was a woman! And black! Yeah? The good old days? Everyone deserves a second chance, Kate.' He now closed his eyes for special emphasis. 'Everyone.'

She looked at her old colleague with something approaching fondness. 'Some people do,' she said evenly. 'But not you and not me.'

Something in Charles's brain finally lit up. He greeted

the insight with abrupt rage. 'You can't prove anything. Your access to the system is revoked. Effective immediately.'

'Charles, you don't know how to do that.'

'Effective immediately!'

He picked up his desk phone and stabbed a button. 'Colin, I'm revoking Kate's credentials immediately. I want you to . . . no, not Kate from accounts, Kate Marsden. I want you to lock her out of the system and deny her access to everything. And I mean everything . . . Colin, are you listeni—? Yes, Kate Marsden! . . . Don't give me that IT bullshit, Colin, I'm not talking Chinese here. Just make it so her computer doesn't work. Throw it out of the fucking window if you have to.' Charles slammed the phone down. He sat and leaned across his desk, snarling. 'You needn't think you can blackmail me.'

'Charles, it was only last month you asked me to hack MI6. It's not fair to tell Colin to lock me out of the system. Colin has talent but we both know that guy couldn't lock me out of a Ford Focus.'

'You don't know what you're dealing with. You don't fuck with a man like Nestor Petrov.'

'Good advice for any teenager.'

'Whatever's in that video, he won't allow it to go public. He'll hurt you.'

'You just haven't been listening. I'm already dead.'

She took out her chewing gum and pressed it into the 'H' of Charles Hunt's silver nameplate, which he claimed had been a gift from Lucian Freud. She started to fashion the gum into a 'C'. She wasn't much of an artist but concentrated on doing the neatest job she could manage. She talked quietly and deliberately as she worked.

'You were quite a sweet boy when I met you, you know? At York, we all thought you were redeemable. We pretty much made you our project, remember?'

She'd never seen Charles so angry. She was pressing a thumb into every bruise and the results were spectacular. His jaw jutted out, baring his lower set of small teeth. 'You smug fucking witch. I don't remember a "project". I remember you and Luke and Amy and Kes and Toby taking the piss out of me in the bar as I got the rounds in. I remember a bunch of freeloading lefties.'

'Yes, that's exactly what we were. But then, all your posher mates used to pick on you for not being related to the Third Duke of Arsefordshire. At least we made you laugh, Chuck. That's why you hung around. And you thought we might be useful to you in the future. In my case, you were dead right. But now you're dead wrong.'

Charles searched for the most hurtful idea he could think of. 'Luke was the worst. Luke was a scumbag.'

Kate breathed through her mounting fury and put the finishing touches to 'Charles Cunt'. She placed it back on the desk and turned it to face him. Charles looked at it and snorted with derision.

His remark about Luke boomeranged in Kate's head and it was lucky that her thoughts were interrupted by a knock on the door. Mainly it was lucky for Charles because Kate had detailed training in how to break his nose and was already picturing herself leaping over the desk.

Colin popped his head round the door. 'Sorry to bother. Problem.'

'Get in here,' Charles snapped. 'What is it?'

Colin Laidlaw, Kate's IT deputy, was a large and large-breasted man in his early thirties with a long beard and a much-worn black t-shirt reading BECAUSE JAVASCRIPT HAS FEELINGS TOO . . .

He closed the door behind him, carrying Kate's computer under his massive arm: the 'power' part of her PowerPC.

'Hi, Colin.'

'All right, Kate! How are you getting on?'

'Not too bad, Col. How's lovely Carly?'

'Aah, she's seven on Friday, mate. She still talks about Go to Work with Daddy Day. You were bloody lovely with her, Kate. She goes, "When's Kate coming round for a playdate?"'

'Well . . . can't make any promises but give her my love and tell her to keep practising the home keys.'

Charles shifted in his chair as if a baby scorpion had just climbed up his arsehole. 'What is it, Colin?'

'Yeah! Thing is, skipper, I can't actually get the windows open. As you probably know, they're not manually activated. Some of them are in the rest of the building . . . I mean, Doug from Aztec on the second floor tells me . . .' Colin noticed the white-lipped impatience of his boss. 'Well, I'm saying that when you guys took the office, Kate made a decision about the regs and put the windows on a circuit. Probably to do with not twatting with the air-con and keeping it all harmonious and ecologically sound, so to speak . . .'

Kate said, 'I regret that, to be honest. People should be able to open their own office window, just in case they want to throw themselves out of it.'

'Exactly,' Colin agreed. He turned back to Charles. 'Trouble is, Kate put the override on a PIN so I'm not actually able to throw her computer out of the window as suggested.'

Charles started to say, 'For Christ's sake—'

Kate interrupted: 'Colin, it's 1832.'

Colin gave her a shrewd look. 'Great Reform Act?

'Cholera pandemic.'

'Nice.'

Charles shot to his feet, the paler parts of his face suddenly matching his rosy cheeks. 'COLIN, you idiot! I don't literally want you to throw her computer out of the window! I just want it disabled! Hit it with a fucking spanner if you have to!'

Colin raised his eyebrows and looked down at the machine under his arm. 'Yeah. The thing is, what we're dealing with here is what's known as a fusion drive. So a spanner, even a heavy spanner . . .'

'Just put it down . . .'

' . . . even a monkey wrench . . .'

'Put the fucking thing on the floor and get out!'

'Right you are, skipper.' Colin set the machine down respectfully on Charles's carpet and turned to leave. Over his shoulder: 'IT drinks tonight, Kate. Don't suppose we can tempt you? It's been ages.'

'Sorry, Colin.'

'All right, mate.' He left.

Charles stared miserably at Kate's computer as she got to her feet and headed towards the door. 'Okay,' she said, 'I'll leave you to it. You might have more luck with a screwdriver than a spanner. Watch out for residual currents, though – I wouldn't want you to get a nasty shock.'

He looked up at her with genuine loathing as she stood at the door. 'You've already taken what you need, haven't you?'

She ignored the remark and said, 'Make the transfers, Charles. Do something good for once. You might even like it.'

'You've stolen confidential material.'

'Report me to the police then.'

'We both know it won't be the police who come looking for what you've taken.'

Kate walked out calmly, leaving the door wide open. Her heart raced with fear as she summoned the lift but no one came after her. Low as Charles had sunk, he hadn't yet installed a private army of thugs in the building. But she had certainly underestimated his fear of Petrov and began to wonder if all this might have been rather a bad idea.

'I suppose this is what people do when they're quietly going round the bend,' she'd thought as she entered the lift.

They plan a very long sleep and then, just as they're ready to doze off . . . they start a war.

Chapter 3

Kate replaced the coal-tar soap in its dish and dried her hands on her jumper. Downstairs, she squinted at the clock on the oven: 10.23 a.m. Much earlier than usual – no wonder she felt like shit. Sunshine from the patio window illuminated the kitchen in all its squalid glory.

Up yours, Charles. Come and get me and see if I care.

She skidded over the discarded laundry and ready-meal sleeves, nearly retching as she felt the cold contact of an ancient linguine between her toes. She bent and wiped her foot with a stiff tea towel and felt her head ready to explode. The hangover was growing in confidence now, summoning reinforcements of nausea and heartburn to bolster the headache. She opened an eye-level cupboard and reached for the blessed silver box of painkillers. As her fingers made contact with it, she saw a paper bag from the local pharmacy on the shelf above. These were the antidepressants that her GP had prescribed four months ago, after her friends had mounted their only successful intervention. She had gone along with it just to shut them up. The obviously overworked doctor was given the minimum information as neutrally as possible. He asked a few questions over those ten minutes and his expression had turned from a stock performance of concern during which he kept interrupting her to say 'Mmm' to an expression of badly concealed alarm. The pills he gave her were of a type and dosage that Kate's friend Amy – a lifelong handler of anxiety and depression – described in her broad Sheffield as 'fucking hardcore'.

'Kate, that bloke is an idiot,' Amy had said. 'You need to bin those buggers and see someone else. What's stopping you?'

Kate had nodded in full agreement and did nothing of the kind. The second doctor's opinion remained unsought, the pills untouched. Tonight she would do more than touch them. Her eyes lingered on the paper bag.

Not yet. At least not this morning.

She brought down the Nurofen and closed the cupboard.

A few moments later she had cleared a space just big enough to nestle her mug of coffee within the mountain of junk that used to be a kitchen table. She flipped a discarded bra from the chair and sat down heavily. The spring sunlight glinted off her house keys, half-stuffed into a dead jade plant.

The memory stick.

She reached for the little plant pot. Why had she stuck her keys in it? Some colossally drunken notion of a security measure in case Petrov had sent a bunch of heavies to burgle the place. She surveyed the encircling crap-heap. Maybe they had burgled the place already. It was difficult to tell. She took her keys and inspected the memory stick dangling on the Tiffany keyring Luke had bought her years ago. The drive itself was just a cheap little 16GB she'd picked up somewhere in the office. She extended it the centimetre out of its Union Jack plastic casing and instinctively looked behind her. Just the window onto the tiny urban garden. She was tempted to watch the stolen video again.

No, not now. Hide it. I'm hiding.

She tossed the keys into a bowl half-lined with fossilised rice and turned it over as if trapping a wasp. She tapped the space bar of her open laptop.

Something of a post-sacking session here last night, she surmised. Another evening spent in the tranquillising embrace of Spotify's *Easy 90s* playlist. And the photos, of course, some of them old enough to be scans – the latest binge with Luke in 2D. Since literally everything reminded her of Luke, she could at least choose certain times to remind herself deliberately. Better to jump willingly into the vortex than to be sucked in by a TV weather report, or the conkers on the ground outside, or the smell of cinnamon, or any overheard mention of the words 'cancer', 'tumour', 'dishwasher', 'collapse', 'pulse', 'panic', 'ambulance', 'hospital', 'DOA', 'sorry' . . . The deliberate seeking of memories didn't lessen the frequency of those that came unbidden, but it gave Kate an inkling of control.

Here he was, then. Luke posing over a huge saucepan of student Bolognese; Luke gesturing with pride to a single string of green tinsel pinned to the ceiling of his room at the end of their first term at York; Kate and Luke in the same room giving a solemn military salute while dressed in each other's clothes. Who had taken that? Probably Toby.

Luke in a bandana, the prat, playing his guitar – topless in his parents' Wiltshire garden, his shoulders absurdly golden in the late afternoon sun. Kate and Luke on their graduation day in 1995; Kate and Luke in Brighton; Kate and Luke in Ibiza. Luke frowning with concentration at an old school textbook of *The Tempest*, his six-foot-two frame folded awkwardly into the tiny bath of their first flat. A sneaky shot of Luke asleep on the morning of his thirtieth birthday, his wavy dark hair cropped to an Action Man fuzz, his eyelashes ('Wasted on a boy,' Kate's mother had said) quite black against the pillow. Kate and Luke on their wedding day outside St Nicholas Church, Deptford; their friend Toby standing to one side, resplendent in his kilt and velvet jacket.

Kate closed the laptop gently and sipped her coffee.

Toby. The shiny sixpence we lost down the back of the sofa.

A movement interrupted her reverie and she held her breath as a mouse made its way casually through the garbage tip of the table: a house mouse, light brown with a white belly, about two inches long not including its hairless tail. Kate fought down a mild wave of revulsion and formed an 'ooh' shape with her lips, breathing out calmly. 'Who breathing,' her first karate instructor had called it.

'Hello then, you,' she said in a soft monotone. 'Sorry, you won't find me very good company. I mean, you'll be nice for a while but you can only spend so much time with depressed people. Eventually we just annoy you and you go away. Or we go batshit and you give us the sack.' She brought the coffee to her lips but put it down again. 'I wonder where you came from?' she asked.

The mouse had found an upended box of Ritz Crackers and immediately got to work on the spilled crumbs. It emitted a squeak in between mouthfuls.

'Sorry, I can't place your accent,' Kate replied. 'I assume you're local. Not one of those North London mice. They can be a bit snooty. You're not from my neck of the woods, are you? Deptford way?' The mouse ignored her. She dropped an elbow on the table to rest her face in one hand and the movement sent her unbalanced phone clattering to the floor. The mouse vanished in an instant. 'Bugger, sorry.' She slowly leant down to reach the phone, groaning and seeing multi-coloured emojis with the effort of putting her head under the table. To her delight she found an unopened bottle of Merlot lying on its side. She heaved herself up and plonked the bottle down on the table, inspecting the time on her phone. The echo of her personal standards had left her with a vague 'wait until lunchtime' rule, even though lunchtime would seldom involve any actual lunch. *Fuck it*, she thought as she unscrewed the cap and took a swig from the bottle.

The order of business as usual was to get drunk enough to go back to sleep.

The mouse reappeared, now scrambling onto a dirty plate and sniffing the dusty remains of a microwave risotto.

'Aren't you a bold one?' she said and then, glancing at the wine, added, 'You'll have to excuse my boozing at this hour. Hair of the dog, you understand.' She took another swig, tired and inaccurate, the wine spilling down the left side of her chin.

'Of course I'd never say that to a dog. That may well be doggist and we can't have that.'

The action of swigging from a red wine bottle and having a one-sided conversation with an animal reminded her of a movie she and Luke both loved. She followed the thought.

What happened to Withnail after those credits rolled?

She replaced her elbow on the table more gently this time and palm-settled her face, sighing with the greatest fraction of sadness that she allowed herself these days.

'"I have of late,"' she recited slowly, '"but wherefore I know not, lost all my mirth, forgone all custom of exercises; and indeed, it goes so heavily with my disposition; that this goodly frame, the earth, seems to me a sterile promontory . . ."'

She gazed around the room. 'Actually I know exactly wherefore. It doesn't mean "where", by the way, it means "why" as I'm sure you know. Not "Where are you, Romeo?" but "Why are you Romeo?" Like, why do you have to be

Romeo? Why couldn't I fall in love with someone . . . safer?' She nodded at the dishwasher. 'Anyway, it was right there.'

That's where the hidden tumour had finally announced itself. A slow-growing meningioma, the pathologist had said. A remarkably slow-growing cancer.

'About this size by the end.' She made a circle with her thumb and finger about the size of a grape. 'He'd been dying since before we met. And I didn't notice. I did nothing.' She found an empty mug amongst the rubbish on the table, wiped it almost clean with the sleeve of her jumper and then filled it with wine.

'Do you know how many days it is since I met him?' she asked the mouse, whom she now loved for being incapable of giving the first toss about whether she lived or died. 'Since the most gorgeous man alive walked into the college bar and we talked for three hours and then I got him to strip his clothes off in a student room that night?' The mouse was sniffing a hard hillock of chewing gum. 'Well, I'll tell you. I've been counting, obviously, but I could work it out in my head from scratch. I'm quite good at sums, you see. And computers and languages and all sorts. Always have been and I'm afraid it doesn't make me popular. Certainly didn't at Deptford Comp. Hate me for being a coward if you like, but don't hate me for being a freak.' She took a large sip of wine and closed her eyes as she swallowed, welcoming the acid against the back of her throat. Taking a breath, she resumed. 'Anyway, it's exactly ten thousand days. I met him ten thousand days ago today.'

The mouse scurried to another part of the table but Kate kept talking.

'The dream always goes wrong. But it didn't go wrong that night. We were in my room, not his. And he took his top off and then I said, "Sorry, I can't draw trousers or socks either – you're really going to have to help me out. Look, there's a loo just through there." I think he knew what I was up to by then but went along with it. He came back from the loo wearing just his flags-of-the-world boxer shorts. Bit of tension going diagonally down to the left. Norway, Finland and Denmark taking most of the strain, as I recall.'

She sipped her wine and found a pack of cigarettes under a lost cardigan. Since the funeral she had gone to considerable trouble to take up smoking again. It had been tough work but she had managed it. She lit a Marlboro Gold and saw with disgust that last night she'd been using one of her old karate trophies as an ashtray. Oh well. What did any of it matter now? There was no ash yet but she rehearsed a flick onto the floor.

'Hope you don't mind the old lady telling you sexy stories, my young friend. Bit grim, I suppose. I was young too then. I'm only forty-five now. It's just that I feel a million.'

She had pretended to ignore the beginnings of Luke's Scandinavian erection as he shyly padded back into her room and retook his position on the bed. 'Oh yes, that'll be much easier,' she said.

All men are created equal. It sounds plausible until you're sharing a small room with Luke Fairbright in just his pants. It wasn't so much his beauty that staggered her as the fact that he seemed completely unaware of it. Maybe slimmer, a touch less muscular than Michelangelo's *David* but Kate didn't think the comparison ridiculous. And unlike David, Luke breathed. He had a scent and a spirit and an attitude: nervous, golden, diffident. He was alive.

Kate had made a few swift marks on the A4 pad for form's sake. 'So I bet you've had loads of girlfriends, right?'

'Yeah, one or two.'

Kate smiled into her drawing. 'Is that one . . . or two?'

'Two,' he said solemnly. Their eyes met again and they both laughed. 'Well,' he added, 'if you mean "sexual partners", it's more than two. But proper girlfriends – yeah, exactly two.'

'Same here, more or less.'

'Sexual partners?'

'Stop saying "sexual partners". I'm trying to concentrate on my art.' They sat in an enjoyable silence for a moment, the atmosphere charged with irony as well as the wooziness of their three hours in the college bar.

'It's about trust really, isn't it?' Luke said.

Kate stopped drawing and looked at him. 'Trust?'

'Well,' Luke shifted position slightly, 'when someone you like turns into someone you love. Or when . . .' His wide hazel eyes searched the orange curtains of her window as he found the words. '. . . you share anything intimate, like your secrets. Or your body.'

'Or the secrets of your body.'

'Yeah,' he said simply.

'You're quite mature, Luke, if I may say so. For a boy.'

He slightly bristled at that but his smile was never far away. 'Boy? Excuse me, I am nearly twenty, you know.'

'Oh, your advanced years are not in question. I meant for someone of your sex.'

'Stop saying sex. You're concentrating on your art.'

She raised a hand in solemn apology.

'Well,' Luke shrugged. 'Yeah, fair enough. Girls do seem to understand mysterious stuff in a baffling kind of way. Why do you think that is?'

Kate wasn't sure if she was being humoured or if this guy was the real thing. She replied, 'My mother would call it women's intuition. I call it paying attention. Women are interested in how men's funny minds work because we might need that knowledge to survive. So we end up anticipating things and it looks like a magic trick.'

His expression didn't falter – another encouraging sign. He could take a bit of feminism on the chin without moaning. Just about. 'I see – all is revealed! You're the Girl from the Future.'

Kate smiled ruefully to herself and murmured, 'All girls are.'

She had encountered the boundaries of her artistic talent. Which is to say she had drawn a stick man with an acid-house smiley face and a massive knob and balls. She was considering the exact moment to reveal her masterpiece.

She said: 'Actually, you're almost elderly – I only turned eighteen last week.'

'Happy birthday. Hang on, so . . . in your year, you must have been . . .?'

This was a mistake. Kate didn't mind telling guys about the karate championships – they were usually more fascinated than intimidated and most of them didn't believe her anyway. But York was a clean slate – these new students didn't need to know about her early A-levels. She was determined that no one here was going to call her a freak.

'Dunno,' she said, 'some kind of admin thing when I started school.' He had been charmingly open and she regretted the evasion. She thought he deserved a secret of her own. 'Anyway, you're right about trust. The fight stuff we were talking about in the bar . . .'

'The Deptford Karate Kid!' Luke exclaimed.

Kate wrinkled her nose but went on. 'Indeed. Well, that all started as a self-defence thing after an unpleasant experience with a man that I trusted.'

Luke's face fell a million fathoms. 'Oh Christ, I'm sorry.'

Kate wondered what the hell she was doing. Rule number

one of getting laid was: Don't Tell Boys You've Been Assaulted. 'Thanks. It's all right.' She sensed him trying to control his alarm and came to his rescue. 'It was just a groping: nothing serious. I mean, it *was* serious – you're really not supposed to feel up a thirteen-year-old on a Geography field trip . . .'

'Bloody hell . . . a *teacher*?'

Kate nodded. 'But nothing horrifying. At least I didn't think so but maybe I was playing it down.'

'Maybe you still are.'

Kate inspected the blunt point of her pencil. There it was again – his emotional boldness. There was considerably more to this boy than a pretty face. And chest. And legs.

'Sorry, that was . . .' he started.

'No, you might be right.' Kate liked to think of herself as being difficult to offend: one of the few qualities she admired in her mother. 'Anyway, Dad was all for killing the bastard.'

'Naturally.'

'I couldn't tell Mother. She'd have just said, "Darling, this is what comes of wearing scarlet leg-warmers." But I could talk to Dad. He was going to run the fucker over in his taxi.'

Luke compressed his lips to stifle a laugh.

'I know,' she grinned. 'Anyway, I said that would be a bad idea and asked him to get me some sort of self-defence lessons instead so that he didn't have to worry. All for his sake and very silly. You can be Rambo but still freeze in the moment if you get blindsided by . . . well, by a betrayal like that.'

That didn't seem to compute in Luke's head: why wouldn't she fight? But she watched him reach out for it with his imagination. 'Yes . . . yeah, I think I see.'

'And I know it's corny but I did love *The Karate Kid*

and David Carradine on TV so I spent weeks with Dad and the Yellow Pages, driving around in his cab after he finished a shift. We must have covered half of London before we found a sensei who would teach a girl.'

She was quietly pleased to see that Luke was now gazing at her like he was sharing a room with Debbie Harry. 'Anyway, blah blah, me me me. But you're right: it's all about trust.'

'I trust you,' said Luke.

Kate stared at him. 'Why on earth would you trust me? You've only known me for three hours.'

He shrugged good-naturedly but his innocence was invincible. 'I just do.'

They looked at each other then – both allowing a pause to open up. A long one. Kate dragged her eyes away from his and they wandered again over his body. She said softly, 'I'm afraid I can't do boxer shorts either. You're going to have to take those off too.'

Luke hesitated. He looked down at his knees and a vulnerable smile played around the corners of his lips.

Kate asked, 'Do you really trust me?'

Luke met her eyes and answered by slowly hooking both thumbs into the waistband of his underwear. He took a breath and leaned back, suppressing a shiver as his shoulders made contact with the cold wall behind him. His heels found the edge of her bed and he levered himself up for a moment, the flags of the world sliding forwards towards Kate as they passed up his thighs, over his knees, down his shins and off the ends of his feet. In a moment of bravado he chucked them to one side like a shy stripper but they landed on her pillow, which he immediately thought inappropriate so scrambled to toss them onto the floor. Kate laughed, chewing the end of her pencil. He sat up against the wall, his right leg still arched, his wavering semi-erection emerging from dark pubic hair, finding a temporary resting place against his left thigh.

He said, 'Sorry, I think I've changed position, haven't I?'

'What?'

'I was supposed to stay still.'

'Oh yes! Well, that's okay,' said Kate, rediscovering some composure. 'Not . . . *all of you* has to stay completely still.'

Luke's lips parted and his breathing became faintly audible as the astonishing girl he'd just met leaned forward and stared frankly at his nakedness. She saw that he was still fighting his own modesty but stayed where he was for her enjoyment, his hard-on growing and climbing towards his navel with languid throbs. She crossed her legs in response to her own arousal but then uncrossed them and stood, moving towards him and slowly hitching up the skirt of her denim dress. Careful not to tread on his bare feet with her oversize boots, she straddled him on the bed, her knees either side of him and her fingers wrapping around the hard warmth of his cock. She leaned in to his ear as she felt his hands on her breasts and uttered the first serious thing she ever said to him.

'I trust you too.'

Chapter 4

Kate's eyes drifted over the ruins of the 10,000-day kitchen. She noticed a card wedged between a stack of box files. It was the invitation to Luke's funeral. She'd designed it herself – one of the many practicalities she'd been grateful for in the early weeks. The undertaker, the bills; the decisions on what to do with Luke's possessions, clothes, the manuscripts of his endless, unpublished novel. All this had kept her distracted from the reckoning she knew was waiting for her down the road. She expected grief, but grief wasn't the problem.

In the pathologist's office, he had explained about the tumour. 'There's nothing you could have done,' the doctor concluded. 'The problem with this kind of thing is that it's almost symptomless.'

Kate froze like she had just been casually introduced to a mortal enemy. 'Almost?' she asked.

'Yes,' he went on, 'you can hardly ever tell.'

Kate said, 'But there *are* symptoms? Sometimes you *can* tell?'

The doctor broke his finger-steepled pose and lightly touched the surface of his desk. 'In the interests of your own peace of mind, I'm not sure that—'

'Symptoms like what?' she insisted.

The doctor blew out his cheeks and sat back in his leather chair. 'Well, for example, migraines? Frequent headaches?'

'No migraines. No more headaches than most people.'

'Okay, well . . . did Luke ever show excessive irritability? Mood swings?'

Kate frowned as if she'd just been asked the stupidest possible question. 'He was a *writer.*'

'I see, yes, fair enough,' said the doctor. 'I've a friend who's an authoress and she can get very . . . anyway. Um, frequent numbness in the same area? Pins and needles?'

Pins and needles!

'Yes,' Kate said slowly. 'He . . . he complained of pins and needles in his right foot.'

'When did this begin?'

Kate shook her head in confusion. 'Always,' she said. 'I mean, only from time to time when we first met but . . . well, it's been more frequent in the last few years as he . . .' The ground was starting to give way from beneath her. '. . . as he got more tetchy, but I thought that was the book. The stupid book! And you don't go to the doctor with pins and needles, do you? I mean, do you!?'

The doctor looked down at his desk. 'No, of course you don't.'

10,000 days since we met and he was alive for the first 9,732. That was 9,732 chances to tell him to go to the doctor. That was 9,732 days when I didn't notice he was ill.

She turned the funeral invitation in her fingers. It reminded her of an airline boarding pass – the vital document that crosses a certain threshold and turns instantly into annoying rubbish. She had expected the funeral to be some kind of cathartic gateway – some escape into a new world of healing. The reality was just a shit party – one where the fun people suddenly didn't drink any more and the serious people overdid the eye-contact and made jokes for the first time since childhood.

Since then, and until she discovered the Petrov file, she had merely gone through the motions at work. Most of her energy was invested in hiding from her friends.

Kes was the easiest. He was a TV actor and the artistic director of a London theatre. He got drunk one night and sent Kate a 3000-word email mainly about his dead aunt. He apologised on the phone three nights later and Kate made sure that her end of the conversation was warmer than polite but not so warm that he could possibly miss the offence. She wasn't offended: she just wanted to be alone. He had then taken to sending her amusing postcards. Fine.

Amy was much harder. The loyalty of a Yorkshirewoman is difficult to wear down but not impossible. For three months she made regular appearances on Kate's doorstep with homemade soups and broths. She would arrive with news of her NGO job and the latest way her boss had screwed up, as well as back-issues of *Smash Hits* and tickets to musicals that she couldn't really afford. During one unbidden lunch visit, Kate waited for Amy to go to the loo and then glumly hacked her phone so she could track it. She used a bit of sticky plastic separating layers of smoked salmon to trace a thumbprint from Amy's wine glass and activated her iPhone to give herself location permissions. After that day, Kate tended to be out when Amy was within a couple of miles of the house. Kate felt bad about this, especially when she got a text saying, 'Do *you* know why my phone smells of fish?' But the intrusion had become intolerable. In her more old-school moments, Kate just didn't answer the door. By month five, Amy had given up.

And then there was Toby. He was no sweat because he just wasn't around. He was a civil servant and his life had disappeared into the Brexit bin-fire. For her wedding day, many years ago, Kate had asked him to take the place of her dad and walk her down the aisle. But that level of intimacy seemed to belong to the same place as all things Luke – the vanished world of her younger self.

If Kes, Amy or Toby had any idea that Kate was blaming herself for Luke's death then the response would have been swift and unanimous: a) that's ridiculous, b) come to think of it, that's probably quite common, and c) did we mention that drowning yourself in guilt over this is still disastrously misplaced and wrong?

He was my husband. He trusted me. I was supposed to look after him. My clever, beautiful man could have married anyone but he married the freakazoid from Deptford.

'You shouldn't blame yourself,' Kate's mother had said, as if she'd heard the phrase somewhere and was trying it out for the first time. To Kate's ear it was an accusation. A perfectly good point – on which she had now impaled herself.

On an impulse she took out the memory stick. Opening her laptop and disabling the wifi, she mounted the disk and pressed 'play' on the encrypted video for the eighteenth time since she'd stolen it.

A medium-sized hotel conference room with about fifty people seated. The camera was aimed at a small podium from a fixed position in the middle of the room. The audience applauded as the Shadow Foreign Secretary, Fiona Moncrief, took to the little stage. Kate didn't have strong feelings about this politician, although she disliked the way the fifty-nine-year-old managed to comport herself with the permanently wounded dignity of a duchess in a chippy. The camera zoomed in to a mid-shot of Moncrief at the podium, speaking without notes. She trilled through the usual formalities and then noted that, 'It's fitting that I'm here in Newcastle this morning, on the seventy-fifth anniversary of D-Day. Many of the ships involved in that momentous operation were manufactured here in this great shipbuilding city. It was the spirit of Tyneside the Nazis were dealing with on that day and as we all know – they didn't like it up 'em!'

It wasn't the tone-deaf appropriation of a line from a beloved sitcom that got Kate's attention. It was the oddly jarring mention of the time and place. Because here was the thing: Kate had established that on that particular morning Fiona Moncrief was nowhere near Newcastle. She was in Bayeux. There was live news footage of her sitting in the cathedral for one of the D-Day commemoration ceremonies. Her presence there was easily confirmed by a dozen news reports with precisely no reference to Newcastle to be found anywhere. She *had* spoken before in Newcastle, and she had spoken in many rooms like this one. But not this room on this day. So what the hell was going on? And then, about halfway through the speech, Moncrief segued into this passage:

'. . . why we honour our proud history. And that's also why I love semolina. I just can't get enough of the stuff. Sometimes when I'm in the kitchen and my pervert husband is feeling aroused, we smear each other with semolina and lick it off each other's genitals and laugh until we vomit. That's how we get our cheap thrills. It's fucking sick, isn't it? But that's just what we're like. And Britain should also look to the future. Not resting on our laurels but engaging with the challenges of . . .'

The rest of the speech returned to the anodyne but with one more gratuitous reference to the time and place.

Moncrief then turned her back to the audience, lifted up her tweed skirt and mooned her naked arse. It was to wild applause she then faced the audience again, gave them the finger and performed a teenager's mime of fellatio. Only then did she wave like a normal politician and leave the stage.

Kate still had her hand over her mouth as she stared at the final frame. The video was, of course, impossible. The whole thing was manufactured. Kate forced herself to eliminate the other possibilities. Moncrief had lost her mind: it can happen to anyone but then what of the audience? One might rather expect word to get around. And was it possible that they would laugh and cheer at such a display of utter madness? What about the insistence that she was in a place that she could not possibly be on that day? No, it was the most awesome demonstration she'd yet seen of deepfake video: where previously captured footage of a subject is rendered to make them say and do something quite different. As far as Kate was aware, up until now the necessary AI had been unequal to the challenge of fooling the human viewer at this level. But this was different.

Kate took a gulp of her pre-lunch wine and tried to remain calm. The technical brilliance was dazzling but the implications filled her with alarm. Whoever had created this wanted the viewer to fully comprehend its artifice. This wasn't a bit of fun. This was a warning. If they could do this, they could do anything: Robert De Niro secretly filmed at a party making racist jokes; a video conference call in which George W. Bush planned the destruction of the twin towers; paparazzi footage of the German chancellor on holiday slapping the pool boy; an admission of murder here, a declaration of war there. The mind boggled. The message was unequivocal: all bets are off – you can never trust anything you see on a screen ever again.

If no one trusts a news bulletin in a dictatorship then that's no problem because nobody seriously expects the truth in the first place. But in a democracy, if suddenly *everything* is possible and *nothing* is true . . .

No wonder Petrov was keen to recover the file: the embedded metadata tied it to his organisation like a pair of concrete flippers. It was clearly a cock-up: the team behind the video hadn't even got round to disguising the original IP address – a server which happened to be located in a Mayfair office leased by one of Petrov's subsidiary media companies. What she was looking at was a work-in-progress which Petrov's team had inadvertently shared with BelTech. If it was made public that Petrov – who owed his wealth and position to the Kremlin and was heavily rumoured to be one of its more active proxies – had people working for him who were capable of this, then he was finished. The technology was unstoppable but only effective if nobody knew where it came from. If Kate blew the whistle then every dodgy video from now till the end of civilisation would come with an accompanying finger pointing squarely at the Russian state, whether they created that particular lie or not. That would not work out terribly well for Mr Petrov. It wasn't just Charles who was crapping himself.

Kate ejected the disk and gazed at the memory stick, lazily twisting it on its keyring. 'Do I dare disturb the universe?' she mumbled. Grief stricken, suicidal and half drunk, she tried to fathom the deeply unwelcome responsibility that had fallen into her lap.

Charles was peripheral to this particular outrage but more generally he had become an enabler of thugs and crooks: tyrant-curious and wank-happy in his proximity to violent men. He was intoxicated by the money, yachts and gold-plated vulgarity. No, Kate thought with bitter self-

reproach, Charles Hunt was not about to donate £50,000 to Camden Women's Refuge.

What hurt her most was that it all centred on London: a tumour of lies growing unseen in her beloved city.

She should just do it. She should shove the memory stick back into her laptop and send it to five newspapers with a brief tutorial on how to open it, who made it and what it meant.

Her head sank into her hands as the kitchen seemed to turn into an oppressive greenhouse.

'Why won't they just let me die in peace?' she muttered. She jerked her head up and opened the private journal on her laptop, trying not to look at the final few words of last night's entry.

. . . because he's gone he's gone he's gone he's gone.

and began to type, the slowness of her fingers at odds with the energy of her thoughts.

Anyway, why is it my job to save liberal fucking democracy? We've had a good run, haven't we? Seventy-odd years since the last global outbreak of genocidal barbarism? Three score and ten? What is this, 'the seventy-year itch?' Go on then – scratch it. It's nothing to do with me. I mean, well done everyone but good things don't last, do they? Come, friendly Blackshirts, and fall on Clapham! Put a fascist in the White House. Put children in cages. All the good men are dead so, yes . . . let's just get it over with.

She paused to light a cigarette, finding a grim comfort in her own cynicism. She knew she was just egging herself on. Where had she read it? 'A homicide kills one person.

47

A suicide kills the whole world.' She balanced the cigarette flat across the lip of an empty karate trophy and continued.

Anyway, it's not as if Charles or Petrov will get away with it. They always screw themselves eventually, these people. Someone will find the memory stick. Probably by the time Wallace or whatever I called him is feasting on my earlobes one morning for breakfast. It's not my responsibility. I'm busy doing nothing. Or at least busy summoning the courage to become nothing.

It was hopeless. She would find an envelope and post the memory stick back to Charles. Let history take its course. She wanted no part of it. She wanted to sleep.

All the same, she picked up her phone and pondered.

Who was she?

Suddenly it lit up with an unidentified caller, startling her half to death. The cigarette rolled off the trophy and landed silently in a pair of tights, where it began to smoulder. Kate sighed impatiently, putting out the small fire with one hand while answering the call with the other.

'Hello, Mother.'

'Kate, darling, it's my kidneys.'

'What is? What is your kidneys?'

'They're next. The woman doctor in the headscarf confirmed it yesterday.'

'Right.' Kate was incapable of ignoring a call from an unknown number and her mother knew it. Some neighbour whom Kate would dearly love to throttle had taught Madeleine the knack of swapping cheap SIM cards into her phone. She must have bought a job-lot from WH Smith and was steadily working her way through them.

Madeleine continued. 'She says it's nothing serious but we've all heard that before. That's what they said to Roy

Castle. Lovely man, I met him of course, absolute gentleman and surprisingly well-furnished in the trouser region but I didn't stare. What with the endless liver trouble, I just knew it would be the kidneys next. They've never given me a day's peace since that wretched paella in Clermont-Ferrand . . .'

Kate settled in for the latest version of the familiar monologue. She called it 'the organ recital'.

'. . . because as we know my pancreas has been missing in action since Princess Diana. The doctors are all quite useless, of course, and just tell me to cut down on the brandy like I'm some sort of street derelict from *L'Assommoir*. Anyway . . . you must be wondering why I called.'

Kate tensed slightly. This was a highly unusual question. Madeleine never needed an excuse to call and there was an ominous mischief in her tone. 'Erm, not really, but do go on.'

'*Somebody* had a visitor yesterday afternoon,' Madeleine warbled with a girlishness that had Kate reaching for another cigarette.

'Oh yes?'

'Oh yes. A handsome visitor bearing flowers.'

'Monty Don?'

'Someone from your past.'

'Heathcliff? She-Ra?'

Undeterred, Madeleine put on an excruciating Scottish accent. 'A bonny young man from the Firth of Forth!'

Okay, you win this one.

Kate was genuinely astonished. 'Toby?'

'The very same! Wonderful Toby. Carnations. All white, hand-tied. I can't bear a mixed bouquet, as you know. Someone like Toby understands these things instinctively.'

'Well, that's nice,' said Kate slowly. She was having to think rather harder than she wanted to and tried not to be distracted by her mother's snobbery. If her dad, Bill, used to like Toby for his prospects and common sense, her mother liked him for his correct use of the subjunctive and the fact that his father was a vice-admiral in the Royal Navy. It had always been hard to blame Toby for this kind of thing. He didn't apologise for his background but neither did he confuse it with 'merit'. There were plenty who did, and Charles Hunt was one of them.

But what the hell was he playing at? She had last seen Toby Harker at Luke's funeral but since then he'd performed one of his customary disappearing acts. Strictly high feasts and festivals, our Toby. Funerals and a few birthdays . . .

And weddings, of course.

'Stay there!' Toby said, and she watched as he darted round the front of the car to open the door. In 2003, they were just young enough to still find the formality of a wedding ridiculous but just old enough to get the thing done well. 'Thanks, Keith,' Kate said to her dad's old mate in the driving seat.

'The honour's all mine, Katie. You look fackin' beautiful, if you don't mind me saying. The old man would be proud.'

Toby opened the door of Keith's black cab, which had been polished to its shiny bones. He did so with mock-military precision and offered his hand with a broad smile. She took it and stepped out of the cab to the sound of the bells of St Nicholas.

Toby stood back as a gaggle of Kate's bridesmaids materialised to start fussing with her simple off-white dress. Amy adjusted a shoulder strap and glanced down at Kate's waist. She leaned in to say, 'I told you not to bother with knickers.'

'I can't not wear knickers in a church.'

'Why not?' Amy said rather more loudly. 'It doesn't

bother Toby.' She gestured at their friend's splendid green tartan kilt.

Toby was well-used to the quaint English preoccupation with his genitals at times like this and was content to play along. 'You'll never know.'

'That right, Tobes?' Amy replied, inspecting Kate's shoes and taking both hands in hers. 'I reckon Toby might lose his mystique if we get him doing the conga later.'

Kate raised her chief bridesmaid's hands and kissed them both. She grinned, fighting down her nerves and glad of the distraction. 'I'm not sure that a gentleman does the conga.' They both looked at Toby.

'You'd have to ask a gentleman,' said Toby and offered Kate his arm. 'Let's go and find one.'

Moments later, Kate and Toby stood inside the entrance to the church, waiting for the wedding march, or in this case 'Today' by the Smashing Pumpkins. 'Any last-minute instructions?' Toby asked.

'Just don't say anything my dad would have said. I don't want to cry.'

'Right.' They faced forward, both smiling at the nearby rows of the congregation who were looking back and throwing double thumbs-ups and kisses. 'So, what might he have said? That I absolutely must not say at a moment like this?'

'I'm obviously not going to tell you,' Kate replied, slightly craning to see Luke at the front. He was facing resolutely forward, slightly bouncing on the balls of his feet while Kes talked animatedly to him.

Toby spotted Madeleine giving them a regal wave from the front row and returned it with a humorous little bow. He continued: 'So I mustn't say anything like, "You look lovely today and I'm so proud of the extraordinary woman you've become"?' he asked. 'That's the kind of thing I really

51

mustn't say in case it makes you feel in future like your father was somehow present on your wedding day.'

Kate understood what Toby was trying to do but found it bloody inconvenient. 'He wouldn't have said anything of the sort,' she announced, maintaining some semblance of reserve even though Toby's words had touched her. 'You were good at distracting me in the cab with your terrible Russian but you mustn't feel that you now have to channel Bill.'

'Absolutely right. Sorry.'

'No problem.'

Toby was still waving at well-wishers as if he was the Queen Mother. 'It was stupid of me. I've never seen you interact with your father and I have no idea of what he might have said.'

'Well, you have and you probably do but . . .'

The pretty introduction to the Smashing Pumpkins' offering to the marrying wing of Generation X echoed through the church speakers and the congregational hubbub subsided.

At which point, Kate froze.

Toby glanced at her and said, 'By the way, I think Luke is literally the nicest guy I've ever met.'

Kate turned to him in a daze. 'Yes.'

'And infuriatingly good-looking.'

'Well . . . there is that, yes.'

'And he loves you like mad and needs you like a flower needs sunshine.'

'Yes.'

'Shall we go and see him? I mean, there seems to be a party happening down the other end and he can be quite good company. What d'you reckon?'

'Yeah,' said Kate, recovering herself and pulling Toby's arm in just a fraction tighter. 'That's a good idea.'

'Jolly good,' he said. And then just as he leaned gently to take his first step: 'Best foot forward, Katie.'

Kate's ribs juddered for a second but the sheer rightness of what she'd just heard emboldened her. Only a maniac and a weirdo wouldn't collapse at that but luckily her great friend knew she was both a maniac and a weirdo. She took a breath, holding on to Toby as they walked. She smiled to the guests on her side of the aisle and ventriloquised to him: 'Toby, you're such an appalling shit.'

'Aye, true enough. But the world needs appalling shits like me.'

'And what did Toby have to say once he'd found a vase for the flowers and heard all about your duodenum?'

Madeleine replied, 'Well, I asked him about work and he was full of news. Some very funny stories about people in his office and the restaurants in Bonn and the workload in the civil service, which sounds outrageous by the way . . .'

Kate resented being sucked into this but had heard quite enough of Toby's career in 'the civil service'.

'Mother, sorry to interrupt but it's been perfectly obvious for years that Toby is a spy.'

'Oh Kate, not again. You and your imagination! Not everybody who works for the Foreign Office is a spy!'

'Agreed. And not all spies claim to work for the Foreign Office. Toby, however, is quite clearly a spy. Nobody else disappears for months because of "work" and then comes back with chronologically perfect and memorably amusing stories about what they've been up to. Nobody from a military family with Toby's sense of purpose would be content to shuffle papers about exactly how to ruin the country.'

'Oh Kate . . .'

'And more than anything, a single man in his forties on

53

what he claims to be a great salary does not drive a Skoda Octavia. Nobody needs a boot that big unless they've got kids with buggies. I'll take any odds that he has a bright red MG in the garage which he doesn't take to friends' funerals because that would make him look like a *spy*. Which is what he is.'

A note of acerbity came down the line. 'He's told you, I take it?'

'No, of course he hasn't told me. He wouldn't be a very good fucking spy if he did, would he?'

'That's circular argument and I'm surprised at you.'

There were moments when Kate got a sharp reminder of her mother's intelligence. Madeleine was only in her early seventies but the loss of Bill had contracted her horizons. She had many friends, as well as a brisk procession of unchallenging 'gentlemen callers', but the truth was that nobody argued with her any more. These days, she liked it that way.

'Okay, maybe I'm wrong about Toby,' Kate said with her eyes closed.

'I think you are, darling, but we can't all be right all the time, can we?'

'No, Mother.'

'Anyway, I can tell I'm disturbing you and you'd rather be doing anything than talking to me.'

Now that the usual passive-aggressive sign-off had been initiated, the comment was suddenly and implacably true. 'That's not true,' said Kate.

'No, I don't like to bother you at work. Give Charles my best. Such an impressive man.'

Kate stubbed her fag out on the table with her eyes still closed, grimacing as she scorched the front of her index finger. 'I can see him through the office window and he's blowing you a kiss.'

'Oh, now that's sweet. He once told me his father used to be David Cameron's fencing instructor, you know.'

Kate was defeated. 'Yes.'

'Yes, he was. Oh, before I go, darling: Toby said that he would call round to see you today. About lunchtime.'

Kate opened her eyes wide. Also her mouth.

'Maybe you'll get carnations too!' Madeleine exclaimed, adding, 'But then you've never really cared for flowers, have you, darling? Oh well.' There was a tiny click as Madeleine hung up.

Kate stared at her iPhone as it reverted to the home screen featuring a sepia picture of Luke playing the trumpet.

And the time: 11.24 a.m.

She tried to think through her rising anxiety: 11.24 a.m. was surely nobody's idea of 'lunchtime'. She could get out of the house. She didn't want to see Toby. Not like this: half naked, a third pissed, surrounded by all the evidence of utter decline and total surrender.

She could pretend to be out? But Toby was absurdly persistent when set on an idea. He would lean on the doorbell for a day. She could easily disable the circuit but that would be pointless. He'd just knock at the door or throw gravel at the window until the end of the world.

She twisted in her chair and gazed up through the kitchen window at the sky and unfocused her eyes.

She was being trolled.

'The world needs appalling shits like me,' he had said on her wedding day. And now, once again, he was trying to be the indispensable appalling shit. He had waited until all her other friends had been dismissed. And now he would prestigiously swoop in to make the World's Best Intervention. No, he was never going to just turn up on her doorstep with a pained look and a homemade cock-a-leekie. Yesterday he had visited her mother in the full knowledge that she would announce his imminent arrival with exactly the kind of snobby fanfare that would annoy the hell out of Kate. He would spike her aggression, rouse her from torpor; send her into the shower.

'Well, fuck you, Toby,' she said out loud. 'Nobody makes me wash.'

Even Luke had sometimes called her a soap-dodger and she had reluctantly joined in with the teasing while privately thinking that personal hygiene was some kind of patriarchal construct.

'Bring it on then, Mr Harker,' she said. 'Come and see me in my shit-pit. Witness the freak show. I'll let you through the door and then sit right back down again, right here, putting one leg up on *this* chair, flashing you my vag and watching you cope. Make a witty remark about *that*, you . . . my . . . nice friend. You . . . shit.'

She took another slug of wine.

She checked the time again.

She looked around the kitchen.

'OH, FUCK YOU, TOBY!' she yelled at the top of her voice. She got to her feet, rolled her eyes at the pain of her immediately inflamed throat and headed upstairs to the bathroom.

It was all perfectly logical. She was not at home to visitors. The house would remain a disgrace but no one would see that because she herself would be out. Going out to anywhere except stupid BelTech might involve making herself presentable. But she wasn't doing that for some bloke. She might, for example, go to the bookshop down the road. It would be disrespectful to turn up at a little independent bookshop looking and smelling like a Dickensian grotesque. Danielle was the owner of Northcote Books and Kate liked Danielle. She was an older woman with a nice line in mocking her ruder or stupider customers on Twitter while serving them with impeccable manners. Kate would wash for Danielle. Sort of. It was only reasonable. *Yes*, thought Kate as she gingerly stepped over the side of the bath and felt the hot water on her feet and hair for the first time in many days, *I'll go for a very long walk.*

Her body seemed to love the shower; the water and soap and shampoo – the attention. She imagined it saying: 'This feels good, right, Kate? We're a team again, yeah?'

'Don't get carried away,' she replied to her hopeful friend. 'I'm still going to kill you tonight.'

She swiftly dressed and found an envelope. She addressed it to Charles Hunt at BelTech and marked it CONFIDENTIAL. She parted the memory stick from Luke's keyring and dropped it into the envelope. She sealed it and pushed it into the pocket of her jacket. It was none of her business. Life and everything in it was none of her business.

Luke had been a mistake. She'd been right the first time. She wasn't a 'sympathetic' person. She was disgusting. She needed no one and no one needed her. In the hallway she noticed a postcard in a clipframe featuring humorous cartoons of cats – a souvenir of a trip to Paris. Without thinking, she took it from the wall and shoved it in her bag. Danielle liked cats.

What would Dad say about all of this? He wouldn't understand. He's not here.

She went through her front door, slamming it hard behind her.

Chapter 5

'Danger in front of you, danger behind you, danger to the sides.'

Kate was fifteen and taking her first driving lesson. She was sitting in the driver's seat of her mother's Mini Metro with Bill beside her. He had driven them to a disused aerodrome in Kent.

'Blimey, Dad. I mean, by all means make it sound as terrifying as possible.'

Bill chuckled and opened a bag of crisps. 'If I had my way, driving a car would be the most dangerous thing you ever do. That said, it really is bloody dangerous.' Bill allowed himself to mildly swear in Kate's presence as long as Madeleine wasn't around. It had opened up yet another conspiracy between father and daughter. There seemed to be an assumption that she was 'courting strong' with Pete Lampton. And that Madeleine had given her some kind of 'sex talk'. Actually, Madeleine had done no such thing. Kate had been content to cobble together the gist from the older pupils she sat in class with, as well as a BBC *Horizon* programme and a breathless combination of D.H. Lawrence and Jilly Cooper.

Seat belt fastened, mirrors adjusted, engine running. She'd been watching her parents drive for years and understood the function of the pedals in theory. Bill had a typical physique for a crisp-loving cab driver and squirmed uncomfortably in the tiny passenger seat. But all London taxis had automatic transmission and Bill was determined his student begin with the awkward mysteries of a manual gearbox. Kate was disappointed not to be behind the wheel of her dad's sleek new FX4 Fairway. For the last year and with just a London A-Z map as her guide, she had insisted her father set weekly route tests for her. In theory, she was nearly halfway through the Knowledge.

'She's not going to be a cab driver, Bill,' Madeleine had objected one Sunday afternoon. Kate had just confidently explained the best route from Whitechapel to Marble Arch on a weekday lunchtime.

'I should hope not!' Bill agreed.

'Maybe we should ask Kate,' said Kate. She didn't really want to be a cab driver but the gigantic challenge of her A-Z task, coupled with its homely normality (there is nothing so reassuringly dull as what your father does for a living) was currently one of her chief pleasures. That and Pete Lampton's tongue.

'Right,' said Bill, 'clutch all the way in, into first, right foot on the footbrake, handbrake off, right foot to the gas, feel where the revs are . . . there they are, that's where you'll find your bite . . . not too much, Nigel Mansell . . . that's better, and gradually let the clutch out . . .' The car juddered violently and stalled. 'No problem. Get it wrong: that's what we're here for.'

'Well, it's *one* of the things we're here for.'

'Heh! We'll get it right in due course, my dearest.' Bill munched happily on his cheese and onion. 'I shouldn't need to tell the likes of you about the egregious value of practice.' Kate went back to the beginning of the starting-off procedure. She hated correcting her self-educated dad but felt not to do so was patronising. They had a code for it. 'How are you using "egregious" there, Dad?'

'By the sound of that question, Katie, I'd say I'm using it . . . wrong.' They both laughed. 'Go on, then.'

Kate was easing the clutch out again. 'It means outstandingly bad. But you're right in a way, because it used to mean outstandingly good.'

'How far out of date was I? Mind those revs.'

'About four hundred years.' Kate managed a wonky transition to the accelerator and the car started to move forward.

'They think she's driving a car!' Bill exclaimed like a posh football commentator. 'She is now!'

Kate moved into second gear.

'Best foot forward, Katie.'

She smiled to herself and nudged the gas.

Bill went on. 'So if I'd told Mr William Shakespeare that I thought his plays were egregiously good, he'd have been pleased, would he?'

'He'd have bought you a pint.'

'Of your finest mead, sir! Watch the speedo and keep it under thirty for now.'

Kate slipped awkwardly up into third and sensed her dad glancing at her. He said, 'Keep your eyes just a bit further down the road, love. Nasty surprises everywhere but not so many if you're looking ahead.'

'Is that some kind of life lesson?'

'No, it's some kind of driving lesson, Mrs Metaphorical.'

She focused further along the track and felt an immediate gain in control.

'To be fair,' Bill continued, 'it's really just a working-the-car lesson. Proper driving is about other drivers. Who's about to cut in, who's about to act like a lemon, who's about to signal left and then turn right. All that.'

'How do you tell? By the cars, you mean?'

'Well, sometimes it's the cars but sometimes you can see the actual driver. I mean, a young lad in a secondhand Cortina is almost guaranteed to be driving like a pillock. You want to give them a bit of room. It's the testosterone.'

'I've got testosterone.'

Bill said through a mouthful of crisps, 'Y'telling me!'

'No, seriously. Men and women both have testosterone. Obviously most blokes have a lot more than most women. But it's a spectrum.'

'Where d'you get this, then?'

'Library.'

'Right. Well, I won't argue.'

'So maybe I've got more than most girls.'

Bill pondered this briefly. 'Yeah, but wouldn't that make you all hairy?'

'Erm . . .'

'No offence, love, but you don't seem that hairy.'

'Well, no.' Kate frowned and Bill noticed the car beginning to slow.

He said, more softly, 'What's on your mind then, Kate?'

'I dunno, just . . .' Kate struggled to find the words. She'd never really admitted this worry to anyone. 'Y'know, all this driving and maps and computers and fighting. It's all supposed to be boys' stuff, right?'

Bill put his bag of crisps in his coat pocket and waited.

'And well, sometimes I worry that it's not very . . . feminine. That I'm not doing feminine properly.'

Bill exhaled with relief. 'Oh, thank God. For a minute there I thought you was worried about something important.'

'Well, it's important to me . . .'

'I'll tell you what you're doing properly,' Bill interrupted firmly. 'You're doing Katherine Jennifer Marsden properly. In fact, you're doing that to a tee and always have.'

The road began to blur in Kate's eyes. Bill continued. 'You've always felt drawn to certain things, love. And you've followed them with all your heart and not given a monkey's. And I know you don't like talking about it, but you're gifted. Brighter than your mother and me put together and then some. People think that makes life easy but we know different, don't we? It sets you apart and that's been bloody 'orrible for you at times.' A tremble had entered Bill's voice and he saw the tears in his daughter's eyes. 'All right, pull over. Rule number one: you can't drive if you're having a cry.'

'I'm not crying.'

'Well, I am. Let's have a break and a good old cry.'

Ten minutes later, they were side by side, leaning against the car and looking out across the wheat and maize fields of northwest Kent; the crops yielding to woodland and a golf club in the distance. Gravesend and the Thames were going about their business behind them. Kate felt a pleasant, post-weeping calm in which anyone could say anything and it didn't really matter.

'They still call me a freak, Dad.'

Bill fought down his usual reaction to the news of anyone bullying his daughter. The violence and mayhem he had imagined over the years – the injustice Kate attracted, not just because of her tomboyish hobbies but because of her extraordinary mind. She was only fifteen but it felt to him like she'd taken a crash course in bad news about human beings far too early. She was free at home – he and Madeleine took her talent for granted. Madeleine had taught her French from an early age but if Kate wanted to teach herself Russian from a book when she was seven, well, that was just Kate. But Bill knew that at school she had learnt to dissemble: that she kept a private rule of raising her hand only once every ten minutes and sometimes got answers deliberately wrong. The incident with Blanchard the gropey geographer had given ammunition to Madeleine's ongoing campaign to have Kate privately educated despite her knowing perfectly well that they couldn't afford it. Bill's socialist principles notwithstanding, his wife had no answer when he said, 'What, so she can attract a better class of groper?'

Kate had come to accept her isolation with a grim sense of inevitability. She knew that it must be deeply annoying for her classmates that a piece of text that they would puzzle over for half an hour could be taken in by her with a longish glance. The teachers, though – the ones who needed to 'take her down a peg or two' – they were not to be forgiven.

She had pounced on the physical demands of her karate training and practised at home with religious devotion. Here was a place where it was okay to excel: it was already so peculiar for a girl to be doing this stuff in the eighties that her swift progression through the grades and belts was almost beside the point. The insistence on discipline and mutual respect gave her a space to compete without apology, and her sensei Jerome had become an admiring/admonishing second dad. Kate found this inconvenient because what she really needed was a second mum – but then nothing's perfect. Jerome made Kate's training his personal project, giving her extra lessons for free, entering her for London-wide and then nationwide tournaments. In a few months from now, she would be competing in the 9th edition of the World Karate Championships (Girls, Under Eighteen) in Granada, Spain, with Jerome essentially working as her private coach.

It was a lifeline. But she knew at the same time that she was just adding to the list of transgressions, the rap-sheet of otherness.

*

By the car, Bill kept his temper and said, 'Freak's just a word people use when they're scared, love. Jealous people, frightened people set in their ways.'

'It could be worse. I've got Jerome. And I've got you.'

Bill swapped his crisps and gave her hand a squeeze with his non-cheese and onion fingers. 'Poor old Jerome. No wonder he loves teaching you. He's got three daughters and they all want to be Princess Di.'

'Nothing wrong with that,' said Kate. 'The royals could do with a black princess. I think that would be cool.'

Bill gave a chuckle. 'Cool for you, maybe. Blimey, can you imagine what the *Daily Mail* would do to her? Come on. Let's have another go.' Kate eagerly climbed into the driver's side and restarted the car.

She said, 'It's fun but it's all a bit redundant, really, isn't it? Probably in the future we'll all have jetpacks or cars will be driven by robots.'

'Sounds horrible. "If the bus is going to Utopia, let me off one stop early."' This was one of Bill's favourite political sayings and, as far as Kate knew, his own. He was so pleased with it, she could almost hear the quotation marks.

'Neil Kinnock's not heading for Utopia, is he?'

Bill was used to her lateral jumps. 'Nowhere near it, love. He's a socialist all right, but no Utopian, no Commie. That's the main reason I can vote for the ginger gasbag.'

Kate opened her mouth to defend the redheads, thinking of Pete, her strawberry-blond boyfriend. But she thought better of it, remembering that Pete's hair was at its gingerest in regions she didn't want to discuss with her father. Instead she said, 'You used to love old Neil. You haven't gone off him just because he lost, have you? That's not like you.' Bill took the compliment but looked out of the passenger window as Kate raggedly moved the Metro off again. The result of the 1987 election was a recent and painful memory.

'I never loved him,' he said.

'Bollocks. When he did that speech giving Militant the boot you literally danced around the kitchen table.'

Bill had finished his crisps. As was his habit, he started to fold the empty packet into a neat triangle. 'There was a pendulum, Kate. And now it's broke.' She'd heard a version of this speech before but only when Bill was a few sherries down on a Sunday night. She waited for the sober version but Bill was never quite sober when it came to politics. She steered the car in a wide loop, allowing him to talk.

'It used to swing between Left and Right, love. Not gently – nothing gentle about it. But reliably. Predictably, so to speak. Bit of compromise from time to time. Labour more about the good of the people. Tories more about the public good. I can't really stand the Tories, as you know, but these were decent people, some of them. Trying to do what's best. So you've got a pendulum, swinging back and forth. Then the union leaders got cocky and started taking the piss. And now Thatcher. She's smashing them to pieces and she's smashing the pendulum too. That's why you need someone like Kinnock, pompous prat though he is. Fix your own house first, get rid of the nutters. Otherwise the other side respond in kind and you've got fucking Blackshirts marching around London. *London*, for crying out loud! We don't need that again, Katie. Believe me.'

Kate kept her eyes on the asphalt ahead, a pattern of pressed grey endlessly repeating itself. It always came back to this. Cable Street. Grandad Marsden had been there in October 1936, in solidarity with the Jews of the East End, seeing off Mosley's fascists. But somehow Bill took no pleasure in it. There always seemed to be something he was holding back. Between her parents, the subject of William Marsden Senior was a matter of tight glances and rapid changes of subject.

Bill combined his crisp packet triangle with another two examples he found in his coat pocket. He slotted them onto his middle three fingers and started to animate the opening titles of *Dad's Army*. The invading triangles of Nazi forces entering Kate's field of vision made her laugh and she joined in with the song.

'Who do you think you are kidding, Mr Hitler,' they sang, 'if you think we're on the run?'

We are the boys who will stop your little game.
We are the boys who will make you think again.
'Cause who do you think you are kidding, Mr Hitler
If you think old England's done?

Chapter 6

*S*crew you, Toby.

Kate stalked down her road bitterly resenting how clean, renewed and exhilarated she felt. Even the exercise was helping. Stupid exercise. And now she realised she was extremely hungry. If she wasn't careful, she could wind up in her favourite café having a delightful lunch which would make her feel even better. It was intolerable.

Toby. How *dare* he? She turned up the Sex Pistols on her phone, glancing around and half hoping that Petrov had sent a gang of hoodlums to steal the memory stick. She would beat the living shit out of them and then hopefully get stabbed to death.

'Morning, Kate!'

'Morning, Vicar.'

Father Lawrence was already slowing down for an exchange of pleasantries. Oh joy.

'You're looking very determined!'

Kate took her hands out of her pockets and removed her earpods. 'Oh, you know – things to do.' She paused the track and readjusted the shoulder strap of her bag the way she'd seen local mums do. Tall and rangey in his dog-collar and black shirt, it was generally found that Father Lawrence had a faint foxiness going on. Kate found her own curiosity doubly inappropriate as he seemed to be remarkably young. Twenty-six, tops – and in charge of a big London parish. A prodigy of some kind. Kate wondered if it had isolated him. 'Did they call you a freak too, Lawrence?' she always wanted to ask. 'And how do you get to be outstandingly good at Jesus Christ anyway?'

Lawrence said, 'I just wanted to thank you for helping out with the Christmas jumble sale. I think your book stall made more cash than all the fairy cakes put together!'

Of course it fucking did, Kate did not reply. Instead she said, 'Oh well, I needed to do a bit of downsizing so . . . win-win!'

'Win-win indeed!' exclaimed Father Lawrence. In public he only really talked in exclamations and it was infectious.

She had cleared the house of the books she knew she would never read again. It was all of them. She had thrown herself into bookselling with a ruthless lack of sentiment. 'What, this F. Scott Fitzgerald paperback that Luke bought me between bouts of mad lovemaking on that wet weekend in Swanage? Sure! Have it for two quid.' Kate had never run a jumble sale stall before and it had been a good day, full of contact and conversation. Later, she had knocked back a pint of Chardonnay and cried herself to sleep.

Kate said, 'I'm just off to the bookshop now!'

'Oh good! Stocking up again!'

Kate thought of the pills in the kitchen cupboard and her plan for the evening. It reminded her to get a bottle of vodka on the way home. 'That's right,' she said, 'although knowing me I'll probably just buy something I won't have time to read!'

'Often the way!' laughed Lawrence, shaking his head mildly and waving to a parishioner over the road who was taking the bins out. 'Well, I'll let you get on with it.'

'Thanks.'

Kate wondered if she could start walking away now. But suddenly Lawrence seemed to be looking straight into the back of her head. 'Luke must have been a great reader.'

'Well . . . yes, he was.'

The young cleric with the demeanour of a kindly grandfather said casually, 'No biggie, but you know our doors are always open.'

Kate looked down and readjusted her bag again. 'Yes.'

'I mean, not literally. Sadly we have to lock them between services for insurance reasons but you get the idea.'

'I do!' said Kate. 'Maybe I'll call in later.' Of all the lies she had told this morning, this was easily the wildest.

It was so brief, his look. Almost a glance. But his eyes contained a depth of compassion that had her wishing she had never left the house.

'God bless you, Kate,' he said, touching her lightly on the shoulder. And off he went.

Kate moved unsteadily on her way. *Jesus*, she thought, *what is this, some kind of a parable? Or a Mr Man book? Little Miss Topherself? Do I now have to bump into a friar, a monk and a Mormon? Are they all going to bless me? I mean, if God gave that much of a toss he wouldn't have . . .* But she had been down this road many times before. She would get more sense out of Johnny Rotten's jubilee tribute to Her Majesty.

She marched into the post office and sent the memory stick back to Charles with all the bathos of a guaranteed next-day delivery. At the counter, she politely removed her earpods as the transaction was carried out. By the time she put them back in, her playlist had shuffled to Del Amitri's 'Nothing Ever Happens'. Leaving the post office she pulled the wire out of the phone and out of her ears, and tossed the little white snake into a bin. She hated that song. She hated walking around in a bubble. She would listen to the world instead.

Kate walked down Northcote Road reviewing her decision and finding it to be flawed. The world was shit. Whatever was good about it was nothing to do with her.

Lunch. Fuck off, lunch. She had avoided the excellent little café where she was known to the staff – they might say something thoughtful about Luke. Instead she dived through the door of an anonymous pizza chain.

She ordered a Fiorentina, taking a guilty pleasure that Luke wasn't there to object. He was firmly of the view that, for all their virtues, eggs had no place on a pizza. Kate thought he might be right but could never pass up the opportunity of a fried egg, whether in the middle of the night or the middle of a pizza. Maybe this is what life could be like. All the everyday irritations of a long partnership amusingly redressed. Did she not have ten thousand days' worth of minor grievances?

Yes, Luke occasionally snored but the idea that he deprived her of more sleep alive than dead was a joke. Kate didn't used to have to swallow a vineyard before daring to close her eyes.

Yes, he was a pain in the kitchen: fussy and proprietorial. He earned very little – therefore he had taught himself to cook. And he cooked like an angel, albeit an angel who frowns and scratches his head irritably every time you start chopping an onion. But the truth was that Kate used to have a healthy interest in delicious meals and a distinct aversion to making them. Would she swap a little camaraderie over a saucepan between the hours of 6 p.m. and 7 p.m. for half a lifetime of being beautifully fed by a beautiful man?

Forget it.

Anyway, the camaraderie would swiftly follow as they

ate in front of the TV and Luke turned back into a normal human. Somehow he left all his vanity in the kitchen.

And yes, speaking of vanity, there was the small matter of his work. Was she relieved not to live any more with a tortured and chronically unsuccessful writer? No, not if the writer was Luke. A week of speed-reading would end with two or three capsule reviews for broadsheet newspaper supplements. He took no pleasure in the reviews and Kate quickly learned not to praise them. What her salary mainly supported was his novel. His vast, fatally unfinished, entirely indecipherable novel that nobody but nobody wanted to publish. Yes, she admitted to herself. She was glad to be rid of that bloody book.

For years, his working title for it was *Whatever*. Kate wondered if that projected to potential readers a kind of who-gives-a-shit? attitude which they might not enjoy. In 1998, she was browsing in a Brixton bookshop when she came across a book called *Whatever* by Michel Houellebecq. 'There's no copyright on titles,' Luke had sniffily observed. As the French author's fame grew for reasons that perplexed them both (Luke was jealous and Kate just thought the guy was a douchebag), Luke began an artistic journey that would see him grudgingly update his working title every few years. From *Whatever* to *Whenever* to *Why?* to, briefly, *Who Cares?* And then triumphantly back to *Whatever*. But Luke worried that he would be accused of plagiarism and that was not to be borne. By the time of his death, Luke's unpublished masterpiece was called *Fuck Off*.

He had asked Kate on a regular basis to read his book. She had done so with increasing concern, gradually transforming over the years into something like helpless dread. She was a wide reader but even as Luke's most supportive critic she felt hobbled and stupid. Luke had an English degree and surely knew what he was doing. She must be missing something. He had talent, she could see that. But as the years passed, Kate had begun to form a conclusion that she had been trying very hard to avoid.

Kate had swallowed the pizza almost whole and now munched on a piece of unripe mango. The truth was that as a writer, Luke had been hampered by just two problems:

1. He hated his readers. His insecurity didn't even want them.

2. He hated stories. He would do anything to avoid telling a story. Stories were for idiots.

He wrote to impress Kate. And also his imaginary professional critics. One day, they would surely praise his beautifully balanced sentences in sentences which were themselves beautifully balanced. But the book was never published and the critics never got the chance. Kate was glad. They'd have killed him. She was almost grateful that the tumour got to him first.

She finished her fruit salad and asked for the bill. No, there was no upside. All this blood-sugar giving her a temporary buzz of serotonin was not to be trusted. You don't abandon a long-planned suicide just because you're feeling happy. That would be madness.

She left a twenty-pound note as a tip. She didn't need money any more. And how had she earned it? At least Luke had tried to *make* something. What kind of person was she? Rejoicing in the absence of her husband whom she had basically neglected to death? She was right the first time. She was a shithead.

She put her purse and phone in her bag, astonished that she hadn't ordered any wine. What was that about? Was mineral water going to salve her conscience? Stupid, appalling arse. Stupid, awful bastard deserves to be found half-eaten by Wallace the mouse.

'Are you all right?' asked the waitress, a woman of about

twenty with a Warsaw accent. Kate fancied practising her Polish but was instantly engulfed by another wave of futility. Practise it for what?

'Oh yes, of course! It was all delicious, thank you.' Kate rose from the table in a flurry of apologies and jacket- and bag-flapping.

'You are hitting your head with back of dessert spoon?'

'Was I? That's right, yes. I'm a drummer. I was practising.'

The waitress creased her brow and started to clear the table. Kate edged round to get out.

'This tip is mistake?' the girl said, discreetly holding up the twenty.

'No, that's for you.'

'You are very kind lady.'

'I'm really not.'

'Good luck with your drumming.'

'Yep. Cheers.'

Young people. She walked along Northcote Road with her self-loathing temporarily reflecting outwards like an evil lighthouse. Young people being nice. What did they know, anyway? Vicars and waitresses barely out of puberty. With their lightness and innocence. They'll learn. She thought a hefty dose of Danielle's worldly sarcasm might cheer her up. Did she want to be cheered up? *Oh, stop asking questions. Go away, head.* She crossed the road and entered the bookshop.

'Well, it's one or the other, isn't it?' Danielle was explaining to a middle-aged customer as if he was seven. Her eyes darted to Kate as she walked in and then she continued. 'We don't do deals on audiobooks because we don't sell them. So you could actually read . . .' She swiftly moved her dangling half-moon glasses up to her eyes. '. . . *60 Movements of Shame* by F. Windsor-Loveridge or you

73

can buy the audiobook elsewhere and have it read to you . . .'

'It's actually for my wife.'

'No doubt . . . Or she can have it read to her by Helen Mirren.'

'Ooh! Is it Helen Mirren?'

'Yes, Dame Peggy Ashcroft was unavailable and Joanna Lumley recently sustained a head injury while shark-fishing off the Great Barrier Reef.'

The stern bookseller in her late sixties looked at the man with stone-cold gravity.

He hesitated. 'Well, I'll probably . . .'

'Lumley can still talk but only with a heavy Australian accent.'

'Right. I'll probably get the audiobook.'

'It's ruined her voice career but I believe she's secured a lucrative television commercial for a leading brand of Australian lager. So that's a happy ending of sorts.' Danielle handed the book back to the customer with the full implication that it was now his job to return it to the shelves.

'Yes,' said the man. Kate had been pretending to peruse the foreign reference section. She straightened her face and turned to see the man carefully leave the book on the bestseller table and head sheepishly towards the door.

Danielle suddenly beamed at him. 'Have a lovely day, sir, and hope to see you again.'

The man smiled back. 'Yes,' he said. And then, as he opened the door, 'I could probably get the audiobook from Amazon, could I?'

Kate took in the full glory of Danielle's immovable smile as she replied, 'I insist that you do.' The customer nodded with relief and left.

Kate replaced an updated version of *Learn Russian Today!* and wandered towards the counter. Danielle regarded her with a wry twinkle, scratching her head through her mass of curly grey hair.

'I wonder if you can help me?' said Kate as if she hadn't been a regular visitor to the shop for fourteen years. Danielle leaned both heavy arms on the counter, raised her eyebrows and gave a slow, camp blink of anticipation.

Kate went on, 'I'm looking for a book called *How to Destroy Your Business Because You're a Luddite and a Literary Snob and You Obviously Should Have Gone into Teaching Instead of Retail*. Do you have it?'

'I'll just check.' Danielle disappeared under the counter and rose up again with her middle finder extended at Kate. Both women cackled with glee and Danielle came round the counter to give Kate a hug.

'That jolly well hurt my knees,' Danielle said into Kate's ear. 'I'm extremely cross with you.'

'Sorry about that,' said Kate, not minding the embrace. Danielle smelled of lavender and civilisation. They parted and Kate glanced round the almost deserted shop. 'So, business is booming?'

Danielle turned with a studied nonchalance and followed Kate's gaze down to the far end of the shop, a distance of about seven metres. A mother and child were chatting happily over a picture book in the carpeted kids' section. 'Not exactly,' she said. 'But then you and Luke were the only customers I could tolerate.'

The hug, the instant mention of Luke – to Kate, it all seemed rather bold. Was it? Or was this just what friends did? She couldn't remember. 'What was so special about us?' she asked, keeping her gaze on the little family and beginning to breathe more deliberately, hoping it was undetectable.

Danielle turned back to Kate and leaned an elbow on her counter. 'Well, you bought 'em by the yard, which is always endearing.'

Kate felt a tiny withdrawal of love. She said, 'So you don't mind turning a profit from time to time?'

Danielle looked past Kate, through the shop-front to the street outside. 'Well, that was a joke, dear, but there are yards and there are yards. You and Luke seemed interested only in the good ones. Betty and I used to refer to you two as "The Goodyards". There's no harm in liking customers for their taste.'

No, this was too much talk of Luke. Kate needed very badly to change the subject. She said quickly, 'That's nice. And how is Betty?'

Danielle pursed her lips and wandered back round to her side of the counter. 'Her arthritis is a continuing embuggerance but she soldiers on in a stubborn kind of Canadian way.'

Kate was sure she had somehow disappointed her friend and now felt about as miserable as she did when she woke up. What was she doing in here anyway? She started thinking of an excuse to leave but Danielle was talking again.

'But I'm not really a literary snob, you know.' She looked over to the paperback bestsellers. 'I've read most of the books on that table and they've all got *something* to recommend them. We can't all be James Joyce, for heaven's sake.'

Kate wasn't sure why but she felt uncomfortable with this line of conversation. She frowned and picked up one of the loo books next to the till: *The 100 Best Things You've Forgotten About the Nineties*. Danielle seemed to take Kate's silence for an objection and carried on. 'Or Shakespeare, for that matter. Not everyone wants to read "Light thickens and the crow makes wing to th' rooky wood". Some people are perfectly happy with "The sun went in and it was all getting a bit tense". Good luck to them, say I.'

Kate flipped through the book impatiently and stopped at a picture of Bret Easton Ellis, one of Luke's favourite authors. It was suddenly incredible that Danielle was still talking.

'No,' Danielle sighed, 'give me a tolerable yarn, a joke or two, some evidence of a brain, some evidence of a heart, and really I'm perfectly . . .'

Kate snapped the book shut and slammed it down on the counter. 'Why can't you just fucking leave it?' she barked. Danielle looked at her in astonishment. 'He had a tumour in his head the size of a fucking kumquat, right? Of course he was obsessive! Of course he'd spend all day figuring out where to put a comma. All of it: random sentences in Latin, characters who talked backwards, whole chapters with no spaces, ten pages devoted to the comparative crown green bowling prowess of David Bryant versus Tony Allcock. He wasn't trying to be James Joyce. He was just ill, right? Sick.'

'Kate, I'm sorry. I really wasn't talking about—'

'At least once a month for twenty-eight years. "Kate, darling, have a look at this, would you?" "Yes, of course, darling, is it your book?" "Yes, it is my book – I think you're going to love what I've done." "Righto, darling – oh, I see you've gone back and re-written Chapter 412 in rhyming couplets." "Yes, I have – it's good, isn't it?" "Yes, of course it is."'

'Kate, dear—'

'Constantly, stupidly encouraging him when all the time it turns out that the appropriate response to reading that stuff was: "You need to see a doctor." Ever tried saying that to a writer? It *really* doesn't go down well.'

'Well . . . no.'

Kate took a breath and searched her bag for a tissue. Danielle found a little pack under the counter and gave it to her. 'Thank you,' she said, drying her eyes and blowing her nose. They both turned to the window. Clapham life went on regardless. A young couple, each holding a hand of their three-year-old in purple dungarees, swinging her up in the air as they ambled by.

More quietly, Kate said, 'He didn't even *like* bowls.'

Danielle allowed a pause to open up and then said carefully, 'I'm almost afraid to ask but . . . have *you* seen a doctor?'

Kate clicked back onto autopilot. It had been silly to take control of the stick, however briefly. Autopilot had a confirmed destination and was much less bumpy. She gave her friend a mouth-only smile and stuffed the wet tissue into her bag. 'Yes. Yes, I have. Don't worry, there's a plan.'

'Indeed?'

'Yeah, I've just been dithering about whether to get on with it.'

'Good. And . . . would it be too much to ask what the plan is?'

Kate straightened the little books on the counter, efficiently putting *The 100 Best Things You've Forgotten About the Nineties* back in place. 'Oh, you know, therapy and exercise and eating well and leaning on my friends. Hanging out with the guys at work, who are all lovely. And my mother's been a real . . . resource, actually, and she's really helped me. Basically looking after myself a bit better, you know?'

Danielle looked like she didn't have much choice but to believe her. 'Well, that all sounds very sensible.'

'It does, doesn't it? Anyway, sorry for the meltdown. See you soon.' Without making eye-contact, Kate left the shop, closing the door gently behind her.

She struggled through her own front door, juggling her keys and a bottle of Smirnoff Blue Label, which she had carried bagless from the off-licence at the end of the road. She bummed the door shut behind her and groaned. Going out had been a mistake. Also, the house was really beginning to stink. She only noticed when she came back from going out, so obviously the solution was to stop going out. She wanted nothing more than to sleep. One more dream of Luke. One that didn't go wrong or end too soon.

How many more final straws did she need? She couldn't bear to think of the mortifying blow-up at poor Danielle. *This is what comes of letting people care about you*, she thought as she slouched down the hall. *Well, no more of that.*

She froze at the entrance to the kitchen.

'Hi Kate!'

Toby was at the sink, the sleeves of his shirt tidily rolled up to the elbows. 'Hope you don't mind. I've got the dishwasher going but it's always best to do the heavy stuff by hand.'

Kate didn't speak for eight seconds, during which Toby lightly whistled 'Ave Maria'. Finally, she managed, 'What . . . *the fuck* . . . are you doing?'

Toby pulled a glass tray from the soapy water and inspected it. 'Erm, well specifically, a pleasingly retro smoked-glass roasting dish.'

'How did you get in?'

'You gave me a key, remember?'

'No. I've never given you a key.'

'No? Oh well, worth a try. I've never been much good at gaslighting.' He nodded at the back door. 'I picked the Yale. No damage, I promise. But it was worryingly easy and I'd suggest adding a bolt for the future.'

Kate advanced a couple of steps into the room. She dropped her bag on the floor and plonked the litre of vodka on the kitchen island, the surface of which she suddenly noticed was clear of junk and recently scrubbed. From the little utility room in the corner she could hear the washing machine at work and there were four bin-liners of rubbish festooning the opposite wall.

'I know what you're thinking,' Toby said. 'You could do with a nice cup of tea. Me too.' He dried his hands on a clean tea towel she hadn't seen for months. He must have found it at the back of the airing cupboard upstairs. Where else had he been? He looked across at her and winked playfully as he filled the kettle. 'Ah!' he chirped as he located the switch and flicked it. Kate saw from the carefully stacked hillock of clean pans on the draining board that the first thing he had washed was a couple of mugs. He righted them and opened a cupboard in search of teabags.

She didn't have the energy for another emotional outburst today but he seemed to be doing his very best to provoke her. 'It's not nice to break into someone's house, Toby,' she said calmly.

'What's that?' His head reappeared from behind the cupboard door and he cupped an ear. 'Sorry – kettle.'

She raised her voice over the kettle but was determined not to shout. 'I don't know how long you plan to keep this up, but for a start I haven't got any milk so you might as well turn the kettle off and get out.'

'Aha! Yorkshire Tea!' he said, producing a box of teabags and refilling the jar. 'Do you remember at York, Luke used to get these because he thought it would endear him to local newsagents? I'm sure Mr Patel was touched.'

Kate was already sick of being on the back foot. 'If you mean the house in our second year, then that particular Mr Patel – Sahir, if you're interested – had lived in York since he moved there with his family from Karachi when he was four. He might well have been "touched". You wouldn't know because you never talked to him.'

Toby finished pouring the boiling water and smiled in admiration. 'Your memory, Kate,' he said, replacing the kettle and locking his blue eyes into hers for the first time. 'What *are* we going to do with it?'

Kate checked her pocket for the memory stick before remembering she'd just posted it to Charles. She felt sure Toby caught the movement as he strolled to the fridge.

Right. So he's definitely a spy. He's after the memory stick. He's after Petrov. He's come to recruit me or kill me. If it's the first, he can fuck off. If it's the second, then he can dream on. The only fucker round here killing me today is me.

Toby spun round with a carton of semi-skimmed milk. 'TA-DAH!' he exclaimed and she started in surprise. 'Ooh sorry! Didn't mean to make you jump.' He opened it on the way back to the brewing mugs. 'I thought maybe you'd be running low so I bought a pint.'

'Why did you break into my house?'

Toby frowned at the mugs and flicked some soap off his watch. 'I'd better give it a couple more minutes otherwise it's not really tea, is it?' He began looking for a teaspoon.

'TOBY, YOU APPALLING SHIT!'

Toby stopped.

Dammit. He's got what he came for.

Toby leaned on the counter top in his white cotton shirt and his pale blue silk tie, loosened for housework duties.

'Yes, Kate,' he said in a tone that was open but watchful.

He was backlit by the sun from the patio window. She felt like telling him that he'd just put his elbow in a patch of dried pesto. At York, he had seemed older than his peers, his skin showing war wounds from a childhood encounter with chickenpox or maybe some recently healed acne. Now, whatever imprints remained brought a character to his face that entirely suited him. He used to seem slightly short and stocky – now, he was still only a couple of inches taller than Kate but lean for a man of his years. Everybody has their time, Kate reflected. And Toby's time was now. It was insufferable.

She said, 'I'm going to ask you some questions and you're going to stop dicking about.'

'Fine.'

'Why did you come here?'

'To make sure that you were all right.'

'But I wasn't in.'

'That became clear.'

'Yes, once you'd broken in to my home.'

'It certainly got even clearer after that.'

'Most people just phone.'

'You don't answer calls.'

'How do you know? I didn't notice you trying.'

Toby took a moment to look down at his brogues and then met her eye again. 'Amy, Kes and others told me that you had cut yourself off. Madeleine said as much when I saw her yesterday. I didn't imagine I would be treated differently.'

Her mouth formed a loose oval and she heard the noise 'Ah' coming out of it.

She wanted to kill him. *Phone calls?* Maybe she would have taken his calls and maybe not. But all she was hearing now was that he didn't bother because his pride couldn't take the rejection.

She took a step closer. 'Listen, *laddie*. I don't care who you work for – MI5 or MI6 or any of those—'

'Kate, let's not do this again . . .'

'No, actually, let's *really* do this again. Since the guy who just broke into my house is standing there making tea and making me feel like a *guest* in my own motherfucking kitchen. Let's do this once and for all. Out loud. Using words.'

82

'Kate, even if you were right I'd hardly be in a position to confirm it, would I? There wouldn't be anything to tell you.'

She glanced at Toby's dark blue suit jacket and waistcoat, hung neatly on the back of a chair. 'No,' she said, 'all you're telling me is that you know where to find a tea towel and you wear a three-piece suit for social calls. You're not going to get out of this by pretending to be gay.'

Toby gave her a toothy grin. 'That's what you said last time.'

At that point, she grabbed the bottle of vodka and threw it at his head.

'Jesus!' He fumbled a painful catch – the bottle frolicking in his hands before he recovered it and set it down on the floor.

Kate stood still and said, 'You've had training.'

Toby tucked some bruised fingers into his armpit. 'What?'

'Those weren't the reflexes of a normal person.'

'Oh, for crying out loud. I used to play a bit of rugby. Remember?'

'Bullshit. Scots don't play rugby.'

'You're thinking of cricket.'

The name of every Scottish player who had beaten England in the first international rugby union match in 1871 flashed across Kate's mind. She had memorised them to impress her dad when she was ten. But okay, yes, she had been thinking of cricket. That was annoying. She didn't feel like giving an inch to the intruder. 'Well, y'know – rugby, cricket. You can't expect a girl to know the difference.' It was a silly remark and they both knew it. But Toby didn't mock her. If anything, that made Kate feel even worse – she was being *handled*.

Instead, he nodded to the mugs. 'That tea should be about brewed by now, d'you not think?'

She gave up. 'Sorry about your fingers,' she said and mooched listlessly round the table and sat while he made the tea.

'Still milk, no sugar?'

She nodded, surveying the unfamiliar calm of her kitchen. Toby had removed any matter which threatened to decay, grow or spawn. Everything else was organised into logical piles. At the top of a bunch of old photographs was a snap from the eighties: square with rounded corners – her dad in a short-sleeved shirt and sunglasses, leaning out of his taxi and giving a thumbs-up. Kate, aged about nine, leaning against the door and doing the same. It had the low-res, washed-out colours that modern phone filters try to recreate. She picked it up and rubbed a thumb tenderly along its edge.

Toby joined her and quietly set down a mug of tea. 'That's lovely of you and Bill,' he said.

'Take it.' She offered him the photo. She didn't know where the impulse came from – part kindness, part masochism. Partly she was still fighting.

Toby sat and settled his own tea. 'No, I couldn't possibly.' His gaze lingered on it.

'He really meant the world to you, didn't he?' Kate said with genuine interest. 'You can't have met him more than five times.'

Toby cradled the mug with both hands in front of him. 'He was just a very nice guy, as you know.'

Kate flapped the photo at him. 'Please,' she said.

Toby looked at her with a quizzical gratitude and took out his phone. He placed the photo on the table in front of him and took a careful picture. 'Just as good, these days,' he half-smiled as he replaced the original at the top of the pile.

'Why did you come here?' she asked again.

84

'I thought you might be in trouble and I wanted to help.'

'Why did you break in?'

'I was worried you were dead.'

Unbearable. This wasn't the plan. Kate rose from the table. 'Well, that reminds me. I'm on a busy schedule, Toby. You need to leave.'

Toby stared at his tea, looking heartbroken. 'I can't do that, Kate.'

She left the table and began to pace around the 10,000-day kitchen. 'What, because you need me to "Choose Life"? You came to give me a pep talk?'

Toby said, 'Look, let's not.' He stood, raising his hands at her in a calming motion of placation.

Kate stopped pacing. 'No, no, no. You don't get to *calm me down*. You haven't earned it. You were nowhere when it mattered. Nowhere.' She watched him absorb the punch. His eyes reddened and flicked to the open back door. She wavered for half a second but couldn't help the follow-up: this time, really going for his nuts. 'I'm a woman alone in a house and I'm asking you to leave. A gentleman would know what to do next.'

She was partly consoled to see him mournfully gather up his waistcoat and jacket.

'There were reasons why I had to stay away,' he said.

'No doubt. But of course you couldn't possibly share them with me now, right?'

He confirmed as much, putting his waistcoat back on and straightening his tie. 'I brought you a present.' He nodded at a perfectly wrapped gift in the shape of a book at the end of the table and started to head towards the patio door.

'Through the front door, please,' Kate said sharply. 'Like a normal person.'

Toby checked his direction with a sigh and turned around,

heading towards the hallway. He paused. 'I know you're in trouble, Kate. I can help.'

'I don't need anybody's help.'

'I'm here. I'll wait for you.'

'Well, you've had plenty of practice.'

By some distance, these were the unkindest words she'd ever said to him. Luke . . . Toby . . . twenty-eight years and nobody had said it out loud. Nobody talked about why Toby was still single. Nobody talked about what a close-run thing it had been back in 1992. It wasn't as if Toby had competed for her. He'd taken one glance at Luke and thrown in the towel.

He did the same now. She saw that his hand was trembling as he took his jacket and slung it over his shoulder. Those who knew him less well would have bought the performance of manly detachment. But what was left of Kate's heart fell through the crust of the Earth. She mumbled, 'Sorry. That was stupid and not fair and I—'

He interrupted, 'I'm not waiting for you to fall in love with me, Kate. If that's what you meant. I didn't come here to *pounce*.'

She wanted to reassure him but didn't have the words. She stared at the floor and the voice within took possession of her thoughts. This was exactly right. This was what she did. She took fine men and reduced them to nothing. She didn't deserve love. She didn't deserve the truth. She was a freak and a monster. Always had been. She needed to push them away for their own good. 'Go,' she said. 'Please go and never come back.' She didn't have the courage to look at his face as he left the kitchen.

The front door opened and closed.

Enough, enough, enough.

In a daze, she walked back to the table and picked up the gift – a slim paperback of some kind, wrapped in plain brown paper. She felt nothing but a numb incuriosity. Some witty message or maybe a self-help book. She tossed it back on the table and picked up the vodka. She casually took the box of drugs from the cupboard and headed upstairs.

At least Toby hadn't touched her bedroom. Bad enough that he'd been rootling around downstairs with the fag packets and takeaway trays. At least she didn't have to imagine him organising her underwear drawer and frowning with concern as he noted Dirk the Dildo had run out of batteries. Caring bastard would have probably replaced them. She flopped onto her bed with her phone in hand. 'Hey, Siri,' she said flatly as the phone beeped to attention. 'Wake me up around four so I can do myself in.'

'Sure thing,' replied the female voice, 'I've set an alarm for four p.m.'

Kate tapped the icon and the phone chimed again. 'Just for the record, Siri, I've always thought you were a cold-hearted shit.'

'I'm sorry, I don't understand what you're—'

'Whatever.' Kate tossed the phone aside and then picked it up again. 'Oh, and if you can arrange it so the last 10,000 days didn't happen, I'd be very grateful.' She stared at the pills and the vodka.

Toby, Danielle, Petrov, Charles, the memory stick, her city, her country . . .

Leave me alone leave me alone leave me alone.

One more dream of Luke. One more. She didn't deserve it. She'd been dreaming her whole life. She deserved nothing. And nothingness.

Kate took his shirt from beneath the pillow, held it to her face and closed her eyes.

Part Two

COME DANCING

Chapter 7

S he woke in darkness.

No, that can't be right. What time is it? She reached for her phone but her hand hit the cold wall. *Hang on – wall? What wall?* And it wasn't even the right kind of darkness. Orange. And somehow blurred. A dawn light glowing through the orange curtains. *Wait, curtains? Drawn? Drawn orange curtains at dawn? What?* And why was the window next to her, not in front of her? And why was she under the duvet instead of lying on top of it? And the duvet was wrong too. Light and insubstantial. A single. She tentatively reached out again and pressed her fingers against the impossible wall, her other hand finding the edge of the mattress. This was a single bed. Her heart began to beat faster and she calmed her rising panic with 'who breathing'.

Who? the word throbbed in her mind. *Who am I? More to the point – where am I?*

She was Kate Marsden. *It's okay*, she thought, *I haven't got amnesia, I haven't lost my mind. I'm Kate Marsden, a forty-five-year-old woman from south-east London. Katherine Jennifer Marsden, born in 1974, daughter of Bill Marsden and Madeleine Theroux; partner of Luke Fairbright for twenty-eight years, married for the last seventeen,* widowed for nearly one. *That much is clear. It's pretty much the* only *thing that's clear but it's something.*

Had she been kidnapped?

Seemed a bit unlikely. She wasn't tied up, she didn't feel like she had been drugged. In fact, apart from almost crapping herself with disorientation she felt physically great.

She couldn't see much but she sensed the proximity of the other walls, the ceiling. Had she got so monumentally arseholed that she had rented a bedsit without remembering? Could *even she* get that wasted without noticing? It would explain the blurry vision. But where was the hangover?

She sat up in bed.

Jesus. That was easy.

What the hell was she wearing? These weren't the clothes she had gone to sleep in. This was . . . this was a long t-shirt. Worn like a nightie. The way she used to sleep when she . . .

She swept her legs out of bed and stood. Bare feet, wrong floor, carpet not wood. Total and bewildering absence of even the first flicker of pain or effort as her feet took her weight. And what weight was this, anyway? Was she suddenly made of balsa wood? She might as well be floating.

She took a step towards the curtains and felt the fabric – thin, rough, cheap, orange, orange, orange . . .

She realised that in the ninety seconds since waking up she had been avoiding the certain knowledge of where she was. She could try to go back to sleep and maybe it would go away. But this was like no dream she had ever experienced. It was a thousand times more physical. If her body was sleeping, she couldn't reach it – there was no remembering it and rising back into it. It wasn't there. It was here.

Her hand was still on the curtain and she boldly parted it aside. The familiar scrape of the metal runners rushed at her. What she saw now through the window was only the confirmation of the inevitable.

This was Benedict College, York.

And this was the view of it from her first-year room.

Opposite was the concrete grey of the north wing of the college. Three storeys below her, the footpaths criss-crossing the scrubby lawn. And immediately outside her sliding-door window, the walkway that she had often resented – the one connecting all the other back doors of Level 3, South Block.

As for her blurred vision – the explanation for that was even more disturbing. She held her breath: gazing ahead and trusting only to muscle memory, she leaned down to her left and extended a hand to the bedside table. There. Her glasses. She held them up close and inspected them. Her black-framed, faux Michael-Caine-in-*The-Ipcress-File* spectacles. She needed them because her laser eye treatment of 2005 had . . . stopped working?

She put them on and looked out again at Benedict, revealed now in all its humdrum clarity. A male student out for an early morning run thumped along the walkway and averted his eyes with a tiny wave of apology as he went by. What had he seen? A middle-aged woman wearing amusingly oversized glasses? She looked down at her faded Ride t-shirt featuring the dude with cucumber slices for eyes and below that, the knees, shins and feet of a young woman.

In fact, an eighteen-year-old. In fact, herself aged eighteen.

She staggered back onto the bed and fought for breath.

The giveaway was the nail polish. A shudderingly unwise 'goodbye holiday' that summer in Poole with Pete Lampton had left her with a tan but also her toenails painted turquoise. The nail polish had been one of many presents he had bought her that week when he had changed his mind about the mutual break-up.

'Long-distance relationships can and do work, Kate!' he had insisted. She had accepted his slightly annoying gift (she didn't much care for either nail varnish or turquoise) but gently impressed upon him that the relationship was over.

'Sometimes people just have to let go,' she had said.

The night before she took the train to the University of York for her first term, she had applied the nail varnish on a sentimental whim. It wasn't just farewell to Pete but farewell to competitive sport. She wouldn't be seen dead wearing cosmetics in a dojo or tournament. But now, having done 'this karate thing' properly, she was cautiously ready to attempt 'this acting like a student but also a woman thing' properly. The rules were considerably less clear. And she was rather behind with the skills too. After twenty minutes of making her feet look like they'd been stamped on, she asked her mother for advice. Madeleine was delighted. 'Le moineau quitte le nid mais n'a pas de chaussures!'

'I've got plenty of shoes, Mother. I just don't know how to paint my fucking feet.'

'Don't spoil it, darling.'

In her student room, Kate stared at her mother's handiwork. She knew she had never worn turquoise nail varnish before or since. She knew she had cleaned it off today because she definitely wasn't wearing it on the first night when she met . . .

She looked up and took in the half-lit room. The walls with no posters. The shelves with no books. The open but unemptied suitcase. She had arrived late the previous night, taking out just her toothbrush, contact lens case and – she checked the bedside table. Yep, *Orlando* by Virginia Woolf. She had been reading it alone in the college bar when he first . . .

No, it wasn't that the laser eye treatment had stopped working. She just hadn't had it yet. She was living in the past. This was Freshers' Week, October 1992.

This wasn't Day 10,000. This was Day 1.

She stood and had just enough time to take her glasses off before the floor leapt up and smacked her in the face.

She woke with her mouth forming a single word. 'Shit.'

Someone was knocking at the door. Kate got to her feet. She grabbed her specs and checked for damage, putting them on and pulling her t-shirt down, hopping towards the door. The little spy-hole was still there, still set at the level for a bloke three inches taller. On tip-toe, she peered through.

Oh God. The Australian second-year Christian doing the rounds and trying to swoop on homesick freshers. What was her name again? Kate opened the door a crack.

'Hi there! Woo, late night, huh? You look frazzled! I'm Lauren! Welcome to Benedict!'

Kate blinked at her. 'Hello.'

'HAHAHA! We're all crazy at Benedict so you'll fit right in.' Lauren appeared to grasp that the girl just out of bed peering at her through eccentric specs wasn't about to invite her into the room. She instantly recovered her joie de vivre and handed Kate a tiny slip of paper with some details printed on it. 'So I'm just here to let you know about a cool tea party we're having at four-thirty today for all the anonymous newbies? Meet people? Like-minded individuals? Maybe people you wouldn't normally converse with? Maybe not! Hey, so . . . catch you there???'

Kate took the roughly guillotined bit of paper. A Christian tea party. She slowly closed the door, saying, 'Erm . . . I'm going to say . . . no?'

She heard a mild huff of bewilderment on the other side

of the door and some retreating flip-flops. Lauren, Kate remembered, had written a review of one of Kes's plays in the student magazine, the piece being notable for its passive-aggressive homophobia and lack of commas. But she hadn't known that last time. How had she treated the bubbly Christian Union rep twenty-eight years ago? She sat down with her back against the door, surveying her room in recollection.

An interesting philosophical question invited itself and Kate chose to ponder it rather than screaming herself demented with mortal terror about what the ATOM-FUCKING-UNIVERSE was going on here??? Maybe she would do that later.

What had she done last time, the first time? She had unpacked and put her contacts in. She had showered and dressed, and dithered over which Caravaggio print to put where. Yes, she had invited Lauren in with the heavy warning that she hadn't had a chance to buy any tea. Lauren had yelled some annoying endearment about the English obsession with hot drinks and had then left her to it.

The question was: had she just changed the course of history? Just now, she had been slightly rude to Lauren; certainly ruder than last time. Would that affect Lauren's mood? Would it make her snappier with the other freshers? Or would she bond with them by making bitchy comments about the weird girl in room South 47? What would be the net effect on the Christian tea party attendance? Would people who had first met there now not meet? Or at least not meet in the way that led to that first date? Or maybe there was still a first date but under different circumstances: rain where there would have been sun; the try-hard business tie instead of the open-necked shirt; *Howards End* instead of *Basic Instinct*? And so no second date? No third? What marriage had she undone? What children unborn? And *their* children? The children who grew up to invent fusion power or perfect carbon capture. In short, had she just doomed planet Earth because she had foreknowledge that Lauren was a queer-loathing bellend?

Come on, this was all very well but she had to be dreaming. Kate took her glasses off and slapped herself hard in the face. 'Wake up,' she said out loud. The sound of her own voice threatened another wave of panic: it was half an octave too high and a stranger to herself as well as, clearly, tobacco. She hadn't really started smoking till the end of this year, when everyone was doing weed after preliminary exams. She said, experimentally, 'This is me talking.' And then a weird falsetto: 'This is me talking.' And then as low as possible: 'This is me talking.' Outside, a neighbour across the hall slammed their door and departed with a jangle of keys. 'Okay,' she whispered, 'maybe stop sounding like a mad person.'

She got up and glanced at the door to the bathroom. That would be a challenge in itself. A mirror. Her younger self. Would she have a heart attack?

Well, no, probably not, she reasoned. It was a young, healthy heart and could take almost anything. Physically at least. But her emotional heart was much older – as old as she believed herself to be. How had she remembered everything? The memories in her brain were forty-five years old. That brain was part of her body and subject to change. But the body had reverted to youth and the brain had stayed the same. That was impossible. It was a dream. She took off her glasses again and administered an even harsher slap.

Noop. Still here. She replaced the glasses and got to her feet. Her fingers hovered over the light switch on the little bathroom's exterior wall. *Best foot forward, Katie*, she thought and then instantly retracted her hand.

Her dad was alive. Not just Luke but Dad.

Somewhere in this building, Luke was putting up his Kurt Cobain poster or maybe setting out to Discount Apparel to buy that grandad shirt. And somewhere back in Deptford, her dad was doing a Saturday morning shift and politely torturing passengers with his informed guesses about their football team's chances this afternoon.

Kate's hand returned to the switch. Right. Courage. One thing at a time. Whatever she did next she needed to put her contacts in, have a wash and get dressed. She flicked the switch and heard the familiar noise of the fan wobbling into life. She stepped inside.

And there she was. 'Oh,' she said softly. 'Oh, my word.'

Apart from the flush on her right cheek from all the self-slapping, her skin was absurdly clear. Golden and still slightly freckled from the summer. Her cheekbones seemed oddly pronounced, as if she'd had surgery.

No, this is what the surgery tries to reclaim. I'm not vain and ridiculous. I'm just healthy. I'm just young. This is not to be confused with beauty. Nothing is going on here.

Her dark hair meandered down to the bottom of her ears – unbrushed and unbothered. She took her glasses off and peered closer. Her eyes were the same grey-blue . . . but the whites! The whites of her eyes could blind a Californian. On an impulse, she lifted the left sleeve of her t-shirt. Her BCG scar! The pale circle from her teenage injection was more pronounced among the youthful muscle of her shoulder. She had only recently stopped training.

What else? This body was strange to her but also home – scarily out of time but right now her only friend. What else, though? What else?

*

Showered and fizzing with curiosity, Kate hurried from the bathroom in a towel and closed the curtains again. What next?

Gleefully, she dropped the towel and set about the almost effortless business of twenty press-ups. She sprang to her feet, shrieking with delight, and performed a nude star-jump. 'Oww!'

Okay – don't try that again without a bra. You're eighteen, not Silicon Woman.

She clapped her hands and laughed like a super-villain. This body! For a second she wanted to run around the college, banging on doors and yelling – 'You're beautiful! You're all so beautiful! You've no idea how fucking ALIVE you are! I don't care if you haven't been training like a karate maniac for years – you're still IN YOUR PRIME! Chuck the books in the bin and go for a run! Or just bonk each other! Is "bonk" still the right word? Or was that the eighties? All right, "romp". Everybody romp immediately! I'm ordering you! Take it from me because I'm the . . .'

She sank down on the carpet, catching her breath and slowly crossing her legs. She said faintly, 'Because I'm The Girl from the Future.'

She pressed her thumbs into the arches of her feet, massaging thoughtfully.

Luke.

What the hell was she supposed to do about Luke?

Kate felt suddenly unprepared and stupidly naked. She scrambled over to her open suitcase and fished out some underwear. She shuffled herself into the most comfy knickers she could find and grabbed a bra. The geography of this body presented a few unexpected curves and angles but it was joyfully familiar in this alarming world. She peered into the retro treasure-trove of her clothes. 'I suppose all treasure-troves are retro,' she said, getting more used to her new voice. Her old voice. Her young voice. Yes, this was going to be complicated. She needed her diary. No laptop.

The notebook diary. Made of paper. Yes, obviously. Oh God. First, get dressed.

Her green corduroy mini-skirt: 'Oh, you've got to be joking,' said Kate. Why had she even packed it?

What had she actually worn on that first day? Indeed, that first night? Well, the denim pinafore dress and the massive boots, of course. Did it matter? Did she have to be wearing the same thing? Because – she permitted the question that was both absurd and inescapable . . .

She wasn't seriously going to try and have sex with Luke tonight, was she?

Right?

Just . . . really?

No. No, that would be too much.

Kate wanted to stay in her body and do more jumping around. But there was too much to think about.

Doesn't matter for now.

She dressed and then looked across to another bag, her rucksack. The one that contained her diary. She took it to her student desk.

I will do everything exactly the same. Completely the same. Except this time, I will save Luke.

Kate replaced the red cap of her Berol rollerball and twizzled it in her fingers as she used to. She compared what she had just written to the entry above it – the one she had written yesterday – the yesterday that was twenty-eight years ago. It was the same pen, but her handwriting had since become scrappy and oversized. She didn't even write shopping lists by hand any more. She half-expected her wrist to hurt from even these seventeen words. But of course not

– this hand and its muscles understood pens. This was the hand that could toss off a three-hour A-level exam, as well as Pete when he was drunk. But her mind insisted that she was forty-five and that fluent handwriting was a lost skill.

She re-read the previous entry.

Holy shit then, off we go! One hour till the 18:54 to York. Dad is so much more nervous than me, the daft bugger. About to cab me to King's Cross, like I haven't got the bus into town a million times. Darling Mother more concerned that I'm abandoning her. High opera, mainly in French. Oh, and she couldn't help another Oxford dig. 'I'm sure York will be wonderful in its own unchallenging sort of way. What a pity. What a pity.' BITCH! I never told either of them the truth about what happened at that interview – that I rejected them. Sort of. Anyway, 'nuff said and best foot forward and other fascinating clichés.

What will it be like? Who'ma'gonna meet? Shall I tell them about school? Or about the silver medal? Fuck it, let the chips fall as they may. Let's just go for it. Tall, dark, handsome stranger? Or maybe some lady-action? Everyone except Pete thinks I'm a lesbian in denial so I might as well. This nail varnish still stinks. Whada mistaka damaka. Ooh, Dad yelling from downstairs about the traffic – must dash. Find out tomorrow in The Continuing Adventures of Ms KJ Marsden and Her Totally Doomed Quest for Normality.

Okay, so I'm chirpy, thought Kate. *I'm chirpy and optimistic. I'm eighteen and full of fucking hope. That's not easy to fake but worth a try. On the other hand, I still love both my parents but find one of them a reliable pain in the arse. That's a bit more familiar. Plus ça change . . . Right.*

She popped the lid off her pen and continued with the new entry.

I don't know what has happened or why I'm here. God or aliens or glitch in the universe or a very deep coma. That last one is the most likely but wtf because I'd only had half a bottle of wine, a brisk walk and a nice lunch. Obviously I was also suicidal and paranoid about dear Charles sending heavies to beat me up and in terrible grief and had just insulted and then ejected a very good friend from the house so . . . yes, definitely quite stressed. But this? This is just unreasonable.

Anyway. Look. I'm here. Completely and undeniably here.

She paused and inspected the underside of her left forearm – while she was in the shower she had scored it with the rough plastic corner of her contact lens case, trying to inflict as much pain as she dared in order to snap out of the dream/coma. Carefully avoiding veins, she had dragged three livid parallel scratches. No, she had not woken up. No, she hadn't really expected to.

She wrote on.

And there must be a reason. For now I've decided that the reason is to save Luke. The meningioma is already there. I've got to convince him that he has a tumour growing in his head which is going to kill him. But without sounding like I'm a mentalist. That, to put it mildly, won't be easy. Let's just get this straight – from his point of view, we've never met. We are complete strangers. He doesn't know he's my husband. And he is not forty-seven, he is nineteen.

102

Kate dropped the pen on the desk and stared ahead into the empty corkboard on the opposite wall. This was crazy. This was mission triple impossible. She felt the room beginning to throb. Was she going to faint again? She breathed. Let it come, then. Let it come. She waited.

She refocused her eyes and found some courage. She took up her pen.

If anyone can do this, it's me. I have these fucking 'gifts' which everyone goes on about. They annoy people but I'm better at hiding them now. Definitely. I know things that they don't. I always did, but now – well, now I know even more. Must be careful with that. But the ace in the hole is that I love Luke. That must help.

She stopped again. Was that really an advantage? If she was going to save his life, did it help that she loved him? Or would that get in the way? She shook the thought from her head, looking for other advantages. There was one which she would have been too shy to write when she was eighteen. In fact, when she was eighteen, she didn't even know.

And by the way, I'm beautiful. That should help.

She stared at that first sentence. Had she really just written that down? Her dad had always said so, but that's just what dads say. Pete had said so, but that's what boyfriends say. Her mother had provided a lifetime's rolling commentary of veiled slights or compliments in search of a subject: 'It's wonderful when young women these days can actually dress in a way that's actually *feminine*.' Or, 'You've nothing to worry about, darling. Yes, men go on looks – your father certainly did – but I know you'll make the best of yourself, despite those muscles.' And the

103

returning, 'Remember that your strangeness doesn't make you beautiful. But you are to me, however you look.'

Luke had called her gorgeous on a daily, then weekly, then monthly basis for twenty-eight years. She didn't believe a word of it. She was quite sure that he fancied her, but that was different.

But just now, in the bathroom, she had gazed at her face with all the compassion and judgement of an older self. In fact, older Kate felt an overwhelming need to give the lovely kid in the mirror something she had always wanted. She picked up the pen.

This girl has a proper mother now. This girl is going to be looked after. And so is Luke.

Chapter 8

Kate pulled on her Doc Martens and laced them. Beside her, two piles of paperwork she had collected from the porter's lodge on arrival last night.

Must get used to calling it 'last night'. Not 'half a life ago'.

She had divided the documents: the leaflets and flyers for various clubs and societies formed one multi-coloured heap; the other, the more sober A4 stapled sheets about her course and the various necessary enrolments and registrations. No lectures till Monday. Societies Fayre in Central Hall: tomorrow. Meeting future dead husband: tonight. She glanced at the paperwork – it was enough to dishearten her.

'Queueing,' she muttered grimly, 'the endless queueing.'

She didn't know how long she was going to be here. But if she was to make contact with Luke and somehow save his life, she would have to blend in and do all the regular student things. And this weekend a large portion of the regular student things involved queues – for her NUS card, her YUSU enrolment, her doctor's registration and all the other start-up stuff. But the queueing didn't stop there. All year for three years: queueing for the phone booth, queueing in the college canteen, queueing in Dennington village for the only cash machine that didn't charge a transaction fee.

She was broke, like everyone else. She could have been less broke but she'd never set foot in a casino since her dad had accused her of abusing her gifts.

'You forged an ID, Katie. That's illegal. You too good for the law, is it?'

'No, 'course not!'

'Well, then! And you can take that power drill back to Halfords first thing. Thanks, but I don't want it if you got it from cheating.'

'It was blackjack – everyone counts cards! It's just some of us are better at it than others!'

'Katie, that's not what a memory like yours is for.'

'What's it for, then?'

'We'd all like to find out, love. But it's not that!'

She pulled the second double bow tight on her boot and rubbed her eyes, remembering to be careful of the contact lenses.

Unlasered eyes. Twenty-twenty vision had become 2020 vision. Hindsight. She was staring at 1992 through the back of her arse. This, she had to consider, wasn't necessarily the most reliable view of it.

Where had she gone first? She had delayed breakfast in the canteen and gone for a self-consciously sentimental walk, taking in her new surroundings and thinking of – and Kate blew a low whistle at this – the future.

She had stopped halfway across one of the lake bridges on campus and some kid called Vandra had ruined the moment by joining her and introducing herself. She would scarcely see Vandra again for the next three years but had engaged with her for those ten minutes just in case she had met her new best friend. This was the crackpot lottery of Freshers' Week – one moment you were furiously exchanging room numbers and gap-year stories with people whose names you wouldn't remember even next week; but then you'd find yourself putting down your lunch tray opposite someone whose wedding you would attend, or whose surprise fortieth birthday weekend you would plan, or whose children would call you Auntie Kate. Or you might find yourself sitting next to someone in a bar whose funeral invitation you would design.

Not quite a lottery, Kate thought. York wasn't a big university in 1992 and Benedict wasn't a big college. Sooner or later she would have bumped into Luke. If not that first night then another. But how? And would it have made a difference? What were the chances that those two people would find that connection at that moment? What were the chances that they had been born at all? What were the chances of life on Earth, of the universe forming in the first place? The entirety of human existence was laughably improbable and it was all complete madness. Remembering that, Kate felt oddly encouraged about her situation. A glitch in the Matrix, a kink in the space-time continuum – well, stranger things have happened.

She hadn't met Luke or any of the other big guns – Amy, Toby or Kes – till that evening in the bar. So she would retrace her steps to avoid them today. She vaguely wondered if she should wear a hat and sunglasses as a disguise before remembering that none of those people knew who the hell she was.

Luke didn't know who she was.

'Okey-doke,' Kate said to herself as she stood. For the sixteenth time that morning she looked for her phone. *Yes. No problem. Who needs a phone?*

Texts, emails, websites, Facebook, Twitter, Instagram . . . all gone. All of it.

She closed her eyes and said calmly to herself, 'Nobody else is walking out of their room today missing their iPhone.

107

I am one of them. I'm Generation X. We invented half of this shit. I can do this. I'm with my people.'

She stuffed her tatty silver wallet into the pocket of her army surplus coat, scrunchied her hair into a ponytail with a few artful strands loose at the front the way Sandra Bullock did in a movie that hadn't been made yet, grabbed her keys and set out.

Three hours and several queues later, the campus had made her feel like she was on a movie set where the designers had gone crazy with 1990s overkill. It was all so insistently, so dementedly 1992. There were too many perms; too many boys in long-sleeved tops under Ned's Atomic Dustbin t-shirts; too many rugby shirts and floppy curtain haircuts; too many girls in heel-length pencil skirts (English students); too much pre-GHD-hair-straightening frizz on those heads; too precisely the right number of Goths for this time of day (none); too many James daisies everywhere; too many students making air-quotes at each other; too much Tasmin Archer, Pearl Jam and SNAP! drifting through open windows from radios and bulky CD players.

She approached Dennington – the small, not-quite-picture-postcard village on the edge of the campus. And now, entering non-student provincial England, the movie-makers seemed to have taken a lunch break and the 1980s had crept back in. The massive white satellite dishes clamped in lines along the newer terraces; the gnomes proudly on show in the neat gardens of those more prosperous: the older-bricked and semi-detached. Two English tribes, Kate reflected – and the recession was deep and painful to many. But this wasn't a culture war or an opportunity for race-hate. Margaret Thatcher was gone, John Major was two years into office with another five to go. Britain was entering a golden era of utter boredom. Wrong in many ways but accountable to the truth. Almost no progress but very few regressions. About to fuck up the railways but not about to fuck up the entire constitutional basis of the country and its relationship with Europe and the rest of the world. In short: grey with sunny intervals – the frustrating weather of a functioning democracy.

She inspected the broadsheet newspapers in the stand outside the newsagent – still broadsheet-sized and with black and white pictures. The IRA exploding bombs in London. The government closing the last of the deep coal mines and warning of cutbacks because of the financial crisis. Chancellor Norman Lamont was about to spend more time with his family. So, for different reasons, was David Mellor. Another philanderer, Boris Johnson, was still just a frivolous hack rather than a frivolous prime minister. Kate assumed that between the sheets of the *Daily Telegraph* an admired column of his about 'Europe' trying to straighten our bananas was already pushing its tiny erection into the back of a sleeping nation. She vaguely wondered if she had been sent back in time to strangle the lying bastard. Probably not.

And the taste in the air as every Astra and Sierra chugged by – lead petrol. Deliciously, poisonously nostalgic. It seemed like the back of every other car trailed a zig-zag rubber strap to make contact with the ground: an evidence-free placebo for car sickness that about half the motorists in the country would swear by – until a few years later when they would quietly change their minds. Otherwise, the strange peacefulness of a village on the edge of a university campus – the mild October day held in check by the asphalt Yorkshire sky.

She noticed for the first time the undeveloped land in between some of the older cottages; the faint smell of manure on the breeze from a nearby farm; a rusting manual lawnmower in someone's wild front garden – nettles and primroses growing around and through it; the plaintive echo of an ice-cream van playing 'O Sole Mio' from a distance. Was it the past or was it just the countryside?

Just one Cornetto . . .

She was a London girl. She loved nothing more than the view of her city from Lambeth Bridge. But this was special too. York was her second home and she dared to allow some love for it back into her heart. Just a little – she had work to do.

Kate reached for her wallet as she approached the cash machine. She thought she was just about in the black on her current account. Judging by the quaint prices she'd found in the café next to the central library, that would be fine until her grant came through.

'Grant'. No wonder millennials and zedsters think we're all full of shit.

The Alliance and Leicester card disappeared into the slot just an instant before she realised she hadn't the first clue of its PIN. She had regularly changed the PIN of every card, scoffing at those fools who kept the same number from year to year. She frowned in bewilderment at the four blank dashes. 'Oh Christ,' she said out loud, 'where are your memory powers now, old woman?'

She keyed in the Great Reform Act. No good. She tried Jane Austen's year of birth. Nope. She sensed someone now standing behind her, slightly huffing with impatience.

Suddenly, inspiration: Luke's birthday! Month and year – yes, obviously. She entered 1072.

YOU HAVE ENTERED AN INCORRECT PIN THREE TIMES. YOUR CARD HAS BEEN RETAINED FOR SECURITY REASONS. PLEASE CONTACT YOUR LOCAL BRANCH.

No, she realised. Of course it wasn't Luke's birthday. She hadn't met Luke.

She shut out the resurfacing grief and screamed at the green text. 'What!? What are you talking about, you stupid Dalek!? How am I supposed to remember a number like that in the middle of all this shit? Fuck you!!'

She drew her right fist back and it took all her self-discipline not to plough it into the screen.

'Go for it, love! I've been there! Fucking lamp it.'

A voice from behind her, and a very familiar one.

Kate turned on the heel of her boot.

'Although, bloody hell, don't hit *me*, tiger! Steady now.'

A fringe, Kate thought as she passed out. *Amy used to have a fringe.*

'She literally just *swooned* like a damsel. I thought, "Bloody hell, did I say the wrong thing?"'

Kate chose not to open her eyes. She heard a second voice, male.

'Surprisingly heavy, actually. Lot of muscle. Probably quite sporty, if you ask me. I mean, she's obviously quite fit. In more ways than one!'

'All right, well, thanks for your help . . . Freddie?'

'Yah, completely. Freddie.'

'All right, love, thanks for your help but I'll look after her now.'

'I can totally stay. She might need some TLC, yeah?'

Kate heard a beat of forced patience.

'You've been very good, Freddie, but my sister's a nurse and I know a thing or two. She'll be all right with me now.'

'You're quite fit too, Amy.'

'Freddie, love, do one.'

'Righto.'

Kate sniggered herself awake. She tried to turn it into a cough.

'Okay, the Kraken awakens-eth,' said Freddie, looming

over her in a two-coloured, four-quartered rugby shirt. 'I'll make my excuses.'

'Thanks a lot for helping me carry her, pet.'

'I'm massively at your disposal, Amy.'

Freddie, Kate thought. *Second-year. Hearty. Rugby and Geography. Not a bad sort but clearly trying to score a shag out of a crisis.*

'Yarp,' said Freddie, finally leaving. 'Any time, Amy. Any time.'

Kate turned her woozy gaze to her friend.

Amy, eighteen years old, a younger parody of herself as if twenty-eight years of ageing had been an elaborate hair and make-up job, now peeled away to leave an essential Amy-ness. Her proto-All Saints period, of course. A camo crop-top, her pierced navel, her jet-black hair still undyed and allowed to fall around her shoulders during the day. Kate smiled and her friend smiled back.

Amy spoke first. 'Now then, you. What was all that about? You looked like you'd seen a bloody ghost.'

'Not till later,' Kate muttered.

'Y'what, love?'

'Nothing.' She sat up and tried to collect herself. 'Sorry. No idea what happened. Some kind of weird turn. I'm Kate.'

'Nice to make your acquaintance, Kate, have a drink of water. I'm Amy.'

Kate took the proffered mug featuring the cast of *thirty-something* and did as she was told. She looked around the room. 'Your room's the same as mine but you've made it look nicer.'

'Are you here too?'

Kate nodded towards the window. 'South Block, over there. Room 47.'

'Well, you certainly know how to make an entrance.'

Kate laughed. 'Sorry again. Christ, what must you think?

112

Bloody . . . collapsing like . . .' She wanted to say 'that BBC weather presenter on YouTube from 2016' but rapidly plumped for '. . . Madame Bovary.' Probably because she knew Amy was here to study French.

'Ah! Now then! Interesting fact. She doesn't actually faint. Justin does, but not Emma.'

Kate saw an opportunity for a connection. 'Emma Bovary's a bit of an idiot, don't you think?'

'I think she's meant to be a bit of an idiot in a good way, but to be honest I can't stand her.'

'That's right! I did not know that about you!'

Amy looked at her quizzically for a moment. Kate filled the gap with default courtesy. Her accent was veering wildly between her native Deptford and her acquired middle-class. 'Thanks so much. It's Amy, isn't it? This has been extremely kind of you.'

'You're all right, love.'

Kate felt herself being observed as she took another awkward sip of water and glanced around the room in embarrassment.

Abruptly, Amy rose from the bedside. 'Anyway, you have a rest, I'm not going anywhere for a while.'

Amy did some half-hearted organisation of her desk but then became quite still. Her back to Kate, she seemed to come to a decision. She turned and retook her position beside the bed, tucking some hair behind one ear and clearing her throat. 'Now then,' she began, giving Kate a shrewd but open look, 'I don't know you, Kate, and you tell me to bugger off if I'm crossing a line. But I can't help noticing that you've been hurting yourself.' Amy let her eyes rest on Kate's left forearm.

The three parallel cuts from this morning.

Kate sloshed the mug onto the bedside table and instinctively covered her injuries. 'Right, yep, no – that . . . that's not what it looks like.'

'I've a good idea of what it looks like, pet, and I've been there too.'

'No, it was an accident.'

'An accident with a sabre-toothed tiger?'

'No, an accident with . . .'

With what? A fork? An angry squirrel? A slippery pine-apple? This was impossible. Kate shuffled down the bed and got up. Amy stood too. 'Yes, you're right. I don't want to talk about it. Anyway, you've been very kind and—'

'Listen!' Amy was instantly at her most formidable, hands on hips, subtly plucked black eyebrows creased into a teacherly frown, one foot slightly forward. 'It's up to you. I'm saying that I've been there. And there are people you can talk to. People who can help.'

Kate had been backing apologetically towards the door but on hearing this she stopped. She levelled herself and threw the sentence like a dagger. 'You don't fucking change, do you?'

Amy gasped at the extravagant madness of this remark as well as the venom in Kate's voice. Her hands remained on her hips but she swapped her leading foot and cocked her head. 'Who . . . the *hell* do you think you—'

Kate interrupted. 'I don't need it. I don't need anyone. I don't "hurt myself". I'm fine. I've always been fine. I will always be . . .' She shook her head as the lies, grief, shame and hopelessness started to choke her voice. Amy's face softened and she made a movement that threatened to turn into an offer of a hug.

Kate grabbed her coat and walked out.

She stomped, head down, back towards her room.

Oh yes, that went TREMENDOUSLY well. Nice one, Kate.

She crossed another campus lake bridge, this one at water-level and made of concrete stepping stones; only a few inches between them and she counted her steps. Mind the gap. The gap will find you out.

Geese. The stupid geese everywhere. She remembered that this was the kind of thing that York alumni talked of fondly when they didn't have goose-shit on their boots any more. She imagined doubling back to the bank to kick some squawking fuck into the sky. Why had she been so horrible to Amy? Was it just a habit now? Was this her *system*? Whatever the century, every time Amy offered help she could expect to be roundly insulted? *What the hell is my problem?* she shouted in her head.

This had been a clean sheet. A fresh start. Now her best friend was forewarned and on the lookout for that rude, swooning, angry . . . *ill* person. Who wants to hurt herself. Which obviously she did, in the old life. But now . . . Kate slowed her steps.

Now . . . she didn't want to die any more.

So that was . . . good?

She reached the opposite bank and stopped. Yes, that was good. It was good but there was no one to share it with. Nobody knew her. She turned and watched a little family of geese venturing out into the lake.

No.

No, that would be unbearable.

But wonderful.

Come on, then. Best foot forward.

She found the row of three phone kiosks in the usual place outside the Junior Common Room. Feeling even more furtive now that she had Amy to avoid, she waited for a free booth – studying her bitten fingernails and wishing she had a phone to look at. But then obviously if she had a phone, she wouldn't be queueing to use a phone.

The fresher in front finished her call. She was so

completely random that even Kate couldn't remember her name. She caught sight of the girl's tearful face as she passed by and Kate felt a pang of regret. First time around, she had never understood the first-years needing to hear a familiar voice after barely twenty-four hours away from home. Now – well, her circumstances were unusual but a little more kindness last time wouldn't have gone amiss. *They're only kids*, she thought. *Some of them have never been away. They don't know anyone – they're scared – so of course they want to talk to their folks.* The only difference was that when the other freshers rang home in 1992, there wasn't much chance they were about to talk to a father who died in 2001.

She took a breath. If dear Mother answered then that would be manageable. But that was not her hope. She checked her watch. Nearly two in the afternoon on a Saturday. Madeleine would surely be at a friend's house where they would spend about ten minutes politely daring each other to open a bottle of rosé before necking one each. Bill, though – if Millwall were playing at home, he'd be watching them at the Old Den with Keith. If not, he would either be out working or enjoying some other game on TV. Kate calculated that he wouldn't mind the interruption. Unless he was in the middle of watching West Ham getting thrashed. If so, no problem – because in those circumstances he wouldn't answer the phone.

She picked up the receiver and dialled 100.

'Operator. How may I direct your call?'

'Hi, I need to make a reverse-charge, um, telephone call.' Kate gave the number and waited for the connection. She heard a phone ringing down the line. The 'new' green phone with buttons instead of a dial and an electric *thwerp* that rang like an outraged cricket – the one in the little hall by the stairs, on the antique side-table which Madeleine had bought, with the wobble that Bill had fixed with a folded envelope.

'Hello?'

The sound of her father's voice had Kate leaning her head against the wooden divider that separated the kiosks. She closed her eyes and experienced the sound as warm milk with just a dash of morphine. She felt pleasantly sick.

'We have a reverse-charge call from a York area phone box. Do you accept the charge?'

'Yes, please.'

No more fainting, no more fainting, no more fainting.

'Thank you – you're through.'

Kate heard the click as the operator hung up. She opened her eyes but could hardly breathe.

'Kate? Hello, Katie, is that you?'

'Daddy,' she gasped. There was a brief pause of surprise at the other end. She hadn't called him that since she was nine.

'You all right, love? Has something happened?'

The last thing she wanted to do was upset him. She gritted her teeth and froze half of her heart to let the other half feel the sun. She imagined being physically attacked by a pack of wild hyenas.

'Nah, no, nothing's happened. Just wanted to hear . . . just wanted to say hello.'

'Well, hello back! I only took you to the station yesterday. Didn't think we'd hear from you till Christmas, to be honest. Not that it's not lovely to talk. You sure you're all right?'

'What you up to? Didn't interrupt a game, did I?'

'No, love. Well, yeah, but it was rubbish so I'd turned it off. Spot of reading. Dr Francis Fukuyama, if you please. *The End of History and the Last Man*, it's called. Brand new. I can smell the paper factory.'

'Why do you buy them in hardback, Dad?'

117

'They last longer.'

Indeed they did. Kate had inherited this book, among others, when her mother had downsized to her bungalow. She had kept it back from the church fête book sale.

'And what's he saying, then?'

'Seems to be saying that the cold war's over and we won, *ergo* we've all agreed that liberal democracy is best and so we don't need to bother arguing any more, *ergo* the end of history. What do you think?'

'I think history might have other ideas.'

'Too right. They say tomorrow never comes but it did yesterday, didn't it?'

Kate laughed. A little pause opened up and she sensed Bill was still puzzled by the call. She said, 'All right, well, I'll let you get on. Just wanted to say hello. I might come and visit a bit sooner than I thought.'

'All right, love, that sounds nice.' There was another pause. 'You are making friends and that, aren't you, love?'

'Yeah! 'Course. Batting them off, I am.'

'Good. Well, just don't get pregnant.'

'That's very much not the plan.'

'Glad to hear it. I'm too beautiful to be a grandad.' Kate smiled but had run out of mental hyenas to battle. She couldn't keep this up any longer. She wanted to say 'I miss you' but didn't dare. Ditto, 'I love you.'

Instead, she could keep her voice level enough to say, 'See you soon, then. Take care of yourself.'

'You too, sweetheart. And call any time you need to.'

'Will do.'

'I'm always here.'

'. . .'

'Kate?'

'Yep. I know you are. Bye.'

'Bye, love.'

Kate put the phone down and sank to the floor with her face in her hands. How many more dead men did she have to talk to today? Just one, hopefully.

It was a complicated kind of hope.

Presently she became aware of a stranger (or so he thought) crouching by her side. She looked up and the heaving sobs turned into a choked laugh. *Yes, of course. Who else?*

Kes – concerned and absurd in his red jeans, carefully chosen odd socks and floral shirt with a flared seventies collar. The sight of him restored her, and her mood swung round on a sixpence like a black cab in a cul-de-sac. He seemed ironed and shrink-wrapped like Amy but the reverse-ageing was less pronounced in this face, given the amount of Botox he was going to pump into it, starting in his early thirties. A TV critic would one day refer to him as 'a Welsh John Barrowman'. Kes found that he could just about live with that despite complaining to his agent that it should really be Barrowman who was 'an American Keven Lloyd'.

'All right there, dear? Bad news from home, is it?'

Kate reached out and he helped her up. 'Thanks. No. No, it's actually great news from home. Just a bit over-whelming. Erm . . .'

'Don't tell me – a distant cousin you've always hated has just won the pools and she's going to blow it on that condo in Biarritz right next to yours and then bang goes the neighbourhood?'

'Yes, exactly.' Kate rapidly tuned in to the wavelength of fantasy bitching she used to enjoy with Kes. 'Typical Marcia. She'll stick fairy lights up everywhere. Such a vulgar prick.'

Kes's face lit up with discovery. 'Yes. What the hell *is* it with Marcia? You've been telling her for years but she won't listen.' Next to Kes, Kate recognised a slightly wan-looking

Benedict student who was beginning to frown in confusion. He shifted his weight, momentarily reminding Kes of his existence. 'Oh, sorry – I'm Kes and this is Jordan.'

'Jury,' said Jury.

'Sorry. Jury.'

'I'm Kate.' She shook their hands.

Kes said, 'I've just got to make a quick call to my tailor on Savile Row, but then maybe I could take you for a stiff gin in the city centre?' Turning ruthlessly to Jury, he added, 'Darling, can we take a rain-check with the tea and crumpet? I feel sure Kate here needs my undivided attention. You know how it is with Marcia.'

Jury started to open his mouth, visibly trying to work out who the hell Marcia was and how she had somehow just cancelled the blow-job he'd been extravagantly promised ten minutes ago. Kes went on: 'But I'll see you later in the bar and don't you dare let me forget.' Before there could be an objection, Kes took Jury's sweet face in his hands and said urgently, 'I want to know a lot more about you. A lot more. You promise you'll be in the bar?'

'Erm . . . okay!'

With that, Kes kissed him lightly on the lips and broke away. The boy blushed but grinned.

'See you later, dearest.' Kes uttered this and nodded with an authority that left the slightly younger man in no doubt that he was now required to go away. Which he did.

Kate watched the youth amble off. In her own time, a gay kiss in public was braver than liberals liked to think but in 1992 Kes was making quite a statement, even on a college campus. She looked at him admiringly but said, 'Predator.'

'I know. Thank God you were here to save me.' Kes went up to the kiosk and rummaged in his pocket for change.

'I meant you.'

'Me?! Oh Kate, how could you? After all this time?' He winked at her and held up an index finger briefly as if to say *I won't be long*, before dropping one of the massive old 50p's into the slot and dialling with care. She turned away and backed off a few paces to give him some privacy.

This was all wrong. She had met Amy too soon and now Kes. And the first time round – that night in the bar – Kes had all but ignored her. His dubious talent for instant friendships had been directed elsewhere. Now he was making what he assumed to be ironic jokes about their long-standing intimacy. All because she had conjured the name 'Marcia' and called her a prick.

On the breeze she could hear a conversation being conducted in Welsh. Kes's tone was cheerful but tender, and she guessed who he was talking to. His older brother David had been in and out of juvenile detention centres since they were children. It would be a few years before Kes's TV success would fund a local college course for David and things would begin to turn around. In the meantime, Kes was giving his time and attention to the brother he worshipped but whose path he had managed to avoid. Kes had made himself the indispensable person and it had worked. Kate wondered at it – a happy ending under construction.

Before long, Kes was off the phone. He clapped his hands loudly. 'Right, then!'

'How was your tailor?'

'Hmm? Oh, he's distraught. I wanted a shimmering gold lamé blazer for the Oscars but he made the last one for Keanu Reeves and has now completely run out of gold lamé. He's quite beside himself.'

'Can't you just ring Keanu and ask to borrow his?' They started to stroll towards town.

'That's a thoughtful suggestion, Kate, but it's well known

that Keanu is aggressively right-wing and homophobic. It's a non-starter.'

'And he particularly hates the Welsh, is that right?'

'He hates us with a passion. He turns up in Porthcawl, ostensibly to play golf . . . you know Keanu's a very keen golfer, don't you?'

Kate pictured Keanu Reeves with a sun-visor and white slacks. She confined a laugh to her abdomen. 'Actually, I didn't know that.'

'Oh my God, he *lives* for golf. But of course he only plays it in Wales so that by night he can go out in disguise and slaughter us one by one with his bare hands.'

Ah, the uncomplicated pleasure of listening to Kes talk bollocks. This was surely what the doctor ordered. 'What's his disguise?'

'His disguise is a matter of controversy. Some say he wears his mother's wedding dress with a veil but I think they've seen too many horror films. My own view is that there's been a terrible misunderstanding. He hates us but he also wants to help us. I think it was his involvement with *Bram Stoker's Dracula* that induced the psychosis. He's conflicted, you see. He tries to lay on his healing hands but he doesn't know his own strength. That's when the bodies start to pile up. It's all deeply regrettable.'

'Is that what brought you here? To escape Keanu's lethal embrace?'

'Yes. That, and the fact that fucking Oxford wouldn't have me.'

Kate chuckled. 'Snap.'

'Ah, a fellow reject.' Kes offered an arm and she took it. 'What's your excuse?'

Kate was glad to be on such familiar territory, looking straight backwards from 1992 with no time-related booby traps to dodge.

'Oxford, right then,' said Kate, happy to tell the truth. 'I lost my shit and was obscenely rude to my interviewer.'

'Oh for God's sake, tell me everything immediately.'

'Well, I'm a computer person at heart and my Computer Science interviewer found that a bit challenging.'

'Because of your provocative ownership of a vagina?'

'I was hoping it wasn't that but it turned out to be completely that.'

'A sexist Oxford don. I find this incredible.'

'He was worried about the hobbies I'd written on my UCAS form.'

Kes was enjoying himself. 'You see, the hobbies I put on my own form were a glorious pack of lies. But I get the sense that yours were truthful.'

Kate took the compliment. God, she had missed him. 'They were. I mentioned my interest in karate.'

'Ah. The violent arts. Is this a casual interest? I mean, do you—'

'I'm a seventh dan black-belt and world silver medallist.'

The eighteen-year-old Kate would never have put it so boldly. She watched Kes absorb the information. He looked at her for the first time in a few minutes, his huge face and teeth set into a wide and helpless smile. All he said was, 'Who got the gold, you appalling loser?'

Kate laughed. 'Her name was Mischa Filatova. Very nice girl, and we were pen-pals for – I mean, we still keep in touch. But the Hungarians were doping their team to distraction. The poor cow looked like Tom Selleck.'

'And our Oxford friend found your achievement too much to bear.'

'He was weirdly aggressive for half an hour. Computer don with egg on his tie and a goatee beard. At the end he suggested a fancy-dress party where I come as Miss Piggy because she also does karate chops.'

'And you took his fancy-dress badinage to heart.'

'I told him he should glue a few more pubes to his chin and go as a cunt.'

Kes closed his eyes to savour the joy of what he'd just heard. 'Oh Kate, I can see we're going to get along rather wonderfully.'

Kate got back to her room at around 5 p.m. after a couple of gin martinis with Kes in the matinée bar of the Theatre Royal. Maxed-out on three credit cards, he had bounced a cheque for the occasion. They had chatted artfully as if they were minor aristocrats slumming it amongst the hoi polloi, or in this case the well-to-do retirees of York lapping up an Ayckbourn. She remembered that Kes brought out the enjoyable worst in her. Years of minding her vocabulary, minding her gifts – making sure she gave nobody the excuse to say she was 'too clever by half' – all released in the bitchy company of this working-class-with-airs-and-graces bisexual funbucket. He had even made a mild pass.

'Lady Katherine, I own that I am not yet one and twenty, but I think I must warn you that I am no mere seeker after the pleasures of the cock. I am also no stranger to the charms of the WOOLWA.'

'Lord Keven of Newport, I appreciate the delicacy of your proposal. But must confess that my WOOLWA is promised to another.'

'Another!? How can this be? Who is this troublesome cad? I shall challenge him to a lethal competition and destroy him instantly.'

'Frisbees at dawn?'

'Razor-edged frisbees at any time.'

'Difficult to throw. Ouch.'

'I hadn't thought of that. But may I be serious – you are attached?'

Kate smiled into her gin. 'Keven, we must have a secret or two between us. Otherwise it gets boring, don't you think?'

Kes was trapped between his insatiable curiosity and the threat of appearing to be dull. They clinked glasses. 'To Kate's lover,' he announced, 'whomsoever they may be. I hope he or she appreciates you.'

'He does,' said Kate. 'He will.'

She sat on her bed, contemplated her unpacked suitcase and then immediately lay down. Her tights and pinafore dress were annoying so she scrambled out of them. *Jeans and a top later. Get comfy. Hmm, bit pissed. This body isn't an alcoholic.* The two gins that would normally serve as a hearty breakfast were now coursing through her blood with a long-forgotten potency.

Her thoughts turned to Luke, vaguely pondering the conundrum of time-travel and monogamy. It wasn't a problem turning down Kes because she wasn't attracted to Kes. But this was surely going to be an issue.

She sniffed sharply and sat up. So then, technically, she was single twice over. She was either a widow who didn't have to be faithful to Luke because he was dead, or she was a young person who didn't have to be faithful to Luke because she had never met the guy. But it wasn't that simple. She couldn't dodge the emotional reality of their twenty-eight years. They had not divorced. They were together. He had died but now he was alive. Her husband was alive. And she could save him. What was lost had been found.

The slight problem was that he didn't know he was lost.

Kate relaxed back into the pillow.

I will play it cool. I'll play it real cool. When Luke walks into that bar? I'll be totally cool.

Chapter 9

She stalked into the room as if returning to the scene of a crime.

The bar of Benedict College resembled an airport departure lounge endured by its unlucky passengers with a British blend of stoicism and alcohol. It was a large, L-shaped room where the bottom of the 'L' formed a quaint 'non-smoking area', carpeted and shop-fresh through lack of use. The main body of the bar was the setting of a vast, ongoing brawl between broken tiles, strip-lighting and chipped Formica. The walls were brown but with that hint of yellow that gives horse manure its element of drama. Around the edges were a series of semi-circular 'booths' featuring red plastic banquettes and tiny, quivering tables guaranteed to immediately spill any drink they came into contact with. The metal chair legs had all lost their rubber stoppers years ago and the effect of a hundred of them scraping against the 'terracotta' floor was – until you learned to tune it out – what insanity might sound like if it lived with a dentist. It was a room that couldn't hear itself think and which understood no smells but tobacco and last night's beer. Kate felt immediately at home.

For a moment she was tempted to take a seat in the non-smoking area but then remembered that she was apparently eighteen and not supposed to be interested in a nice sit down in a comfy chair. She had passed a shoe shop earlier and had found her eyes lingering on a pair of Scholl's. She turned into the main bar and paused, surveying the field of battle. That was the corner. The table she'd been sitting at on her own when Luke had approached. It was empty. She affected a casual stroll to the bar, trying to tell her heart to calm down.

Good old Malcolm, the impassive and almost entirely silent barman, was modelling his usual costume – a darts shirt and powder-blue slacks. A publican's taste for his own supply and a Lambert and Butler permanently smouldering in the ashtray behind him had prematurely aged Malcolm's hangdog kisser but he couldn't be older than thirty-five. Oh boy – even Malcolm was younger than her. *Be cool. Just get a drink.* Kate had found a tenner in the pocket of these jeans so at least the money problem was fixed for now. Everything else looked normal. The corner was empty, as it should be. Malcolm was ponderously shining a pint glass, as he should be.

And Toby Harker was standing right next to her. As he absolutely should not be.

Kate froze, staring down at the picture of Florence Nightingale on the back of her clownishly large banknote. *No, no, no. Not Toby. Not yet.*

Toby had buggered up his entrance. He shouldn't appear for at least an hour. He should be in his dressing room doing vocal exercises and working on his lines. He wanders over to the corner banquette and bums a light from Kes and they end up arguing about Jacques Derrida. Then they bond over how Kate and Luke – these two 'love-birds' in the corner – are rudely ignoring everyone else and are obviously about to bang each other. And then Kes asks Toby, 'Where exactly is all the cock-fun in York?' and Toby says he's not sure that he can help. No, Toby shouldn't be standing here in his green jeans and white t-shirt and navy waistcoat and his straight arm on the bar featuring his ancient Swatch and his . . . *oh God, his ponytail! His braid!*

Kate stole another glance to her left at the teenage Toby. The single braid of his dirty blond hair limply dissected a strong left cheekbone, ending somewhere around his jaw, where it clearly irritated his spots. The braid agreed with the unwashed hair but was in violent dispute with the velvet waistcoat, which itself had a problem with the perfectly fitting jeans. He was like a newly-regenerated time lord who hadn't yet found his look. At some future point, money would nego-tiate the peace. The crusty would disappear, and the dandy would meet the beefcake in an expensive tailor's on New Bond Street. Not long from now, Toby would re-embrace the traditional signifiers of masculinity as well as the traditional value of shampoo. In the meantime, this was glorious. Kate looked away with a smirk just a fraction too late.

'Hello! How d'you do?'

'Oh. Yes.'

'I'm Toby.'

'Yes. Er, Kate.'

He kept his place at the bar with his Swatch arm and used his other to shake hands in an awkward backward motion that made her smile. Like all the old/young friends she had met today, he sounded like he'd just had half a toke on a helium balloon. And his accent was a little closer to his Edinburgh home than she remembered. Otherwise, this young man was doing a tremendously good impression of Toby. Kate felt encouraged. 'I was just admiring your braid.'

'Och, this stupid thing.' He instantly vanished it into the confusion of his ponytail. 'I keep meaning to get rid of it but . . . Some girls made it for me while I was lying in a field.'

'Were you drugged and tied up?'

He smiled briefly, revealing the gap between his front teeth. 'Drugged but not tied up. Glastonbury.'

'Ah.'

'Were you there?'

'Nope. No, I was . . .' Kate turned over the banknote in her hands for a second. She was what? She was in Grenada winning a silver medal in the World Karate Championships? Let's not do that. 'I was . . . washing my hair.'

The swiftest cloud of uncertainty crossed Toby's brow as he appeared to wonder if this girl was taking the piss and whether or not he minded. 'It doesn't smell, you know.'

'What doesn't?'

'The hair. After a while it doesn't smell of anything.'

'Yes, I'm sure. I wasn't taking the—'

'You can smell it if you like.'

'I'm not going to *smell* you, Toby.'

He blinked in amused surprise. Okay, that might have been just a touch too familiar.

'Can I get you a drink?'

Oh *great*.

'No thanks, I'm . . .' What? Driving? Grieving?

'I'm . . . trying to cut down. I just want a glass of water really,' she said. 'Actually, I'm not feeling too . . .'

'Can we get a glass of water, please, the lady's feeling unwell.' Toby made the request with an authority that had Malcolm reaching for a glass with something close to haste. Kate leaned on the bar. The unutterable madness of her situation came at her in waves and this was a big one. 'Sorry, I'm all right really.'

'Of course you are. But you're also shaking. And I don't usually have that effect on women so I thought it might be something else.'

'Here you go, love,' said Malcolm, roughly doubling the

number of words Kate had ever heard him say. He pushed a glass of water her way and she picked it up and gulped. She listened to her heart, calming it with her breathing, noticing the blood in her veins, the pressure of the floor through her soles, the cold of the metal bar rail in her palm. Toby seemed to figure there wasn't much he could do for now and she heard him quietly order himself a pint of bitter. Dearest Toby . . .

But this was no good. Calmer now, she risked a glance at her watch. 7.38. The time was six minutes to Luke. First time around she had gawped as he walked through the door – that door, the one at the far end near the pool table. And she had looked down at her watch – this watch on this young wrist. It had seemed the obvious thing to do. Just as a doctor records the time of death, Kate had recorded love at first sight. 7.44 p.m.

She had to get to the corner table. 'Thank you,' she said to Toby, 'you've been really kind but I need to go and sit down.'

Toby wiped some beer froth away from his top lip. 'Sure. There's an empty table in that corner. Shall we—'

'I mean on my own.'

'Right. Yes, of course.'

'Sorry. Is that horrible? It's just, I'm waiting for someone.'

'Right.' He took a forbearing sip of beer. She saw him wondering what to say next and had to stop herself from hugging him. Toby didn't invest much of his pride in his looks but the poor kid was now visibly contemplating a haircut.

Kate heard herself talking. 'He's just some bloke really. I mean, someone I used to know. No big deal. But it turns out he's a fresher here. What were the chances? I'd introduce you but . . . well, I'm sure I will but . . .'

Toby was nodding through this but had regained his

usual self-sufficiency. He pocketed his change and said, 'Cool. See you later.'

'I mean, he's probably forgotten me.'

He met her eyes kindly and said, 'I doubt that.'

Kate was silent for a moment. A thought was trying very hard to get her attention. It was an exciting and deeply troubling thought. In fact, it was deeply troubling because it was exciting. But it didn't get a chance to explain itself because it was interrupted by a bellowing Welshman.

'KATE MARSDEN, YOU INSATIABLE WHORE!' The bar had begun to fill and half of it now turned to see Kes striding towards Kate with a face of gleeful teeth. He had the look of a man who'd been drinking since lunch and had no intention of stopping till roughly the same time tomorrow.

'Christ,' Kate muttered as he arrived at the bar. She snatched another look at her watch. Five minutes.

'So this is your secret boyfriend!' Kes announced, clapping Toby on the back.

'Er, no,' said Toby, putting what was left of his pint down and wiping a soaking hand on his jeans.

'Very much not,' she said, 'I mean, not *very much* not but also . . . not. In fact, I don't have a secret boyfriend. Or any other boyfriend.'

'"My WOOLWA is promised to another." You said that not three hours since! I assumed it was this handsome bastard. Oh Christ! I spilled your pint!'

'Yes,' said Toby. 'It's nae bother.'

'It's an unforgivable bother! I can't apologise enough. Barman! A large whisky for my Scottish friend here! A single malt, if such a thing exists in this godforsaken shithole!'

'Erm. I'm sure that's not necessary,' Kate interjected.

A sanguine Toby turned to her: 'I'm actually fine with that.'

'Okay, well, I'll see you both later.'

Kes flapped his exhausted chequebook on the bar and started looking for a pen. 'You're not going?'

'She needs to sit down,' Toby said.

'What have you done to her, you gorgeous brute? Oh, thank you!' Kes received Toby's silver fountain pen and inspected it with admiration as he talked. 'Let me tell you: Marsden and I go way back. It was in the innocent days of just after lunch that she revealed to me—'

It was clear that the only way to shut Kes up and get away was to dumbfound him. Kate glanced at her watch as she began to speak.

Four minutes.

'Keven, this is Toby. Toby, Keven. You both have quite strong views about Jacques Derrida. Kes is a big fan but, Toby, you think he's a fraud and that Deconstruction is just an excuse for English professors to do philosophy badly. Is that right?'

The movement of Toby's pint had frozen halfway to his mouth. 'That does sound like the kind of thing I might say,' he managed.

'Great,' said Kate, picking up her water. 'Apart from that, you don't have much in common except you're both Aquarians and neither of you likes prawns. Excuse me.' She turned and started for the corner, leaving the bar aghast. Luckily Kes was already too pissed to take much of this in. Over her shoulder she heard him say, 'So then, Toby is it? What the *fuck* is your problem with Derrida?'

She dodged and weaved to get to the table, which had now taken on a religious importance. *Double-seat, double-seat, gotta getta double-seat.* The mantra of an old Ben Elton stand-up routine about how the British turn into Nazis when finding seats on trains beat through her head and at this point she would have gladly chopped someone in the throat to get to the hallowed table next to the loo. She wriggled round the trembling table and set down her glass.

Three minutes. Made it.

Surely something would now go wrong. Surely Lauren the Aussie Christian would come and ask her why she was such a weirdo. Surely Amy would block her view of the pool-table door, standing there with her hands on her hips and making another speech about how Kate was a self-harmer in denial. 'A self-harmer in denial.' Maybe that was exactly right. Maybe that's what she had been, back in her 10,000-day kitchen. She focused on the pool table: a game of doubles – three boys and a girl. A third-year lawyer was trying to show a female fresher where to aim the cue ball. If she minded she didn't let it show, laughing and flipping her perm to one side as she got down to the table. *Sandra Milhouse*, Kate recalled. *Sandra Milhouse, the silly fucker with goldfish in her room.*

One minute.

She had lost sight of Toby and Kes. And was Luke actually going to turn up? Why would he? Because other things had been different today and there was no reason to believe that—

There. Standing in the doorway, politely letting someone out, running a careless hand through his dark hair.

Luke Fairbright, nineteen years old, come again.

Chapter 10

He wandered through the doorway and she stared at him as if re-introduced to her own heart. She thought of the times she had watched him from the bedroom window as he left the house. Observed but unaware, vulnerable in his innocence. Luke in his body, ambling down the street – the shape of love.

'You,' she whispered.

He was making his way through the room with no more than his usual saunter, but to Kate it was shockingly fast. In dreams, dead people move slowly, if at all. They wade through sepia. They shimmer like a hologram and say wise things at half-speed.

He moved round the pool table and she half wanted to scream, half wanted to vanish into thin air. She'd never known him to miss a date and here he was, right on time. Dressed as before: black jeans, black boots, black imitation leather jacket from the secondhand shop in Salisbury. A cheap steel earring in each lobe. All in black except under the jacket – his shirt. The blue and grey grandad shirt that she'd found in the back of the wardrobe along with other student treasures that Luke couldn't let go. It was the shirt that she found clutched in her fists every morning. The one that suddenly belonged to him again. What she had understood in her head now finally began to wrap itself tightly around her guts: he didn't know she slept with that shirt because he didn't know he was dead; he wasn't on time for a date because there was no date; he wasn't looking for her because he didn't know who she was. And yet . . .

Alive! Luke's alive! She gripped the table with one hand and wiped her tears away with another. She risked a glance up – he approached the end of the bar, the other end from Toby and Kes. On his way he passed a couple of women, one of whom just openly gasped at him and nudged her friend as he walked by. *Ah, yes,* Kate recalled, trying to steady herself, *that's the other thing. That's going to be a problem.* She remembered a brief period when Luke was in his mid-thirties and he would angle himself topless in their bedroom mirror, dismayed by the beginnings of a beer gut. Instead of telling him to stop whining and go to the gym, she'd claimed to prefer him with a bit more beef. If she was really going to quibble, *this* Luke was too thin. But no one here was quibbling. Kate remembered what a pain in the arse this used to be – he was obviously fucking gorgeous. There were straight men in this room who were looking at Luke like they didn't know whether to hit him or buy him a bunch of flowers.

Kate dithered. Why the hell was she just sitting here?

Don't freak him out. Maybe just go over and buy him a drink. Too much? Yes, clearly *way* too much. Just stay here. He gets his lager, turns around and sees an empty table with a girl reading *Orlando*.

Fuck! Where's Orlando? *Left it in the fucking room!*

He won't see a girl reading a book. He's about to turn around and see a girl staring at him like she's seen a ghost. Or the man in her dreams. And both.

Okay, screw the table. The table will keep. Kate summoned all the courage she had ever needed, slowly rose and walked unsteadily towards her young dead husband. He had popped an elbow on the bar and was apparently whistling to himself. A near-silent rendition of 'Chirpy Chirpy Cheep Cheep', unless Kate missed her guess. That was his 'keep cheerful when the lights go out' tune of choice, inherited from his mother. He was in profile as she approached, fiddling with his right earring – another nervous tell. She thought of the first time around – no wonder he'd headed straight for the girl reading the familiar book. *Orlando* was his only friend in the room.

Kate sensed him glancing at her as she reached the bar but she kept her eyes firmly on Malcolm. She fished in her back pocket for the tenner, trying to ignore Luke's absurd glamour. She wondered at it. This is why it's weird when you meet someone famous, because as far as you're concerned you've already met them. They haven't met you but they're imagining how you feel – because every famous person started out as a fan. So there's a strange intimacy that leaves both parties feeling tongue-tied and mutually protective. It's almost like love.

She was standing right next to him now and dared to take a slow, deep inhalation. He never wore after shave but there was a trace of Lynx Oriental. She felt like saving him a couple of unnecessary years of underarm eczema and telling him he needed to switch to an alcohol-free substitute right now. Also, that he had a brain tumour. But again, that just might be a *tad* forward.

Keep it together, keep it together, keep it together.

Kate glanced round at the corner table and saw that a bunch of third-year medics had already settled themselves and were opening bags of crisps on the table to share. Christ, it was all going wrong.

She caught Malcolm's eye as he shuffled over and jerked his chin to her imperceptibly. At least she could get the same drink as last time.

'Pint of Scrumpy Jack, please.'

'Scrumpy's off.'

Kate blinked at him as if he'd just told her the Earth was made of Lego. 'No. That's not right,' she announced.

Malcolm looked slightly hurt. 'Well . . . it is what it is.'

'The Scrumpy can't be off. Not tonight.'

Malcolm shrugged and looked along the bar. 'We've got Strongbow.'

Kate panicked as yet another slice of the Luke and Kate Creation Cake appeared to eat itself before her very eyes. 'Strongbow!? How can I *possibly* drink Strongbow?' *Ooh. That didn't sound good.* She realised she sounded like a middle-aged, middle-class woman making an entitled dick of herself. Malcolm reached behind for his lit cigarette and regrouped. He had clearly seen this kind of thing before with cider drinkers.

'I know what you mean. Strongbow really is piss.' He took a drag and exhaled thoughtfully. 'We've got some bottled stuff in the chillers.'

Kate sensed Luke sipping his beer and listening to every word. She said, 'Sorry, yes. Fine, no, I'm being a total bellend. Strongbow's fine.' Malcolm replaced his fag complacently and reached for a glass.

Kate stole a glance at Luke, who was looking right at her with a half-smile. He averted his eyes and watched Malcolm pour the pint. Kate did the same, biting her lower lip so hard she nearly drew blood. She turned back to Luke.

'Hi,' she said.

'Hi.'

'You must think I'm crazy.'

'No, no. You've just got some very strong views about Scrumpy Jack.'

This was hardly the impression Kate had been hoping

to make but at least it was an impression. She went with it. She went with it a lot.

'Ha ha! Yes, I take cider *incredibly* seriously. The thing you have to understand about the way they make Scrumpy Jack is . . .' Kate realised that in the great cathedral of her memory there was absolutely nothing to be found under the subject heading, 'the way they make Scrumpy Jack is'. She just liked drinking the stuff because it helped her forget that she could remember basically everything else. Fortunately Malcolm arrived with her pint so she styled-out the pause by handing over her warm ten-pound note. Malcolm received it with a frown. She looked back at Luke, hoping he'd forgotten what she was talking about.

'You were saying . . .' he prompted, annoyingly.

'Yes,' Kate said. She took a drink and watched Malcolm open the till and sigh at the meagre state of the float, before mournfully closing the till, taking a massive Bell's whisky bottle full of change and starting to slowly and rhythmically shake silver and coppers onto a bar towel. 'Yes,' Kate continued, 'it's made from very special apples.'

'Special apples. Right.' Luke wasn't even bothering to keep the satire out of his voice and had arranged his face into the kind of nodding sincerity he would use a few years later for charity workers on the doorstep.

Kate suddenly felt like slapping the little shit. Standing there, smugly innocent of the nine months of torment he'd put her through. She hadn't been dragged back to the 1990s to be mocked by this *child*. And not even the fun bit of the 1990s but the shit bit where white boys thought nothing of spraying their armpits with deodorant calling itself 'Oriental' and the word 'chairperson' was a joke and 'recycled loo roll' was a joke and Malcolm was sparking up another Lambert in a public place and 'global warming' was something that may or may not happen in the 'future' where we would all be living on Mars anyway and . . .

But it was now a matter of pride that she persevere. She looked at him squarely. 'Special apples. Yes, that's what I said. They grow them in a climate controlled dome just outside Salisbury. I don't know if you know the area? I'm a big fan of Wiltshire generally but Salisbury itself can be full of facetious twats. So they get the special apples and instead of just pressing them in a machine like an idiot would – like an idiot doing an English degree but hasn't even read *Middlemarch* would – they separate them into special *groups* of special apples – thank you, Malcolm.'

'Sorry about the change.'

'That's no problem whatsoever.' Kate began stuffing the half-ton of massive coins into her pockets. 'They get groups of apples, separated both by size and genetic compatibility according to European Union – by which obviously I mean European Community – regulations, and then basically fry them.'

She took a swift drink of cider and looked up at Luke, daring him to challenge her. Luke's sarcasm had been quickly replaced by a rising anxiety. He took a drink and said, 'I see.'

'Do you, though?'

'I think so.'

'You heard me say that they fry the apples.'

'I did, yeah.'

'And you've nothing to say about that.'

'Actually, I do have one thing to say.' Luke looked around the room as if he didn't want to be overheard.

'And what's that?' Kate asked.

'I've missed you.'

Chapter 11

'Marsden does seem to faint on a regular basis. Could it be vaginismus?'

'I just ran over. I mean, she basically lives here now. I might as well open a B&B.'

'You've been very good to her, Amy. My God, Marsden is deeply troubled. I salute her!'

'D'you not think this is just a wee bit odd? She looked like she was five seconds from an aneurysm when I offered to buy her a drink.'

'My dear Toby, that's the natural reaction when—'

'Please don't make a joke about Scots and money.'

'I wasn't going to.'

'Yes, you were.'

'Yes, I was.'

'Lads, you don't have to stay.'

'We'll leave you in peace if you like, Amy, but I don't see why Kate's your responsibility.'

'Because I'm the girl.'

'Nonsense.'

'We won't hear of it, Amelia! Toby, pass the medicinal brandy.'

'Oi! This is my room and that's for Fainting Fanny when she comes round.'

'Quite right, Amelia. The Karate Child does have remarkable powers of recovery, mind. She was on the floor crying her eyes out when I met her near the phones. And then she . . . well, she perked up no end. It seems fanciful but it was as if she knew me already.'

There was a thoughtful silence. The next voice was Amy's. 'If anything, it's not what we're doing for her but what she's doing to us.'

Toby now: 'Go on? Kes, put her cider down.'

'Sorry.'

'Well,' Amy continued, 'how long have we all known her? Kes had a drink with her in the theatre but that's not exactly *This Is Your Life*. You and me can't have spent more than five minutes apiece with her. That tall bloke who caught her scampered off to the off-licence to get us all booze. I mean . . . here we are. Eight o'clock on the first night of Freshers' Week holding a bloody vigil.'

'Seems only decent.'

'Don't get me wrong, Toby, I don't mind. It's just . . .'

'No, I know what you mean. By the way, Kes, I saw that.'

'Sorry. Marsden can have the brandy.'

'For Christ's sake!'

'But you're both right,' Kes said through a cidery burp. 'I don't know what it is about this Kate Marsden. She seems to have an aura.'

Kate felt bad about eavesdropping on her friends but had taken the last minute to gather her wits. She felt a presence at the side of the bed. Toby. 'I'm not sure I believe in auras.'

Now Kes again, from the corner of the room: 'Me neither, come to think of it. But there's something going on. We must have all loved her in another life.'

Another pause. Kate decided it was time to wake up.

Here was Toby, pulling the little student duvet protectively over her shoulder. Her eyes were only half open as they met his. She said, 'Where's Luke?'

'Who?'

Amy joined Toby by the bed. 'She means the tall bloke.'

Toby kept his eyes on Kate. 'He's gone.'

'To the offy!' shouted Kes from his chair.

'I need to talk to Luke,' Kate said, swinging her legs out of Amy's bed and finding the floor.

'Which one's Luke?' Kes asked.

'I just said. The tall lad that went to the offy.'

Toby withdrew to Amy's desk chair and Kate heard him mutter to himself, 'He's not *that* fucking tall.'

It was at this point that Kate realised she wasn't wearing any trousers. 'Erm . . .'

Amy handed over her jeans. 'Sorry, love, I took your jeans and boots off. Don't worry, the fellas stepped outside.'

Kes lit a cigarette. 'I was all for having a good old stare but Tobias here literally pushed me out of the door with his gallant biceps.'

Toby found the ceiling in embarrassment and said quietly, 'Oh, shoosh yer face.'

Kate took her clothes upside down and all of Malcolm's change spilled onto the floor. 'Oh, bollocks.'

'Look at that, Marsden's a millionaire!'

Kate pulled on her jeans, causing Toby to take a sudden interest in Amy's lava lamp. She said, 'Sorry I've been so shit. I didn't mean to spoil your first night here.'

'It's your first night too, Kate,' Amy said, taking Kes's fag from him and stubbing it out in a cactus plant.

Kes watched the action with equanimity and said, 'Absolutely. Anyway, we brought our drinks.'

'I brought the drinks,' Toby corrected, 'you carried Kate.'

'That's it. You brought the drinks, I carried Kate.'

'And I just organised,' said Amy, lighting a joss stick.

Kate couldn't help being amused that her oldest/newest friends had rescued her again but without being so careless as to leave their booze in the bar. They were students after all.

'Let's go back to the bar!' she announced. 'I'll get a round in.' She glanced at the constellation of change on Amy's carpet. 'I've still got eight pounds, twenty-five pee. We're in for a hell of a night!'

Toby looked at the huge pile of coins and frowned.

'Jesus Christ, not Benedict bar again!' Kes almost shouted. 'It's a screeching fuckhole beyond imagining.'

Toby knelt down and began collecting Kate's money for her. She pursed her lips as she realised he was secretly counting it. Surely a spy in the making. He said, 'Maybe find a pub, then?'

'I'll go with the flow,' Amy said easily, 'but we should really wait for the tall bloke. He'll be back any minute.'

Kate was suddenly in no hurry to be in Luke's presence again. 'Okay, just text him.'

Toby's hands stopped and he looked at Kate. 'Just what him?'

'I mean, just leave a note on the door for him.'

Kes let out a semi-discreet fart. 'Who are we talking about?'

'"Luke", apparently,' said Toby. He had stacked Kate's change into columns and now looked up at her. 'It's exactly eight pounds, twenty-five.'

Hmm, not much of a spy then. Spies don't just announce the results of their spying.

Kate knelt down opposite him and began to pocket the money. He handed her a pile or two of silver and she noted his bitten nails and the surprising warmth of his fingers as they brushed against hers. 'What can I say?' she grinned at him. 'A girl on a budget knows the price of cider, right?'

Toby returned the smile. 'Evidently.'

There was a knock at the door.

'Oh, that'll be Luke,' Amy said on her way to answer.

Kate and Toby didn't move. She found herself listening to Amy at the door and her gaze wandering freely over Toby's hands, Toby's watch, the fine blond hairs of Toby's bare arms.

'That's nice of you, love. What do we owe you?'

'Oh, don't worry, my grant came through early.'

'Come on in.'

Stiffly and automatically, Kate stood. Physically impressive in the small room, Luke advanced into the space like the world's most hesitant panther. There was a brief round of re-introductions during which Kate had time to collect herself. Behind her, she sensed Toby returning to his seat.

Luke held up one of two plastic bags from Oddbins. 'I didn't know whether people liked red or white so I got both.'

Kes was immediately on his feet, relieving Luke of both bottles. 'That's the kind of decision-making I can do business with.'

Luke regarded Kate warily. 'And I . . . sorry, it's Kate, isn't it?'

'Yes,' she said. 'It's Kate.'

'I thought so. Anyway, I got you this.'

From the second bag he produced a litre bottle of Scrumpy Jack. In her t-shirt and jeans and bare feet, Kate took a couple of steps towards him and took the bottle in silence. Looking at the label, she asked, 'Why did you say that you'd missed me?'

There was a level of awkwardness that a student room containing five British humans was not built to cope with. Luke blushed and started to babble. 'Yeah, I'm so sorry about that. I didn't think you were going to – it's just a stupid line.'

'A line?'

'Yeah. A chat-up line. Sorry.'

Amy handed a corkscrew to Kes and Kate caught them sharing two pairs of raised eyebrows. Toby was still inspecting the lava lamp but this time as if he might hate the lava lamp and everything lava lamps stood for. Amy cleared her throat and started to put on a CD.

Luke went on. 'From a film. Sorry. That makes it even cornier, doesn't it? From *Sammy and Rosie Get* . . . well, *Get Laid.*'

'Ah, yes.' Kes came in swiftly as he made short work of opening Luke's bottle of Spanish plonk. 'Roland Gift and Frances Barber. La Barber.'

'Film Four, 1987, directed by Stephen Frears,' Toby flatly informed the lava lamp.

'Yeah, exactly,' said Luke. So . . .' He looked around but there was nowhere to sit. Kate was now staring at him and Amy's speakers sounded the first notes of REM's 'Losing My Religion'.

Luke carried on: 'So . . . yeah. Roland Gift meets this girl and says "I missed you" and she says "We've never met" and he says "If we'd met, it would have been worse."'

'I see,' said Kate, swaying slightly.

'So he's kind of cheekily assuming a pre-destiny, where in fact—'

'I get it.'

'Sorry. Really cheesy. People don't normally faint.'

At this, Toby turned his attention directly to Luke. 'It's something you've said before, then, I take it.' He said it with his most charming smile and the lightness of tone that public school boys deploy when they want to call someone an arsehole just to see if they notice.

Luke did not. He shrugged affably and said, 'Well, only once. And it didn't really work, but . . .'

Kes and Amy chuckled indulgently and started asking Luke friendly questions about what course he was doing. Kate sat slowly back down on Amy's bed and regarded the boy with whom she'd shared her life. She saw how easy it was for him. He was going to shrug and self-deprecate his way through it all. He would bat off compliments and insults in exactly the same way – by simply not hearing them.

So this is how you did it. This is how you subsisted for twenty-eight years without getting an actual job.

Luke elected to sit next to her on the bed. Kes had apparently been holding forth on the subject of literary novels. 'It's exactly the same with Ben Okri,' he concluded.

In a long day of surreal moments, Kate reflected that this was an extraordinary wind-up. The man whom everyone in the room knew had just tried to chat her up was now sitting next to her and talking about Ben Okri. She marvelled at how these young people just accepted the weirdness and rolled with it. They were so light.

'The thing about Ben Okri,' Luke was saying, 'is that he needs to go back to short stories to refresh his style.'

If Kate's eyeballs were capable of swivelling as far back as they suddenly needed to, she would now have a close-up view of her own brain. 'Ben Okri needs to go back to short stories to refresh his style' was one of Luke's *Greatest Hits*. He wheeled it out every time he thought he needed to say something that sounded smart about books. It was right up there with '*Ulysses* is actually amazingly conventional' and 'I prefer Ian McEwan's earlier, darker stuff'. The fact that Luke hadn't read *Ulysses* or a single word written by Ben Okri was beside the point. He was yet to meet anyone willing to call out his bullshit. He was, in other words, yet to properly meet Kate Marsden.

Kate crossed one leg over the other and tried to look

out of the window but it was dark now and all she saw was her own reflection.

Give the kid a break. He's a fresher and an English student – of course he's lying about books. You, on the other hand – you're lying about everything.

She found Toby's gaze in the window – a look of quizzical concern. Whatever she was doing with her face, it didn't look normal. What would be the normal thing to do now? *Join in. Must join in.* She heard what she had to say – she was saying it in an unnaturally loud voice. 'So, Luke – what's your *very favourite* short story by Ben Okri?'

He turned to her in surprise but kept his composure. 'Oh God, so many, so many . . .'

'Yes, of course,' she sympathised.

I've so had it with your bullshit.

'Well . . .' He picked soulfully at the loose thread of his ripped jeans. 'Oh God, you're not really going to make me pick just one?'

'Yes, I am,' said Kate, beaming at him pleasantly, 'I really am going to make you pick just one.'

Luke gave a brave little smile and looked deeply troubled. It was surely very unfair that someone who loved Ben Okri as much as Luke should be expected to choose just one story. He waited patiently for someone to rescue him. It took about three seconds.

'There are good things in *Incidents at the Shrine*,' Kes ventured, as if agreeing with something Luke had just said.

Luke nodded painfully. He shrugged in a worldly manner. 'But the reviews . . .'

'Oh God, yes, the fucking reviews were—'

'Hang on,' said Kate.

Kes continued, 'Well, critics are all wankers, as we know.'

'As we know,' Luke repeated, as if giving his magnanimous blessing to this powerful insight.

Kate wasn't giving up that easily. 'Yes, but *Incidents at the Shrine* is the name of a collection, isn't it? What's your favourite story *within* that collection, Luke?'

Luke – unfazed and apparently quite used to young women insisting on his opinion of such matters – turned to her. 'Well, the first one in the collection, the one that's . . .' His head spun quickly back to Kes and he frowned as if the trifling matter of a title was something his new assistant might help him with.

'"Laughter Beneath the Bridge",' Kes obliged.

'Yes, that's . . . is that . . . that's not the first one, is it?'

'I believe it is. I might be wrong.'

'No, sorry, I think you're right. Well, it has this lyrical quality that . . .'

Kate didn't listen to the rest of Luke's content-free speech. That little hesitation he had feigned, that reflexive gaslighting of Kes to find out which story came first – it chilled her. She started to pull on her socks.

Luke was still talking. '. . . qualities which get confused with Zola but I think that's a false opposition. I suppose I have an affinity with French literature anyway, y'know, what with my name.'

Kate shook her head and tied the laces of her Doc Martens with abrupt movements. Toby couldn't resist the bait but managed to keep his tone neutral. 'What is it about your name, Luke?'

'Well, it's actually spelt L-U-C. Something in the family going way back. My dad thinks we're descended from Eleanor of Aquitaine, but I don't really believe that.'

Kate finished knotting and reached for her coat. It was fucking unbelievable. Of all of Luke's first-term affectations, she'd forgotten this one: the guy was still pretending to be

French. She stood and announced, 'Anyway, I'm going back to the bar.'

Luke, or apparently 'Luc', retracted his long legs but she stepped over the vacated space anyway. There was a volley of baffled objections but Kate was already at the door when she turned back to Luke with a look so severe it silenced the room. She spoke softly to him. 'You shouldn't tell someone you missed them when you don't know who they are.'

'I know. Sorry. Like I say, it was just—'

'Don't ever do it again.'

She closed the door carefully behind her. At that moment the CD track ended and Amy's low voice was just audible: 'That girl needs help.'

Chapter 12

The October air had turned sharp and Kate hugged her coat around her. She headed towards the centre of the campus, unwilling to return to the busy bar or her empty room, although neither could make her feel as lonely as the boy she'd just left.

It was as if her favourite movie was lost and she'd been forced to sit through its shittest imaginable prequel. As if someone had recorded over the only copy of *Casablanca* and replaced it with two hours of Rick Blaine standing in front of a shaving mirror, combing his eyebrows and failing to get his bow-tie straight; rehearsing his coolest lines and getting them all slightly wrong. 'Here's looking at you, krid' and 'We'll always have Doris' and 'I think Ben Okri should go back to short stories to refresh his style.'

Why hadn't it annoyed her the first time round? Luke's weird lies and affectations? The goose crap on the path glistened and she looked up at the full moon for inspiration.

Well, the first time it was charming because she was in love. And being in love is when you truly live in the present: when every moment is a discovery, every tiny detail is pregnant with meaning. Grief though . . . grief is the opposite of meaning; grief is where the present can't breathe; where the past is everywhere you look; where every new moment is dead on arrival. Grief is Groundhog Day.

Oh yes, that and the fact that she was furious with him. Furious for the dumb line about missing her. Just for that second in the bar she had imagined a glimpse of the man she knew was trapped in the body of the boy in front of her. But no. Luke really was a stranger and the man was yet to grow around him. And not just grow – the mature Luke would take work to build and Kate had a pretty good idea that it was she who had laid about half of the bricks. No, we don't lie to people to sound cool. No, sounding cool isn't very important in the first place. No, we don't expect the person we live with to clean the flat because she was born with a uterus. No, we don't go into a two-hour sulk when we're upset and wait for someone to ask us what the matter is. No, being very serious does not make you clever. And being clever is less important than being kind.

Yes, I'm the Girl From the Future. I always was. I knew things. Why didn't you?

And was she supposed to do it all again? For another twenty-eight years?

Kate took a left past Derwent College. The pendulum of her thoughts took the inevitable swing back to self-reproach. So how kind had *she* been today? How *wise*? What was she doing right now if not sulking? Okay, maybe these were extraordinary circumstances, but aren't they always? Do you wait until you feel kind before you behave kindly or do you do it anyway? Does a fire fighter hang back and watch a house burn because he's 'not really in the mood today'? Do you love your partner only when they're at their best?

Kate realised she'd arrived at the Still Spot: a miniature secular college chapel where students could come to find

151

some quiet. It centred on a cute Georgian gazebo, a two-storey brick building with one room on each floor. Kate and Luke had once had sex in the top room, which was very much not in the spirit of the place. Even Kes had been shocked. She had sworn Luke to secrecy and it was a promise which he had kept by telling only one friend at a time.

Between her and the building was a sculptured garden consisting of many giant free-standing shrubs set out in an asymmetrical grid but planted close enough to give the effect of a maze. She wandered towards them, the huge bushes taking on a benign mystery in the darkness, like sleeping gods.

Passing silently between the outer trees, she stopped at the sound of weeping. Someone in the garden was crying. They would be sitting on the bench set in the centre. Kate's opinion of her own compassion was something she would consider another time: for now she moved swiftly towards the sound of distress, her softening heart forgetting itself. As she got closer she realised the unhappy person on the bench was a man – the sobs were being furiously suppressed but the occasional bark on an in-breath was unmistakably male.

What she found when she rounded the central bushes was indeed a man sitting on the wooden bench but not the kind of man or the kind of sitting she had imagined. He was certainly a student, or of student age; but instead of sitting forward with his head in his hands, he was slumped back at an awkward angle with his arms held unnaturally behind him. That was the third most surprising thing about him. The second most surprising thing about him was that he was naked except for what appeared to be a pair of white Y-fronts. But the real winner in the Surprising Things About the Weeping Youth Contest only became apparent when the boy sensed Kate's presence and looked across to her, squinting at her in the gloom and instantly turning his face away in shame. That head movement, that skinny pale body, that light hair, that face. Kate felt like laughing. Well, every other acquaintance from Benedict College had shown up today – this one was only a matter of time.

'Can I help you, Charles?'

Charles Hunt turned back to her in astonishment. 'Who are you? How do you know my name?'

Kate ignored the questions as well as the imperious tone. As she approached, she realised why Charles's hands were behind him; indeed why they were behind the bench. Her sympathy for him flooded back and this time with an accompanying glug of anger. 'Who the hell did this to you?'

'Bastards tied me up, didn't they? Bloody bastards tied me to this wretched bench and scarpered with my clothes, the shits.'

Kate moved round the back and found Charles's wrists bound tightly to one of the horizontal bench slats with two thick plastic cable ties. She thought of running to ask a Derwent porter for a pair of scissors but these ties were industry-level and it would take wire cutters to slice through them. Charles was already violently shivering. He spoke through his chattering teeth. 'Bonzo was the one with the plastic things. Said he pinched them from the chaps putting up the marquee for his eighteenth. Thought they might "come in handy", the blumming bastard. Dusty and Laz were no better. Held me down and stole my trousers.'

'Why did they pick on you?'

'I told them it was my birthday.'

'Right. Of course.'

'Can you loosen them?'

'No.'

'Oh, bloody Christ on a scooter!'

'It's okay. I can get you free but you have to keep still.'

'What? What are you going to do?'

'Shush. I need to concentrate.'

Still behind Charles, Kate took a step back and sized up the bench, taking in its dimensions. Solidly constructed but worn with age. She couldn't make it out in the dark but hopefully some woodworm too. Charles's dickhead public-school fresher-victimising tormentors had tied his wrists to just one slat, the third one down. Too low for a punch and awkward for a kick. Still – nothing's easy.

Kate said, 'You're stuck pretty fast to this plank so you might feel a slight jolt.'

'Why, what are you going to—'

Charles didn't finish his sentence. By the time he reached the word 'you', this strangely confident woman in the body of an eighteen-year-old world karate medallist had leapt a foot and a half into the air, her arms lifting and spreading for balance as her right leg coiled back, and with a lightning whip of Doc Marten on ageing pine, smashed through the slat and splintered the ones above and below.

'CHRIST! Fucking ow! You . . . oh, I see. Blimey.' With Kate's help, Charles gingerly slid the tied wrists over the matchwood end of the broken plank. The cable ties were suddenly like bangles for a giant and fell off his hands. Charles's first words of freedom were, 'You're going to get into trouble for that, you know.'

'I don't see why. They should send the repair bill to Gonzo or whatever his fucking name is. Here.' Kate took off her coat and handed it to the vibrating Charles.

'It's a girl's coat.'

'It's a coat. Put it on, you idiot, before you die of hypothermia.'

'It's got a Nazi flag on it.'

'It's the flag of West Germany. We beat them in the World Cup, remember?'

'Were they on our side?'

'In the World Cup? No.'

'But in the war.'

'Shall we start moving, Charles? Which way is your room?'

The coat was three sizes too big for Kate and a surprisingly good fit for her freezing companion. Kate reflected that if there was one member of Benedict College she'd been half-expecting to see in just his underwear tonight, it really wasn't this one.

'Other side of the lake.'

Kate looked down at Charles's bony legs protruding from the overcoat like a child's drawing of a man in a skirt. It reminded her of a kids' TV show called *Bod*. 'Bastards didn't even leave you any shoes. Right, mind your step. Let's go.' She led the way, with Charles gingerly following and trying to do up the coat buttons, most of which were missing. Charles was then struck by another insurmountable problem.

'I haven't got my room key!'

'The porters will have a spare.'

'Oh. Look, I can find my own way. Why are you coming too?'

'Because I'll want my coat back, won't I?'

'Oh. Yeah.'

How, how, HOW did this confirmed idiot become her boss? How was it possible that one of the stupidest men she'd ever met had the slightest influence over her twenty-first-century self?

'How come you know my name? You didn't say.'

'Oh, I must have heard someone use it earlier. Think I was standing behind you in the queue for . . .' She tried to do a Luke. '. . .you know, that massive bloody queue with all the . . .'

'In the canteen at lunch?'

'Yeah.'

'Oh, right.'

It was a long walk to Charles's end of Benedict. Kate reflected on this 'Bonzo' person. Jesus. By the end of Kate's first year, the ringleader of Charles's bullies had become well-known to her. Paul Bonaugh, post-grad Economics student – the kind of guy you didn't get drunk with; the kind of guy whose room you didn't go back to; the kind of guy who took the word 'no' as a coquettish incitement. Kate had made a mental list of the men like Bonaugh she'd heard about at this university. Oddly famous for her monogamy with Luke, she had avoided most of their shit. But she had heard things and believed things. Was she meant to do something about that? In the custom of someone vaguely aware that they have a drinking problem, Kate tried not to follow the thought. The trouble with drunks and wayward thoughts is that one minute you're thinking something outrageous and the next minute you're actually saying it or doing it. No, she decided with some reluctance: she was not here to beat up every suspected rapist on campus. She didn't believe that justice was best served by thugs and vigilantes. It wouldn't be right for her to do it now any more than it would be right in a few years' time for a mob to do it when they failed to distinguish between the words 'paedophile' and 'paediatrician'.

That said, if she caught 'Bonzo' so much as grinning at Amy in the wrong way she would obviously break his face.

These men. Charles wasn't one of them but he didn't mind their company. The proximity to male violence was already giving him some kind of hard-on. She tried not to think about that either. Those pants. Eurgh.

She glanced at him, trailing behind her. 'You know, you really shouldn't hang out with those people.'

Charles was miserably scanning the path ahead and behind in case anybody witnessed his walk of shame, even though the shame belonged to his attackers. 'The shits,' he muttered. 'They'll be bloody sorry when my father hears about this. Very bloody sorry.'

Kate pictured Charles's father as he would be now – still in his fifties, still a government minister. 'What does your father do?'

Charles weighed this up for a moment, caught between his wariness of this stranger and a powerful need to assert some status. 'He's a politician.'

'Really?'

'Rather an important one, actually.'

'Sounds impressive.'

'Well. It impresses some people, but . . . you know, it just comes with the territory really.'

'I guess so. My dad's a taxi driver.'

'I'm sorry to hear that.'

He was entirely sincere and Kate had to suppress a laugh. But she wanted to press on: never in twenty-eight years had she got Charles to talk truthfully about his father. 'So he's a powerful man, your dad?'

A beat of silence. 'Yes.'

'You must really look up to him.' She took another look at Charles. His face was hard to read in the dark but there was a quality to the pause that spoke of a terrible longing.

At length, he said quietly, 'He is a hard act to follow.'

There it was. Charles Hunt in seven words. Or at least Charles Hunt's problem. Which he would turn into everyone else's problem. Kate said, 'I'm sure he's very proud of you.'

'Sorry, what's your name?'

'Kate.'

'Right. It's really none of your business, Kate.'

After a mortifying visit to the porter's lodge, Charles let himself into his place and Kate followed. He turned on the overhead light to reveal a tidy room, the walls of which were decorated with only two pictures: a poster of a Harrier Jump Jet and a newspaper cut-out of Margaret Thatcher. Charles went straight to his wardrobe and pulled out a pair of chinos and a plaid shirt. Kate turned to a bookshelf as he dressed, not wishing upon herself another indelible image of Charles's body, which she presumed was still the colour and texture of wet Blu-Tack.

'Um, this is yours, then,' he mumbled as he returned Kate's coat.

'Thanks, I'll be off.' Kate put the coat on, feeling rather proud of herself for rescuing this ungrateful prat. If she could be this nice to her future enemy, surely she could forgive her future husband? Disappointing teenager or not, Luke was still in danger and she still had a job to do. 'I'm off to the bar, actually. The night's still young. D'you want to come?'

'Erm . . .' Though now dressed, Charles was clearly experiencing a new kind of anxiety – the one where you're alone with a woman in a bedroom for the first time ever. He drifted around frowning at the floor and randomly touching the furniture like a bad actor. 'No, I think I'll just . . . stay in for now. Catch up on some reading, maybe listen to one of my compact discs.' He looked sick, as if there was something he knew needed saying but to say it would make him throw up. He did his best. 'Look, um, Kate. You've been . . . that was . . . Why were you nice to me?'

Kate smiled at him. 'Because everyone deserves a second chance, Charles. Everyone.'

Chapter 13

The bar was packed as Kate swerved round the pool table. She reckoned the gang would have repaired here by now: it had been an hour since she left Amy's room and Kes's objections to the bar would have dried up along with the wine. She spotted them at a central table with a few other freshers huddled round. Given her narky departure, it would take some nerve to just stroll up but Kate figured that in their eyes she had already reached a cruising altitude of weirdness and one more weird action would make little difference. She got herself half a cider and approached the table.

Kes saw her first. 'Marsden! She leaves, she returns, she's in, she's out, she does the hokey-cokey and she shakes it all about!'

'Hello! Me again.'

Kes shuffled up along the banquette to create a space, slightly squashing Toby, who raised a glass at Kate and gave her an open smile. Amy was saying something vehement to Luke about the demerits of the Nestlé business model in developing countries. He was doing his sincere nodding routine while his eyes constantly flicked over Amy's shoulder in case there was something more interesting going on elsewhere.

Toby was making himself a roll-up. 'Kes and I were discussing children's TV shows, if you can imagine anything more banal. It's like we're in denial.'

'Oh yeah?' Kate began to take off her student coat, a manoeuvre she'd forgotten was almost impossible while sitting down. She stood. 'What are we denying?' The movement and question caused Luke and Amy to look up at her. Kate removed her coat and sat down, randomly giving Amy an enthusiastic thumbs-up. Without moving her hand from the table, Amy slowly extended a thumb while maintaining an immovable frown. Kate nodded playfully, as if everything was normal. And decided to ignore the baffled expression of her dead husband.

Yep, playing it cool. Real cool.

'We're in denial of our huge academic potential,' Kes continued. 'It's violently transgressive to be talking about *Bagpuss* in an environment such as this.'

There was a loud crash from the far corner and the sound of a dropped tray of drinks and somebody's utter humiliation was greeted with the obligatory massive cheer.

Toby ran the tip of his tongue along the Rizla and added some final touches to his handiwork. 'Yes, the place is clearly an intellectual powerhouse.'

'God, I used to love *Bagpuss*!' said Luke.

Amy folded her arms and looked elsewhere. Kate felt that Luke's comment should be encouraged, since he'd finally said something honest. He really did love *Bagpuss*. How exactly she was going to finesse that into 'You've got a brain tumour' was a bit of admin that probably needed to be dealt with at some future point quite soon.

'I liked it too,' she said, weakly.

Toby was still on Luke's case. 'What was it you loved about *Bagpuss*, Luke?'

'Yaffle,' Luke replied decisively. 'Professor Yaffle. He's a massive pedant. He thinks it's all beneath him but can't help getting involved. It makes the whole thing more real.'

'You mean, he's the benign patriarch,' Toby went on, lighting the rollie and not meeting Luke's pretty eyelashes, now batting themselves to attention. 'He's the grown-up in the room who gives the whole operation validity. So that even as children, we need to be given permission to believe in magic.'

'Well, Bagpuss himself *is* magic.'

'Unquestionably. But you think we need Yaffle to sign the chitty.'

'Chitty?'

'Permission slip. We can't enjoy the impossible unless someone calling himself a professor says it's okay.'

'I didn't say that.'

'Did you not? I thought you said he makes it more real?'

'No, I . . . yes, I probably did say that, but . . .'

Kes sensed something in the air and chose to diffuse it. 'Obviously the boss of Bagpuss is a matriarch. It's Emily's shop. Emily is the prime mover.'

Amy found a principle that overcame her reluctance to join in. 'Oh, for God's sake. Emily's not even in it! Emily turns up in the opening credits and you never see her again! Matriarch, my arse.'

The familiarity of this topic was beginning to oppress Kate. It wasn't like she hadn't happily joined in the first time round – for that whole first term, if it wasn't *Bagpuss* then it was *Rainbow* or *Chigley* or *The Flumps*. But Luke using the word 'real' had bothered her. Kate suddenly felt the weight of her years – by the time she was forty her own childhood felt so distant that she sometimes had to ask herself how much of it had really happened. Reflexively she reached for her left shoulder and ran a fingertip over her BCG scar.

'Yup!' said Luke brightly. 'Nostalgia certainly isn't what it used to be!'

There was a moment's silence for this conversation-stopper and Luke took a swift sip of his beer. Kate's heart bounced for him in sympathy. She had always known Luke's greatest fear, his most secret dread. Luke was afraid that he was boring.

He walked into rooms and his appearance excited expectations that he felt could never be met. He was like David Beckham: a demi-god as voiced by *Sesame Street*. Achilles would open his mouth and everyone would be basically relieved that he sounded like Elmo. There was nothing odd about Luke's voice: an easy contralto and soft as chalk. He just worried about what he used it for. Hence all the posing and bullshitting. Kate had weaned him away from that through a combination of love and sarcasm. She much preferred it when his pronouncements were made of milk and cookies: she liked it when he sounded like Barbara, his mum. And besides, she was intimately acquainted with his inner life, and that was considerably darker and knottier. She had read his book. If a character in Luke's sprawling novel said something as bland as 'Nostalgia isn't what it used to be!', Luke would persecute him for the next five pages and then throw him under a lorry.

'It certainly isn't!' Kate agreed, and tried to think of something to complement Luke's vanilla tone. 'They say flares are coming back but I say that's nonsense!'

Toby looked mildly alarmed. 'Flares *have* come back, haven't they?'

Amy agreed. 'They've been and gone.'

Kes checked the bootleg cut of his red jeans. 'No, I can

162

confirm that they're still in. We're still doing the seventies again.'

'Flares are from the sixties,' Toby objected. 'My dad's still got a pair in his wardrobe.'

'Okay, I was wrong,' said Luke, who seemed to have rallied. 'Nostalgia clearly *is* what it used to be. Everything comes back.'

But now Kate said quietly, 'It does. But it's not the same, is it?'

'I'm not sure anyone's saying it's the same,' said Amy.

Kate felt herself slamming into a wall of utter futility. She couldn't say a damn thing to these people. She knew too much. 'You are, though. You don't know it, but you are.'

Kes detected the hornet's nest of thoughts behind Kate's eyes and decided to give it a good old poke. 'My God, Marsden is having one of her brainwaves and now we're all in the shit!'

Kate ignored him.

'We must shelter from the cataclysm. She's about to destroy us for our idle talk of flares and *Bagpuss*.'

'It's not that it's idle, it's just that the whole trying-to-live-in-the-past thing is meaningless.'

'Why?'

Don't say anything weird. Don't say anything weird.

Kate almost shouted: 'Because obviously you can't do something for the first time twice! Because you can't fake innocence!'

There was a startled silence. Kate went on more calmly but with a measured anger. She didn't even know who she was angry with.

'You can wear flares like it's the seventies and you can make your indie band sound like David Bowie like it's the seventies and you can enjoy *Ivor the Engine* like it's the seventies but it won't be the same because you know things that people in the seventies didn't know. It's like saying, "You keep AIDS and Tiananmen Square, we'll have the space-hoppers." And backwards, it's always looking backwards. "Let's get *back* to basics. Let's take *back* control. Let's make America great *again*." And it's always a mistake. Because nobody remembers anything properly. Let's re-nationalise the trains and forget how they used to be even shitter. Flares, for crying out loud. You might as well be doing the conga in a graveyard.'

Kes timed a pause and then turned to an imaginary camera: 'And that concludes this week's edition of *Kate Marsden Holds Forth*.' The break in the tension left Kate simultaneously peeved and grateful. Kes went on. 'Next week, Kate meets Nelson Mandela and gives him a thorough bollocking about his taste in shirts.'

Kate laughed along. 'Sorry. I didn't mean to go on like that.'

Amy grabbed her arm. 'Don't you dare apologise.' She nodded at the boys around the table. 'They wouldn't.'

'I might, actually,' said Luke with such good-naturedness that Toby let out a small groan, which attracted more attention than he intended. He styled it into a throat clearance.

'Yes,' he said. 'But I'm a bit confused about the railways, though. What do you mean, re-nationalise them? Last time I looked they were in public ownership.'

Kate realised her mistake but was given a moment to breathe by Amy cutting in bitterly.

'Not for long, knowing these bastards.'

'Well,' said Toby, 'Major's talking about it but—'

Kate had found what she was looking for in the giant fresco of her memory and was so relieved she blurted out the correction: 'Nineteen ninety-four. They're going to sell them off in . . . in a couple of years. I reckon.'

164

'I knew it. Marsden is not only furiously opinionated on the subject of nostalgia, but also psychic.'

'No, no, that's—'

'You knew Tobias and I were both Aquarians.'

'That was just—'

Luke joined in. 'So who's going to win next year's Grand National?'

Kate took a sip of cider. 'Er . . . Red Rum?'

Luke laughed. 'I think Red Rum would have to come back from the dead. Sorry, are you okay?'

Kate recovered and wiped the cider from her nose. 'Yup, just went down the wrong way. Look—'

'No, let's stick with politics,' Kes announced to the ceiling, determined that 'Kate the Clairvoyant' was a great game. 'So, Marsden, is John Smith going to win the next general election?'

'I . . . doubt it.'

'Why not?' asked Toby.

Fatal heart attack.

'Too safe,' Amy interjected. 'Now Kinnock's blown it, they need someone from the Left.'

'Well, that's true enough,' agreed Kes.

Five people who would vote for Tony Blair with varying degrees of enthusiasm. Kate was glad it wasn't her job to let them know.

'What's my star sign, then?' said Luke quietly, from under his eyelashes.

Okay – Luke flirting again. That's . . . good?

Kate recalled Luke's absurd weakness for horoscopes and wanted to close down this nonsense as soon as possible. Then again, she was just beginning to recapture his interest, which would be handy if she was going to save his life. She met his gaze evenly and said, 'You're a Libra.'

Luke confirmed she was right by looking at the others

and upturning a palm in her direction. He turned back to Kate. There had been an air of discovery about him ever since her rant. And now she recognised a look on his face. Something she hadn't seen for a very long time.

'Surely that was a one-in-twelve fluke,' muttered Toby, flipping a bar mat and catching it. Kate kept her eyes on Luke, who was looking straight at her. He didn't even care that she could see what he was thinking.

Frisky husband. Oh, you're a bold one when you feel like it.

Luke quickly drained the last of his pint and made rather a pantomime of looking at his watch. 'Right, that's me. Lovely to meet you all.' He leaned over and kissed Amy on the cheek. It was just a peck but also somehow 0.00045 seconds too long. Amy knew instantly that the kiss was for Kate's benefit and raised an eyebrow at the girl across the table. Luke was reaching down for his coat as Kate replied with the briefest of complicit grins and Amy looked away, openly smiling. Kate longed to be alone with her friend. Just one talk with Amy without freaking her out . . .

Outraged, Kes was on his feet. 'In the name of God, man – where are you going? They haven't even rung last orders!'

'I know,' Luke said, slowly raking the dark hair out of his eyes. 'Shameful, isn't it?' With that last comment he glanced again at Kate. And then: 'I'm off to bed.'

'Night-night, Luke!' said Toby loudly. 'Mind the bugs don't bite!'

Luke smiled and made to leave. Amy said, 'If you change your mind, we're off clubbing at chucking-out time.'

Toby looked up. 'Are we?'

'Yeah. I was talking to some fourth-year economist bloke and he said there was a place called Blossom which is a Chinese restaurant by day and then turns into a disco at night.'

Kes considered this. 'Sounds barking mad. Let's go.'

Luke cast his jacket over one shoulder, looking more like a model than ever. 'Well, have fun.' He sauntered off but not before making significant eye-contact with Kate once more on his way past.

Confident little bastard! He actually expects me to follow him.

'Right, my round,' said Toby. 'What are you having, Kate?'

'Oh shit, are we doing rounds?' asked Kes.

Amy too was perplexed: 'First I've heard of it.'

But Kate was on her feet. 'Actually, I'm going to head off too.' Toby had been rummaging in his coat for money: he kept his head down as the rummaging stopped for half a second and then continued. Kate saw his face settle into a look of wry resignation. She shrugged apologetically at the group. 'Bit of a long day.'

Having scraped her off the floor three times since breakfast, the gang could hardly argue with that. Kes relented: 'Maybe see you later at the Beijing Bopalong if you get a second wind.'

'Maybe. Look, you've all been really kind to me today. Thanks.'

Toby stood to go to the bar and put his hands in his pockets. 'Any time.'

Kate nodded warmly to him and then knelt down next to Amy. The two men sensed a private moment and busily organised the drinks order.

'Especially you,' Kate said.

'I don't know what's going on with you, pet,' said Amy, taking Kate's hand. 'But if you need a mate . . . well, you definitely know where my room is.'

Kate rolled her eyes in apology. 'I definitely do.' She looked down at her friend's hand and thought of those first few weeks after Luke had died. 'I had this dream, you see? Not some kind of prophesy or anything daft like that, but . . . it was just very real. And in the dream, I lost someone. Someone very close.'

'Sounds horrible.'

'It was, yeah. And the thing is . . . you were there. Don't freak out – not you obviously, that's impossible. But . . . someone very like you. And we were friends. And you educated yourself about grief. You read as much as you could about it on – in a big library. And you found out that people in "complicated grief" – people who've lost people very suddenly or when they're too young or things like that – that they lose their appetite for a while. So you would make these soups, Amy. Soups and broths. And you would come round with them. Come to the house with a thermos flask and a couple of magazines. And you did it every day. The person like you. You tried to look after me. And I was too poorly to thank you.'

Amy shook her head gently, apparently still wondering whether this girl was best served by giving her a hug or getting her sectioned. She said softly, 'Well, I'd like to think I'd act that way for someone if it came to it, but . . . well, you never know, do you?'

'No. You never know.'

Kate didn't think she could go any further and made to stand before she had one last thought. 'By the way, that fourth-year bloke who told you about Blossom. He wasn't a big hearty bloke with dyed blond hair, was he?'

'He was, yeah. His mates were calling him Bonzo or something. Do you know him?'

'Friend of a friend. Look, don't take this the wrong way. I'm sure you can take care of yourself. Just . . . he's worth watching out for. Bad reputation. Very bad.'

Amy fully understood what she was being told. 'Right, love. Thanks.'

'I always think it's best to be informed.'

'Me too.'

'See you around, Amy. See you again.'

Chapter 14

Kate's grandad shirt was still occupied by Luke when he opened the door. She didn't know what she had expected – Torso of the Decade with a bulge in the front of his jeans? A Terry Thomas smoking jacket and a slow wink? And assuming she had read his expression right in the bar, how would *she* react anyway? He was nineteen. It would be like shagging a nephew.

The short journey to his room had felt like a déjà vu assault course. Up the dizzyingly familiar staircase to his corridor, past the shared kitchen with its aromatic calling card of student cuisine (the rice and stuff, the pasta and stuff, the tuna, the empty cans of chopped tomatoes scattered on a draining board) and past the closed door of Martin Bailey's room with *Achtung Baby* blaring from within. With every step she contended with a hundred precious memories and was fearful of overwriting them. But she had no choice – this was overwriting with a purpose.

It was perfectly straightforward. She was going to convince Luke that she was from the future and he needed to get a tumour removed from his brain otherwise he would drop dead at the age of forty-seven in his kitchen, which was incidentally also her kitchen because she was his wife. Fine.

Kate was immediately crushed not by the fact that he was fully dressed but by his look of astonishment.

'Oh! Hi,' he said.

'Hi.'

'Yes.'

'I, erm . . . I just found myself walking over here.'

'Right. Were you looking for someone?'

Oh, for God's sake.

'Well, yes. For you, actually.'

'Oh!'

She ended a stupendously awkward pause by anticipating his next question. 'I got your room number from the porters. Don't worry, I'm not stalking you!'

Luke chuckled politely but didn't look convinced.

'I mean, obviously I *have* slightly stalked you. A bit. A mini-stalk.'

'A stalklet.'

'Exactly.'

It seemed to occur to Luke that he had to do something. 'Right, well, do come in.' He said it as if to a friend of the family whom he was now required to entertain until his parents got back from Waitrose.

'Thanks,' she said and squeezed past him while thinking that this might well be the stupidest plan ever conceived by Woman.

Luke closed the door behind him as Kate moved into the centre of the room. She noticed his bare feet and suddenly felt like an intruder.

'Can I take your coat?' he said. His alarm had sent him into middle-class autopilot.

'Um . . . cheers.' Kate gave him the coat that had recently enclosed Charles Hunt's clay-like body and sat down in a reading chair by the window. She buried a smile as she watched him wonder what the hell to do with the coat and opt to just fold it up and put it carefully on the floor. He sat down on the bed opposite. It was like her recurring dream but he was tense and hunched forward instead of leaning back under Kurt Cobain. If ever there was a time to say 'Why don't you take all your clothes off so I can pretend to draw you?', this was not it. The universe was laughing at her and even Kurt seemed to be in on the joke.

Very well then – let the overwriting commence!

'Luke, there's something I need to tell you.'

'Coffee!' he exclaimed. 'I asked you to come back for a coffee, maybe. And then I forgot.'

'You . . .? Erm, no, not in so many words . . . Although you did give me a look that kind of—'

'Exactly. Yes. I'm a terrible flirt. I mean I'm terrible at it. But I do fancy you quite a lot so I'm glad you're here.'

'Right. Well . . . good to have that firmly established.'

'Sorry. That was—'

'I'm glad I'm here too.' She gave him a reassuring smile and they both laughed. Yep, this was more like it – enjoyably mortifying levels of embarrassment over a mutual attraction, just like normal teenagers. Kate felt this was something to work with. She was also touched and relieved that the old Luke – the young Luke of old – had finally made an appearance. The second he was out of public he dropped the bullshit. No pretending to be French, no smarmy chat-up lines. Just this frank-hearted young man who said things like 'I fancy you quite a lot' with no idea what would happen next.

'Right. So,' he said, looking around his room for inspiration. 'Certain level of self-consciousness here. We should probably make some small-talk.'

Kate realised that if she were still eighteen she would agree about the self-consciousness and there would now follow a long and ironic conversation about not knowing what to talk about. But she was forty-five and didn't have the time. 'So like I say, there's something—'

'I haven't actually got any coffee,' he interrupted. 'That's not to say it wouldn't be great to have "coffee" but I don't have any actual coffee.'

'That's very flattering but I'm actually fine for both kinds of coffee.'

'Sorry – I didn't mean to assume—'

'No worries. But it's worth saying that we're not going to be doing any banging tonight, Luke.'

'Aren't we?'

'No.'

'Drat.'

'At least I'm not.'

'I see.'

'I'm not really in a banging mood.'

'Fair enough. First night and everything.'

Kate was amused that he was putting this down to her being 'not that sort of girl' when, as it happened, she most certainly was. But this would do for now. 'Yep,' she said.

He looked pleased: the weird but interesting girl had introduced the possibility of sex and her ruling it out was somehow nearly as exciting as her ruling it in. The point was that sex was now in the room. He drew a leg up onto the bed and started to massage his foot absent-mindedly. 'Let's just get to know each other. You're a good talker. You were amazing in the bar. Oh, I know! We can take a short cut by—'

'What's wrong with your foot?'

'What?'

'You're rubbing your right foot. Have you hurt it?'

He glanced down in surprise and reflexively withdrew his hand. 'Oh God, no. Just. It gets numb sometimes. Weird.'

'Pins and needles?'

'Yeah, sometimes. Anyway, I know a good short cut for the getting-to-know-you routine . . .'

Kate took a breath and tried not to focus on Luke's symptomless tumour, now actively trolling her by presenting its one and only symptom. She glanced up at Kurt Cobain, who apparently didn't know whether to laugh or cry. Luke's action was so utterly characteristic it had hidden in plain sight. She tried to give herself a break: she might as well have called an ambulance every time he fingered the mole on his neck or sounded the 'd' in 'Wednesday'.

Don't panic. There's no rush. Let him talk and then gently bring the conversation round to medicine or thinking about the future or . . . anyway – look at him – he's otherwise completely healthy. Nothing to get upset about.

She tuned back in and realised Luke was talking about his English course.

'. . . because you can't be much of a writer unless you're a devoted reader, don't you think?'

She tried to concentrate. 'I expect that's right. I mean, I've never really tried to—'

'So, do you want to read my book?'

Kate swallowed hard. 'Book?'

'Not all of it, obviously. It's not finished but it's already quite long.' He was up on his feet and opening a desk drawer. 'Think of it like a trust exercise.'

'Trust,' Kate repeated as if in a daze.

'Yeah, like the thesps do.' He produced what Kate recognised as an early version of many first drafts of *Whatever* – about two hundred A4 pages of manuscript, written in longhand, bound together with a couple of treasury tags Luke had pinched from school. He thrust it towards her and she received it like a hand grenade with the pin missing. Luke registered her expression but now his enthusiasm was bordering on mania. It was enough to overcome his modesty: 'Of course, you don't have to.'

Kate momentarily wished she was American so that she could take that statement at face value. In the original English, he had just said, 'Obviously, you have absolutely no choice in this matter.'

'No, no – it looks . . .'

'Cool. I'll go and make us that coffee. I'll nick some from the kitchen, rebel that I am.' He marched towards the door and then turned back. 'It's only a first draft – be gentle with me! It's like I'm letting you see me naked, but less disgusting.'

Kate, currently two years older than Luke's mother, looked up from the title page and said, 'I'm sure you look very nice naked. But like I say . . .'

'Understood!' He seemed to have second thoughts about letting her read the masterpiece and said more quietly, 'You only get one chance to read it for the first time, of course. And it really isn't at all finished. You won't take the piss, will you?'

'It's all about trust, isn't it?'

Luke looked relieved. 'Exactly! Couldn't have put it better myself.' He opened his door. 'Won't be long.'

Not for the first time in her life, Kate was left alone in a room with nothing left of Luke save for his awful book. She gingerly turned the title page. Here it was, then: her enemy. The lunatic in the basement. The portrait in the attic. Despite Luke's claim, she knew that this first paragraph had been rewritten countless times already: he had started just after his GCSEs. She was more interested, now, in his handwriting. It was soon – during this first term at York – that he had switched to digital. He wouldn't own a computer for years but this was where he had started to type the thing up on a shared Mac Classic II in Benedict's

175

Computer Room. Naturally you need a Computer Room. Where you keep the Computers.

She marvelled like an archaeologist at the ancient scroll before her. So much of his ink, so much of his hand. Where Kate came from, artefacts featuring Luke's handwriting were a scarce resource. Old love letters, the early ones written from the pad of Basildon Bond probably in the drawer next to her – the same one he had taken the book from. A shopping list or two; the stubs of an old cheque-book. But here were all the sloping 'l's and flourished 'f's – the angry crossings-out and urgent notes written vertically in the margin. All of it in careless abundance, as if the ink would never run out and the hand would never be still.

Kate read, politely ignoring what was scribbled out and trying to re-examine what Luke was currently trying to achieve.

The sky-high heels of Jessica Zed tick across the asphalt, transporting the pneumatic breasts of their mistress and telling their own story as the multi-storied roof shimmers in the heat-blur like a slab of sorbet grateful to melt. Her mind is empty. Light as a plastic turd. Empty like this car park roof; proof positive that Gary Disposal has made the grade. Oh, he's chosen the place to meet alright. He'd abused the sheets of his fetid bed (they wreaked) but he'd hung up the mouthcan exulted. She'd agreed.

And now she comes: clipping toward him.
– featherweight
– jailbait
– checkmate.

Is it her perfume that makes him so digress? JuJu at £80 for 100mls of vinegar tokes. Distressed, he watches with his high and his low, his grey matter and his won't matter: id-dipped and ego-tripped, Disposal's ying and yang are fucking in the sun and you can sniff out the rutstench from Jupiter's moons.

Here she is at last: degged in Ju, dappled in Ju, are the tips of the nips of her tits shown through.

Her vagina is the first to speak—

Kate sighed and mildly shook her head. He wasn't really going to keep this up for two hundred pages, was he? But of course he was. He was going to keep it up for twenty-eight years. She flipped impatiently to the middle. She tried – not for the first time – to look at the thing objectively. So then: there was a sense of rhythm and that was good. There was an enjoyment of language and that was good. There was a total absence of any point to any of it and that was bad. There was a weird misogyny, which was bad. There were idle literary allusions which went nowhere: these could have been half-good if they had anything to do with the story but they didn't and so were fully bad. This was mainly because there was no actual story. Luke wasn't writing a story. He was having a wank. One where neither he nor the reader would ever come. Kate reflected that if Luke taped himself having an actual wank there would at least be a market for that. And at least it would end.

She flipped the pages again. Something caught her eye.

. . . but that isn't the deal with Morlock.

Morris Morlock surveys the playground like what the hell what the hell it's happening again. Not happening but presuming. And always there. Like something growing, brainside. Some tiny cock in his head like an itch, like a stitch you can't scratch. Stealthy and wealthy, like Veronica Void. She made him feel like the chemo had already shaved his strength. Like she'd tied him to a kitchen chair and—

Kate had long forgotten this passage. The image of something cancerous growing in a person's head had been discarded by Luke years ago. She read on.

Presently, a noise at the door made her guiltily turn the page as Luke elbowed his way into the room with two mugs of coffee.

'Think I got away with it!' he said in a stage whisper. 'I'll get them a replacement jar in the morning. I'm afraid it's instant and made by Nestlé. Is that all right?'

'I promise I won't tell Amy.'

'Ha! Yes, phew! God, that woman can talk.' He moved an old exercise book to the end of the desk and set one mug down on it next to Kate, trying to make the movement as natural as possible so it didn't look like he was doing what he was obviously doing: protecting the desk and giving her a coaster. Kate knew Barbara had packed a couple of actual coasters featuring tasteful watercolours of Salisbury Cathedral in his rucksack. Luke was happy to use them when alone.

'So,' he said, sitting on his bed and cradling his mug in both hands, 'did you have a chance to . . . read a few bits?'

Kate took a breath and closed the manuscript. She found herself fighting a muscle memory – a long ingrained urge to protect him, encourage him: to give him what he wanted rather than what he needed. It was the act of a bad parent. But that shouldn't have been the deal in the first place – she wasn't his mother. She carefully put the book to one side and focused on the boy opposite, weighing his mass and dimensions as if he were a bone that needed to be broken before it could be reset. This was going to hurt.

He took her stillness for hesitation. 'It's okay, I'm actually amazingly arrogant so I won't be offended.' He took a nervous sip of coffee. 'What did you think?'

'I think you need your head examining,' she said evenly.

A wry grin took slow possession of his face. 'Blimey. I mean, don't sit on the fence, Kate. Tell me what you really—'

'You're going to die when you're only forty-seven years old. I know because I was there and it broke my heart. Luke, my love . . . I'm your wife. I'm from the future and I'm here to save you.'

Chapter 15

His expression didn't change. He stared at her for a few seconds with an air of sceptical amusement. He took another sip of coffee and placed the mug down carefully by his bare feet, the toes of which had briefly contracted into prehensile claws trying to grip the carpet but which he now relaxed.

'Right. Quite a lot to unpack there,' he said.

'Obviously you think I'm nuts.'

'No! Erm . . . well. A bit, yeah.'

'Yeah. So look—'

'I mean, if you don't like the book then just—'

'It's really not about the book.'

'I mean, it's only a first draft so—'

'Luke, will you *kindly* shut up about the book.'

He did shut up. It wasn't so much the rebuke but the easy familiarity of it, as if she'd been occasionally telling him to shut up for a very long time. And there was something else in her tone – not just intimacy but authority. It was as if he was being told off by a benign teacher or some other figure twice his age.

Kate read as much in the furrows that briefly crossed his brow – the creases appeared and vanished like the shadows of fast-moving clouds across a sunlit field. Like her own, those lines would grow deeper and permanent with time. But in his case, not deep enough.

She pushed on. 'If I was that desperate to change the subject I'm pretty sure I could have come up with something surprising but more plausible. Like, y'know . . . "The book's great but did you know I'm actually Belgian?" or "I like the book but let's talk about my dad, who invented *The Wombles*." That kind of thing.'

'Right?' he said, cautiously.

'But I didn't. I made a series of completely mad claims.'

'I noticed.'

'So you've got to ask yourself – why would I do that?'

'It beats me.'

Kate remembered she was asking the impossible and stilled a ripple of impatience. Surely, he was being rather lazy. She had a nuclear arsenal of facts that could blow this kid's brain apart but she wanted him to meet her at least part-way first. He could do some of the work with logic if he just got off his arse. 'Right, let's play a game. You like games, don't you?'

'Well, you'd know, wouldn't you? You're my *wife*.' Dismally, Luke accompanied the last word with full air-quotes.

Kate didn't know whether it was a good sign that he seemed to be enjoying this, but at least he was still listening. 'Yup,' she said. 'So you get to ask me any question about the future and I'll give you an honest answer. Five minutes only. Starting now.'

Luke shifted position and sat cross-legged on the edge of his bed. He looked off to the side, some humour returning to his lips. 'Okaaaay . . . when in the future?'

'The start of the third decade of the twenty-first century.'

Luke's smile widened. 'So the year two thousand and twenty.'

'Yes.'

'But you're not dressed as a spaceman. Where's your hoverboard?'

'We don't have hoverboards.' She remained patient but began to feel that this was cruel: the more she let him dick around, the bigger the idiot he was going to feel if she convinced him.

'No hoverboards. Bummer. So who's the president of America?'

Kate sensed danger. Answering questions about the future of American politics was no way to convince someone she was sane. Or British politics for that matter. 'You don't want to know.'

'Can't be worse than George Bush.'

She used to love talking to him about politics. She couldn't resist saying, 'He really can. In fact, George Bush's son was worse than George Bush but the current guy makes even him look like Gandhi.'

'George Bush's . . . son?'

'Move on.'

'So who? Who's the current guy, then? You said you'd answer.'

'You won't have heard of him.'

'Try me.'

Kate sighed. 'Donald Trump.'

'Donald . . .?'

'You see? Nobody in 1992 is interested in—'

'What, that American twat?'

'Well, presidents of America do tend to be American but—'

'The property prick with the wig?'

Pleasantly surprised to find a gap in her knowledge of Luke's knowledge, Kate nevertheless found this deeply inconvenient. When the hell had he first heard of Trump? 'Yes.'

'. . . Is the President of the United States of America?'

Kate looked at her watch. 'Four minutes. Let's move on.'

Highly sceptical, Luke was still enjoying himself. 'So what's it like generally? The future where you're from?'

Kate refocused: she obviously wasn't going to get anywhere with the abstract future. She needed to bring it closer to home. 'It's shit. My husband just died.'

'And that would be me.'

'That's right.'

'What did I die of?'

'Cancer. Brain tumour called a meningioma.'

The smile was fading from Luke's face. Whatever the hell this girl was doing, cancer clearly didn't make it to his Top Ten Whimsical Conversation Topics. His eyes narrowed into a shrewd stare. 'Really?'

'Yes.'

'When did I get that, then?'

'You've got it now.'

He blinked.

'Just here.' Kate had never known Luke to be violent but ultimately he was a big guy and she was about to seriously upset him. She kept her distance and demonstrated with her own head, reaching up to a place two inches above and behind her left ear. 'It's about the size of a grain of rice but it grows every day.'

He folded his arms, apparently resisting the urge to feel for himself. 'Very funny,' he said.

'Actually it wasn't funny at all. I loved you very much and I blamed myself. I was devastated and suicidal.' She said it so simply, compressing nine months of agony into a statement of fact. For the first time, a look of fear darkened her husband's face. It was almost a relief when he pushed it away and converted it into dumb sarcasm.

'Yes, it must have been very upsetting for you. It's "Kate", isn't it? Must have been awful, Kate. Because we'd been married for . . . how long?'

'We got married in 2003.'

'Of course we did. It must have been quite an occasion.'

'It was. I won't describe the whole thing but—'

'I suppose you had to *be there*.'

Kate was momentarily winded by that one.

He kept going. 'And when did we first start going out, Kate?'

'Tonight.'

'Really?'

'Yes.'

'Tonight's Kate's big night, is it?'

'It was, yes. And yours.'

'But not any more?'

'No.'

He made a performative big deal of crossing one leg over the other and cocking his head to one side. Kate could see that she had spooked him, and that it was bringing out some of his less loveable defences – the showboating pillock was back. 'Sorry,' he said, 'I'm sure I'm being very dim—'

'That's okay.'

He ignored the interruption. 'But, just going with this – how come you were so keen to sleep with me "tonight" but not so very interested "tonight"?'

It wasn't a stupid question, even though he was now behaving very stupidly. She leaned forward and the insight tumbled upon her as she spoke. She should have seen this coming. 'Because I'm a different person now. But that isn't the problem. The problem is that you're a different person too.'

'I'm sure that's terribly significant but you'll have to—'

'You died, mate. And even though you don't believe me,

you're now and forever someone who sat in a room and had to hear it. You're different now. Right now, you don't even like me, much less want to marry me.'

'Oh crumbs, the wedding's off! Never mind.' Luke stood and affected a yawn. 'Well, this has been fascinating but I'd like you to go.'

Kate persisted. 'And I'm different too. Not just because in my head I'm older, but because I've only just seen how you treat people you don't believe. And it isn't very nice. If you really think I'm mad then you ought to be nicer to me than this.'

'Right, yeah – I'm a crushing disappointment. That must be why, according to you, it took us eleven years to get married.'

Kate rose too. 'That's not why it took eleven years.' She slowly crossed to pick up her coat.

'Oh well, do tell! Don't leave me hanging!'

She turned to him regretfully. 'I was waiting, Luke. I was doing what any woman would do, given a bit of time and the sense she was born with. I was waiting for the bloke to grow up.'

It was an unkind remark but, she now realised, horribly true. The young Luke took it as a debating point. 'I don't see what gives you the right to . . . Hang on, can we just take a step back here? Can we just talk about the fucking INSANITY of what you're saying? Apparently I should be nicer but, look . . . you don't seem to be exhibiting any classic signs of mental illness so what are you doing? What's your fucking game?'

Saddened and defeated, Kate put her coat on. It was useless – she had failed him again. But she refused to leave the room with him hectoring her like this. Just for the sake of her pride, she asked, 'Do you know much about mental illness then, Luke?'

'As a matter of fact, I do. In fact, my parents wanted me to be a—'

'No,' she interrupted. 'Not both your parents. Just Richard. He wanted you to be a doctor, like him.'

Luke had his mouth open to reply but no sound came out. Kate realised she'd been going about this in completely the wrong way. It wasn't a time-traveller's knowledge of Luke's future that was going to get through to him. It was a wife's knowledge of his past.

She stood simply before him, her hands in her coat pockets. 'I know how Richard felt because it was one of the first things he said to me when you took me home to meet your parents next summer.'

'Took you . . . next . . . fucking . . .'

'Katie, that's not what a memory like yours is for.'
'What's it for, then?'

She went on. 'It's a lovely place – 12 Fleetwood Avenue. Big, proper detached house. I'd guessed you were well-to-do but I must say it came as a shock. First time I'd been in a house with two staircases. I didn't know there were such things except off the telly. Lucky boy, growing up there. You were allowed to launch your Evel Knievel off the top of the back stairs but not the other one: the main one with the brass stair rods. And two gardens. Barbara made the front pretty and kept some herbs – rosemary and parsley and mint. You got your Lego spacemen to explore it like it was an alien planet with giant flowers. And round the back – a long lawn that Richard kept in check with his Flymo. You told me that when you were little it used to be your job to pick out any stones before he started mowing. Weekends and summer holidays. And then bring him a bottle of Batemans ale halfway through. You'd sit down together and he'd quiz you about the periodic table or get you to name all the bones in the human body. You almost always got the answers right. But then when you were a teenager you'd rather be down the bottom, talking to the big goldfish in the pond, thinking up stories. You'd named the fish – all boys, of course: Rodney and Del Boy, Hannibal and Murdoch.'

Luke looked like he had entered some kind of trance.

'Luke, you told me these things. And I'm quite good at remembering, you see? One day you found Murdoch floating on the surface. You were upset and you walked back into the house and your mum had Radio 2 on in the kitchen. You remember what song was playing, right?'

He had taken half a step back and now his eyes were glazed with reverie. He said hoarsely, 'Yes.'

'You didn't mention the dead fish to Barbara. You walked straight past her because you were fourteen and boys don't cry. But you remember the song. It struck you that the song was sad all right, but was too cheap and shit to fit the occasion. You couldn't believe that the world just carried on regardless, even though Murdoch had died.'

'It was—'

She had to interrupt. 'It was "Every Loser Wins" by Nick Berry.'

There followed a moment where the two of them could have burst out laughing as they contemplated the gravity and magnitude of 'Every Loser Wins' by Nick Berry. Kate wished, as Luke had wished before her, that this pivotal track had been Mozart's Requiem or at least something a bit thoughtful by Sting. But the moment passed and Luke seemed to make a decision.

'Okay, listen to me,' he said steadily. 'I don't know who you are, or what you want, but I need you to get out. Now.'

'Luke – just *think*! How could I know these things? And

187

why would I say them? Why would I lie? What do I get out of this?'

'HOW SHOULD I KNOW!?' he yelled. 'How should I know how your fucking sick brain works?'

'I've thought about it. You could pretend that you're having seizures. That would at least convince them to give you a scan or—'

'GET OUT! JUST GET OUT!' He made a sudden movement towards her and she put her hands up in surrender and backed away.

'Okay! All right!' she said. 'Fucking hell, no need to blow a gasket! Jesus!' Intending to leave, Kate instinctively checked her pockets for her phone and was exasperated for the eightieth time that day to find it missing. If she couldn't help this idiotic boy, then what the hell was she doing here anyway? She turned to the door and then immediately spun back again. 'Fuck it, I'm going dancing,' she announced.

'You're what?'

'I'm going out with the others. I'm going to Blossom and I'm going to score some drugs or get pissed and throw myself at the first bloke I see. You can stay here.'

Luke was poleaxed by this unnecessary order. 'I . . . I fully intend to stay here.'

'Good, then.'

'Good.'

She opened the door and was halfway through it when he called her name. 'Kate!'

'What is it?'

Calmer now and slightly abashed, he approached and addressed his question to the doorframe. 'Will you be all right?'

She thought of her recurring dream and how this was the assurance he gave her. *You're going to be all right.* For a moment she couldn't speak. 'I mean . . .' he went on, 'tonight. Going out on your own.'

She managed a business-like nod. 'Thanks, but I won't be alone. I've got friends.'

Chapter 16

She heard them before she saw them. Kate rounded the corner onto Coney Street and approached the queue for Blossom. From near the front came the sound of Kes at full pitch. 'No, no! You're all too tuneful! It has to be one note! You in particular, Toby, are singing like a choirboy. It's giving me an erection but it's completely wrong!'

Kes's robust, twentieth-century attitude to paedophile jokes would never change but this wasn't the thing that caught Kate's attention. She remembered this perverse project of his. Kes, bound for a performing career in West End musicals, was currently obsessed with the idea of becoming a millionaire impresario by mounting a series of productions where all the songs were sung on one note. Just one. In every other respect, the musicals would be the same: the production values would be high, the sets and costumes, starry cast and glitzy marketing would be exactly those which West End audiences had come to expect. But every word of every song would be sung on the same note. G sharp, to be precise. Because, according to Kes, it was 'a criminally neglected note and easily one of the funniest'.

'It will be magnificent,' he was saying – not just to Toby and Amy but to at least a dozen freshers and regulars in the queue whom he had been leading in non-song. 'To begin with, the stupid London audience will be baffled. Then, they will find it hilarious. Hysterically, dangerously so. Some of them will literally soil themselves and the ushers will have to dive in with mops and commodes. Towards the end of Act One, the good people of Shaftesbury Avenue will hate it. But then they will love it again. Then they will find "I Whistle a Happy Tune" being sung on G sharp intensely upsetting. But then transcendent! At the interval, most of them will leave. But then . . .'

From Kate's perspective, this plan had not yet come to fruition. In fact, Kes would be pretty much over the idea within the next eight days. But she remembered the soundtrack to her Freshers' Week featured large tracts of *Oliver!* And *The King and I* being spiritedly droned at the instigation of Keven Lloyd. The more people joined in, the funnier it became. But if you weren't one of the people joining in, it sounded obnoxious and awful. The experience was not unlike being friends with Kes himself.

She found them in the queue, slipping her arm into Amy's. She checked Kate's expression and then just accepted the gesture with a smile and patted Kate's hand without comment.

Here's to the friends who don't ask questions!

Kate felt immediately ashamed of the thought. Friends get to ask questions when they need to. Friends get to intrude. And their own friends let them.

Toby looked especially pleased to see Kate. 'Save me, for God's sake,' he said.

Kate scratched her nose briefly and asked, 'Save you?'

'From this. From the enforced rehearsal of this man's crazy dream.'

'The exact musical doesn't matter,' Kes exclaimed. 'But surely, on a night like this, we simply must do "Getting to Know You".'

Amy gave Kate's arm a rough squeeze. 'We have been,' she said quite loudly. 'For example, I've just found out that Toby's got a girlfriend back in Edinburgh that he plans to break up with by writing her a letter!'

'Oh Toby!' Kate exclaimed. 'You can't do it by letter!' Kate knew perfectly well that the girlfriend at home was an imaginary character that Toby conjured whenever women he didn't fancy came on to him. He really was tremendously fussy. And Amy, Kate realised, was leaning quite heavily on her arm.

'I didn't say that, Amy,' Toby objected mildly. 'I just said we're thinking things over, y'know? Taking a spell.'

'Very grown-up,' Kate said.

Toby had been swaying slightly but suddenly found his balance. 'I like to think so,' he said to her. He looked away with a flicker of a frown as if he wished he could have thought of something wittier.

'Right then, almost there!' Kes bellowed. 'One more song to mark the occasion of our very first visit – and very possibly *last* visit – to . . . what the hell is it called again?'

'Blossom, y'student tosser!' somebody called out. There was a genial chuckle from the regulars.

'Thank you, member of the public!' Kes replied, shitfaced. And then conspiratorially to his friends, 'I love my public, you see. Love them.'

In they went, past the bouncer, through the unprepossessing door, up the steep, greasy staircase.

'Mind your step there,' said Toby. 'It smells like the whole of York has thrown up on these stairs every night for two hundred years.' Instinctively he offered Kate his hand but then withdrew it and immediately muttered, 'Sorry.'

To her own surprise, Kate reached up and took it. 'Thanks,' she said.

Toby paused and now they were walking up the narrow staircase side by side. 'Yup, I daresay you're capable of walking up a flight of stairs unaided.'

Kate smiled to herself. 'I probably would have managed. But it was nice of you anyway.'

'You're not one of those scary feminists then, Kate?'

'Actually, Toby, I'm one of the scariest feminists you'll ever meet.'

'Oh Christ. Now I'm in trouble.'

'Nah, I'm just kidding.' Her smile faded as she thought of the times she had picked her husband's THIS IS WHAT A FEMINIST LOOKS LIKE t-shirt up off the bedroom floor; the way – along with the rest of his laundry – she had washed it, dried it, folded it and put it back in his drawer only to find it on the floor again a couple of weeks later. She said, 'Actually, I'm not sure the sisterhood would be entirely thrilled by some of my choices.'

Toby looked at her in surprise. 'Well, I can't say I'm in touch with the sisterhood but I'm sure it's more forgiving than you think.'

'We'll see.' It felt daring as she gave his hand a playful squeeze. By way of return he gently intensified his hold, the soft hug of his palm and fingers sending tingles of warmth up her arm and through her body.

Oblivious, Toby glanced behind them. 'Well, they let us in so we seem to have cleared the dress code.'

Kate enjoyed the idea that dearest Blossom could have something as grand as a dress code. 'We both look fabulous,' she said.

'You do.' He peeked down at his naff waistcoat. 'This thing has seen better days.'

They came to a halt as the queue bottlenecked for the coat-dumping broom cupboard. Kate gave Toby's waistcoat a more detailed inspection than she had the first time around. She noticed a patch of cotton in a lighter blue. 'Well, somebody loves it.'

He followed her gaze. 'Aye, the moths got together in the wardrobe over the summer and gave it a good seeing to.'

'Did your mum fix it up?'

Toby gave her a look of mock offence. 'How dare you? All my own work, I'll have you know.'

'Really? You darn your own clothes?'

He looked genuinely surprised. 'Most certainly. Who else should be doing it?'

Kate giggled. 'Sorry.'

'No, you're all right. I'm not the only abandoned public school boy with a sewing kit in his trunk.' But then as an afterthought he murmured, 'Although there's probably not many of us, truth to tell.'

And although Kate had been through this Blossom process many times – climbing the stairs, getting the green hand-stamp, dumping her coat, entering the wide, low-ceilinged room with the restaurant tables pushed to the edges – for the first time today she felt something was new. She felt, in fact, as though she was living in the present. She listened to Amy and Kes behind them, giving a rousing G sharp rendition from *The King and I*, and she kept Toby's hand in hers as they made their way to the bar.

> *Getting to knoooow you,*
> *Getting to know aaall abooooout you,*
> *Getting to liiiike you,*
> *Getting to hope you like me.*

She danced like she was eight years old. Not eighteen. Eight. Even Kes couldn't keep up with her, and he was by no means a retiring presence on the dance floor. Kate felt every cheesy beat the Blossom DJ sent her way as a call to life itself: spinning, jumping, headbanging, moshing, grooving, laughing, screaming, falling, dancing like a woman possessed. It should have frightened people but this was Blossom and her joy was unconquerable and infectious. After his second tequila shot, Toby too lost all inhibition – as well as his waistcoat and hairband. His dirty blond locks thrashed around his slim centre of gravity, the sweat of his white t-shirt clinging to him like a groupie to an unlikely sex-god. He and Kate were giving the world a brief refresher course on the meaning of joy: by turns daft and flirtatious; decorous and chaotic; together and apart. But always keeping a space between them when they locked eye-contact that crackled with potential; as if getting too close would complete a circuit and the whole city would blow a fuse. Not since she caught Olga Bhukarin in a crafty shin-sweep and saw that silver medal in her grasp had Kate felt so sure that her body was in the right place doing the right thing. Amy pumped her fist in the air and laughed as Kes struck a rhythmic series of curious poses which threatened to put another dent in the panelled ceiling. Urban Cookie Collective threw out the pounding throb of their gift to the world.

'We must meet this woman!' Toby yelled to Kate.

'What?'

'We must meet this woman! She has not only the KEY but also the SECRET!'

'I LOVE IT that she has both the KEY and the SECRET! I wonder what the difference is?!'

'She doesn't seem to give a shit!'

Kate laughed and moved closer to shout across Toby's left ear. 'Don't go anywhere. I need a piss.'

He pretended to be confused. 'What? You want to give me a kiss?'

'No. I want a . . .' She let her hands rest on his shoulders and they slowed down, losing the beat but swaying together. 'Actually a kiss would be great,' she said.

Toby's courage deserted him and he tried to keep up the joke. 'A piss would be great? Well, we all sometimes need—'

She kissed him. She reached up and pushed the fingers of one hand through his tangled hair; the other hand at his waist and squeezing to find a hip bone moving in time with her. She felt a strong hand round the small of her back as he gently lifted her into him. And under the taste of booze and tobacco – what was that? She nearly laughed as she identified the sweetness.

Strawberries. Fuck me, if this boy doesn't taste of strawberries.

He kissed with feeling and self-control; half the passion was in what he held back. It was the sexiest kind of kiss. It was a promise.

They were snogging in the middle of the dance floor, getting occasionally jostled by their fellow boppers. They broke off and smiled at each other in discovery – she took his hand and led him to a corner.

'Hi,' she said.

'Hi.'

And then, because it was suddenly the obvious question, 'How are you?'

'How am I?' Toby gave a toothy smile and looked out to the room for a moment. 'I must say I've felt worse.' He returned his gaze to her. 'I'm a wee bit dizzy, to be honest.'

'Oh, right. Is that what happens when you dance?'

'No. Apparently it's what happens when I stand quite close to you.'

Kate looked down at her boots and shuffled like a schoolgirl. There wasn't much point trying to be cool about this. 'That's a nice thing to say.'

'It's a nice thing to feel, I don't mind telling you.'

She reached up and kissed him again, more passionately this time. He placed a hand on the side of her face and she experienced a sudden drop in her pelvic region as if she'd just driven a car over a humpback bridge at high speed.

She broke off. 'Ooh, right. Okay.'

'Hmm,' he said. 'My thoughts entirely.'

Kate took a woozy moment to reflect that the sudden change in her feelings for Toby were the exact opposite of sudden. It wasn't that he was different – it was that she now saw what she had first missed. *Of course!* Of course Toby was an unassuming fuck-god. Of course he was self-sufficient and kind. And that kiss – of course it felt rich and tender. Why wouldn't it? It had been cooking for twenty-eight years.

Still, the insight frightened her and she didn't trust her feelings. She needed to take a moment. Luckily her bladder was giving her an insistent excuse. She was glad she wouldn't have to lie to him. There had been quite enough of that. 'Don't take this the wrong way,' she said, 'but I really do need that piss.'

His expression faltered. 'Okay . . .'

'Toby, seriously.' She kissed him again. 'I promise I'm not going to disappear.'

'Go, then. I demand that you have this important piss.'

'You'll be here?'

'I'll be waiting.'

She laid a hand on his warm chest and then forced herself to turn towards the door.

The one-cubicle sensory provocation that called itself the 'Ladies' was back through the main door and past the stairs. Kate made her way round the edge of the room, grabbing a handful of complimentary prawn crackers from a shared bucket on the way. It was a muscle memory: you're at Blossom – you pig-out on prawn crackers. Not just because you're hungry but because you once heard that the fat content allowed you to drink for longer before keeling over. Moving through the crowded doorway, she contemplated the metaphysics of her attitude to the prawn crackers. Her older self – or rather, herself in her future life – would now take a dim view of exposing her immune system to the do-boys-really-wash-their-hands-after-having-a-wee? bacterial lottery of a communal snack bucket. There again, her older self didn't seem to be entirely in charge of this body. This body seemed to have quite strong opinions of its own. For example, the lower-middle part of it was, she was the first to notice, currently having *quite the party* because of a kiss from Toby Harker.

She then wobbled round the corner to a sight that was equally unexpected and considerably less welcome.

Luke had just reached the top of the stairs and wore an expression of unhinged determination. He looked like a man who'd just discovered a neighbour had driven over his display of prize begonias and he was jolly well going to say something. Kate wanted to hide but Luke had already seen her and he stopped her by saying, weirdly, 'Excuse me!'

She was still holding a prawn cracker and sensed that she probably had crumbs on her lips. It was as if she had just been caught red-handed doing something outrageous. She immediately resented a powerful feeling of guilt and tossed her hair, waiting for him to speak.

'I came to ask you what the hell you think you're playing at,' he said.

'I've said everything I had to say. The rest is up to you.'

'And you expect me to believe you?'

Kate took a large and defiant bite of prawn cracker and said through it, 'Yeah, I do actually.'

'That I've got a brain tumour and you're my time-travelling fucking . . . *wife* from the future?'

Kate glanced around, conscious that she didn't want this conversation overheard. The merry patrons of Blossom were toing and froing around them obliviously. Luke registered her unease: 'Oh, what? You don't want other people to know? You think they might think you're nuts?'

She dropped the rest of the cracker on the floor and wiped her hand on her jeans. 'Luke, you're making a dick of yourself. I understand that you're having trouble accepting this, but—'

'How could you possibly understand!?' He was shouting now, an angry flush reddening his face and throat. 'People I care about, a grandmother that I really loved, died of cancer and it's not a funny subject!'

Granny Fairbright. Lilian. Bowel cancer. When he was twelve.

Kate opened her mouth to speak but Luke couldn't allow it. 'And don't say that you knew that! Don't you dare say that you know! You don't know these things about me. You don't know things! I don't believe you! You don't know!'

He was hysterical. He'd obviously spent the last hour in his room knocking up a hot soup of fear and incomprehension. She moved closer and tried to calm him. 'Luke . . .' she said.

'DON'T YOU FUCKING TOUCH ME!' he yelled and lurched to take a step back.

But there was no step to take.

Instead, Luke's hastily reversing foot found the thin air at the top of the stairs. Kate lunged forward to grab him. Already falling, Luke took the movement as some kind of attack and batted her hand away. He flailed wildly with his other arm at the slick wall of the staircase but there was nothing to save him. The momentum of his recoil from Kate carried his six-foot-two body down the stairs with the back of his head leading the way. It struck a middle step and the rest of him followed in a crumpled somersault. Over he went: once, twice.

Clattering down after him, Kate was at his side before he had stopped moving.

'Luke! Luke!'

There was no response from his closed eyes. And Kate fought for breath as a pool of his blood began to form on the ground behind his broken head.

She screamed. 'Help me! I need help!'

Chapter 17

'I can't say I'm surprised. Your aunt Vanessa only lasted one day at secretarial college.'

'Mother, I already told you. I haven't dropped out. I just came back to collect a few things.'

'It was a blessing in disguise, of course,' Madeleine went on. 'She would never have made a typist, not with those nails. Or her attitude to men.'

They sat opposite each other in the small, tidy room that Bill called the living room and Madeleine called the parlour. A modest sunrise was breaking through the net curtains: a Sunday morning in Kate's childhood home in Deptford. A very recent childhood as far as Madeleine was concerned. As for Kate, she had let herself in through the front door for the first time in many years. Since, in fact, her mother had sold the place after Bill's death. Kate was tremulously aware that her father was asleep upstairs.

Kate sipped the Earl Grey her mother had made for them. She hadn't slept. She had ridden with Luke in the ambulance, holding his hand and chanting to herself 'I'm sorry, I'm sorry' as the paramedics improved on her work to stop the bleeding. Once he was stable in intensive care there was nothing to do except call his parents. Barbara had answered with impressive speed given that she must have been in bed. But then, Kate imagined, this is what parents do: the phone rings after midnight and they expect the worst. *Poor Barbara!* Kate had always loved her and had now admired the focused and unfussy way she had taken the details of the hospital from this strange young woman on the end of the phone. She had told Barbara the truth, from a certain point of view: she didn't know Luke well but there had been an accident.

Kate looked at her watch. There were no trains that late and Luke's dad, Richard, would have driven them from Salisbury to York through the night. Kate had felt – perhaps conveniently – that she would only get in the way if she hung around. The truth was she couldn't bear it. She couldn't bear to see Luke's parents in a hospital. Not again. She couldn't begin to imagine the lies she would have to tell them while concealing the full impact of her own re-animated grief. What was she supposed to say? She was some girl who met him a few hours ago and that's why she was at the hospital looking like the world had imploded? That Luke had somehow managed to give her his parents' phone number before losing consciousness? She couldn't do it. He was alive and there were doctors; when he came round he would see his mum and dad – not the witch who might as well have pushed him down the stairs with her broomstick. She had tried never to take the word 'witch' as an insult even when that was the intention. A witch was just an eccentric woman who tried to heal people in ways which too often provoked fear. Yup, she'd been a witch all right.

Above all, Kate needed to talk to her father. She had waited outside York station in the dark and fare-dodged the first train to London. God bless 1992: the ticket inspectors who couldn't be arsed before rush hour and the automated barriers that didn't exist.

Madeleine was a light sleeper and had appeared in her splendid black and gold oriental-style dressing gown before Kate had managed to fill the kettle.

And now, in her parlour, she was inspecting her daughter with a shrewd eye. The dawn had broken and Madeleine reached to turn off a side lamp without taking her eyes off Kate's clothes. 'Your father will be up shortly,' she said. 'You might want to visit the bathroom first and have a wash and a change.'

'Do I smell, Mother?'

'I'm sure it's him you've come to see anyway. Lucky to catch him on a Sunday, but then of course you've thought of that.'

At forty-five, Kate's mother was a state-of-the-art delivery system for laser-guided passive-aggression. In her head, Kate counted to twenty, slowly and in Russian. Madeleine had just entered her dyed blonde phase – a stylish bob, efficiently brushed in the dark while her husband slept. The lines at the downturn of her mouth were less pronounced than Kate was used to, the green eyes were agile and focused. This was vintage Mother – a woman of agency. Kate was on high alert.

'Darling,' Madeleine said suddenly enough to make Kate jump. 'If it's man-trouble, you know you can tell me about it.'

Kate made a rapid mental inventory of people she would discuss 'man-trouble' with before discussing it with her mother. The list started with Dr Susie Orbach and she got down to Anders Breivik before giving up. 'There's really no man-trouble, Mother.'

'Well, then,' Madeleine said, edging forward in her straight-backed chair, 'woman-trouble, then. You can tell me, darling – I was around in the sixties. I'm quite unshockable.'

'Oh God, here we go again.' Kate was already annoyed

with herself for taking the bait. 'When are you going to accept that I'm not a lesbian?'

'It's nothing to be ashamed of. Look at Gloria Hunniford.'

'I understand it would . . . hang on, Gloria Hunniford isn't gay either.'

'Well . . . you say that.'

'Yes, I do say that.'

'Well . . .'

'No, not "well". Look, I understand it would give you great pleasure to tell Estelle and Sheila and all the other Ladies Who Lunch that your daughter is a massive homo and you're bravely standing by her, but—'

'There's no need to mock my friends. They've already been very supportive.'

'What do you mean "already"? Oh Christ, I knew it! You've been dining out on this for years!'

'Is it any wonder? The martial arts! The way you dress! We worry about you, darling.'

'Well, you can take your bullshit worry and shove it up your arse, darling.'

Madeleine's eyes widened at the appropriation of the d-word. Eighteen-year-old Kate could be argumentative but this was considerably more push-back than she was used to. She loved it. This had the makings of a proper fight. 'There's really no need to be so hurtful, Katherine.'

But Kate had one or two things on her mind. 'Martial arts, for crying out loud. Look at you. Going around in the nineteen-sixties with your Little Red Book, quoting tosspot aphorisms from a mass-murderer, and then the first sign that your daughter is into something girls aren't supposed to be into – that's it. She must be queer.'

'I would never use such a prejudiced term.'

'Fuck the terms. The terms change. They're less important than the individuals.'

'Individualism, is it? Spoken like a child of Thatcher!'

'Who you voted for twice, you phoney old twat.'

'Kate!'

'What? I thought you were unshockable.'

'There's such a thing as civility. I thought you understood that.'

This was an instinctively smart move. Kate knew she had an appalling temper and it constantly undermined her arguments. She took a breath. 'I'm sorry. That was rude.'

'All these years . . .' Madeleine shook her head in martyred regret.

Kate understood that she had raised the emotional temperature too high for Madeleine to listen to another word she said. But she finished her argument anyway – something which, ironically, her mother had always taught her to do.

'I apologise again,' she said. 'But it's not cool to tell girls who like karate that they're lesbian. They might be, and that's fine, but they might not be and that's also fine. The point is, girls don't get into boys' stuff so our parents can find an excuse to feel good about themselves. We like it because we like it.'

Madeleine had her hands in front of her eyes and was beginning to vibrate. 'I can't believe a daughter of mine is such a homophobe.'

'Mother, please don't cry.'

Madeleine was crying. Or rather, as Kate wearily recognised, Madeleine had actively summoned the necessary feelings which would allow her to cry. The feelings were real but they had been accessed with precision: she was a consummate actor. Kate offered a silent prayer of thanks that her mother would never really get the hang of Twitter. This talent for willed grievance would have made her a star.

There was a creak from the floorboards above them. 'And now you've woken your father,' she moaned. 'Perfect.'

Kate was reminded that even Madeleine wasn't going to live forever. Whatever victory this was, it was worthless. She tried a peace offering – at least a morsel of gossip which could be expanded at a future 'luncheon' with Estelle and Sheila. 'All right, Mother. Look. There *is* a boy.'

Madeleine stopped crying and found a tissue. 'There's no need to humour me,' she said bitterly. 'It's perfectly clear the matter is beneath your dignity.'

'Actually, two boys.'

Madeleine interrupted her nose-blow. 'Oh . . . Kate!'

'I know,' said Kate flatly. 'Outrageous.'

'You've only been there twenty-four hours. Are you *determined* to die of AIDS?'

'I haven't shagged them, Mother. I'm just a bit confused. That's all I have to say about it.'

The loo flushed upstairs. Kate said, 'And I'd appreciate it if you didn't tell Dad. I don't want either of you worried about me.' Kate had never tried this before – bringing her mother into a conspiracy that excluded Bill. The woman opposite uttered a non-committal 'Hmm . . .' but she was clearly considering whether or not to feel flattered. Kate went on: 'But like I say, I came back to collect some stuff. That I forgot to pack. There were some things that I missed.'

'Hello, hello! I know that voice!' Bill popped his head round the door, his thick, greying hair madly unbrushed; the collar of his pyjama top sticking up. He looked like an Elvis impersonator with twenty minutes to sober up before a show. Kate stood and approached him as calmly as possible. Which was not very calmly. She hugged him close.

Warmth. Peppermint. Cigarettes. Yesterday's after shave. A touch of BO. All present and correct.

'Looks like somebody missed me, then!' She released him

and laughed, wiping her eyes. Bill turned to his wife. 'I told you, Maddy. I said Kate can't go two days without our scintillating company.'

Madeleine drained her teacup and stood. 'You said no such thing, Bill. You and your stories.'

Kate sensed her dad's surprise at the tightness of the hug but he stayed on the surface for now. 'Right,' he said. 'Let's have a cup of tea.'

'There's one in the pot,' said Madelaine, crossing to the door. 'I'll pour it.'

'Oh yes please then, love.'

Kate had recently recovered the power of speech. She said weakly, 'I came back to collect a few things.'

Madeleine had just gone through the door but now instantly reappeared. 'That's right. Kate came back to collect a few things. Also, she's overwrought because she entangled herself in a *ménage à trois*. For all I know, she's working as a prostitute and has got herself pregnant three times over. But it's a women's issue and it's between ourselves. She'd prefer not to talk about it and I for one respect that.'

Bill turned his big face back to Kate. 'Blimey.'

Kate looked from her dad to her mum with a resigned smile. 'Thank you, Mother.'

'Not at all. And you're staying for lunch, I take it?'

'I don't want to intrude.'

Her parents were united in the same astonishment and the same word: 'Intrude?'

'Tell me how you met,' Kate said as Bill handed her another saucepan to dry. They were side by side in the little kitchen, looking out onto the back yard.

Earlier, Kate had helped her mother chop vegetables, relieved that she didn't have to conceal any new-found twenty-first-century skill in this area because she didn't have any. The pair managed to restrict their conversation to literature and the weather. After lunch, Madeleine retired for her nap. Bill's nap would be later, of course. It was a routine which Kate had to admire for its easy predictability. And although the division of domestic labour was largely traditional – which is to say Madeleine did basically everything – both parties seemed largely content with the arrangement. The husband went out to work; and if this particular wife felt she'd had a rough deal from the universe (or in her case – God) then she didn't seem to locate her resentments in Bill. Madeleine Theroux was angry about a lot of things and with a lot of people. But not the handsome rocker she found in that dance hall in 1963. And presumably – and Kate still didn't like to conjure these particular images, no matter how grown up she was supposed to be – well, they had separate naps but not separate beds.

Bill patiently scrubbed a roasting tray. 'Oh gawd, you must have heard it a thousand times over.'

'I think I've heard it twice. Go on. I like the way you tell it.'

He did an impression of a Northern Irish stand-up which was reassuringly dated even for 1992. 'It's the way I tell 'em! It's a cracker!'

'Go on.'

He didn't need any more encouragement. 'Well, it was a Saturday night down the Mecca in Hammersmith. The Palais de Danse, no less. Joe Loss & His Orchestra, hundreds of youngsters. Packed, it was. Magic. And I see this lovely-looking girl sitting on her own. Beautiful light green dress she was wearing, classy as you like. You'd think she'd be getting a lot of attention but nobody dared – half of us thought it was flamin' Princess Margaret. Anyway, I go up and ask if she'd mind me spending a few moments telling her all about my new boots. Shoes, actually. Creepers.

Bloody stupid idea but I couldn't think of anything better to say. But I did know that beautiful women never want to hear that they're beautiful because either they know already or they don't agree. Either way, they've heard it all before. As you probably know, love. Anyway, she says she'd been admiring my new shoes from a distance and couldn't believe it had taken me this long to come and tell her all about them. Cool as a cucumber, she was, and I nearly wet myself. Anyway, we get talking. She must have liked the look of me, or more likely felt sorry for me. And then I can't remember how but we get on to politics and she asks if I'm Labour and I say yeah. And to my great surprise she says that she's just joined her local Labour club, mainly to stick it to her old man but she's a proper Wilson fan. And I tell her that, no offence, but that comes as a bit of a surprise, what with her sounding quite posh. She laughs at this and then says, "People say I'm this and people say I'm that . . . but I know that I'm just Madeleine Theroux." And I say, "Yeah, we're all just muddling through, love. Anyway, let's have a fuckin' dance."'

Kate cackled at this. But had never understood whether Bill had misheard Madeleine in the noisy dance hall or whether his reply had been a deliberate joke. The tea towel in her hand slowed its journey around the rim of a saucepan as she realised this might be her last chance to ask.

She decided against it. Some stories shouldn't be explained. They should be left alive with their own mysteries and contradictions. But it prompted another question. 'Do you believe in fate, then?'

Bill raised his eyebrows at the soapy water. 'What, as in me and your mother?'

'Yeah. Do you think two people are ever meant for each other? Or is that just what couples tell themselves when they get too old to go dancing?'

'Cheeky mare! We can still dance! You should have seen us at Keith's fiftieth.'

'You know what I mean.'

Amused, Bill took his hands out of the water and leaned on the sink. He looked up through the window at the clouds. 'Nah, not really.'

Kate burst out laughing. 'You old romantic, you!'

'Well, you did ask.'

'No, that's good. It's honest, anyway.'

Still smiling, Bill entered a reverie and unconsciously twisted at his wedding ring. 'It's not fate that counts, Katie. It's love. Could she have ended up marrying someone else if I hadn't gone out that night? Yeah, 'course she could.'

'Could you?'

Bill looked at her.

'I mean, if you hadn't been in that place at that time. If you'd gone out the next Saturday. Or even if you'd been in a different corner of the Palais on the same night . . . It could all have been different, couldn't it? There's no law that says it had to be you and Mother.'

'No, 'course not. No, there's no law exactly. But . . . you don't tend to think about it like that. At least I don't anyway. It's . . . I know you're a bright one, Kate, but it's hard to explain to someone young who's never been married.'

Kate nodded carefully. 'Yeah, I'm just interested. I suppose I'm thinking about the future.'

'Well, all right – so you meet someone. Maybe it's random, but the point is you met them and there's no going back. You can't go back. You all right, love? Don't worry, that's a quality saucepan – I'm always dropping stuff.'

Kate silently picked up her saucepan and placed it gently on the draining board. Bill went on.

'Like I say, you can never go back. And you wouldn't want to, usually. It would be weird. And then if you get married . . . well, that's a choice. That's not fate, that's a choice. You marry them because you love them. And marriage . . . well, it's a long game, at least if you're lucky. You take the rough with the smooth, no doubt about it.'

Kate had to insist. 'Yeah, I know all that, but—'

'Well, you say that you know all that, but—'

'I mean, I can *imagine* all that, but . . . what if you *did* have to go back? What if you had what you thought was a good marriage and a good life but then you're back in Hammersmith Palais and there's some other girl that you didn't notice properly the first time? And she's amazing. Not like some shrinking violet who's good at *looking* like a shrinking violet but is obviously a massively confident English rose – but an *actual* shrinking violet . . .' The national flower metaphor was not helping Kate; there was very little in her latest experience of Toby Harker that involved any *shrinking*. 'I mean, more like a lovely thistle really, but a lot less prickly than you thought, and anyway some prickles are good so . . .'

She took a breath. 'But I'm saying that it's possible to get it right the first time but then, when you know what you know now – which you didn't know then – you still think you were right the first time, but now in the second time there's a whole new first time, and this time something different is definitely right.' She looked at her dad and optimistically added, 'Surely.'

Bill had been frowning through this and dried his hands on a tea towel. 'Katie,' he said calmly, 'what's this all about?'

'What?'

'Why are you here, love?'

'I just came back to collect a few things.'

'Come on.'

Kate turned slowly and walked to the other side of the room.

It is the ambition of many parents that the phrase 'come on', said in the right tone at the right moment, will elicit from their teenaged children an outpouring of truth. All previous evasions and secrets will fall away and there will follow an unbridled sharing of souls in which the parents will have the opportunity to divest themselves of their considerable wisdom and thereby not only make the lives of their children happier but also make their own lives less full of guilt and inadequacy. This was no such moment.

Bill had earned it – he had put the hours in with his daughter – but Kate knew there was no way she could give him even the most general outline of what was going on. She felt her throat beginning to constrict and wiped her eyes as if to warn them to behave. 'There's just some slightly complicated stuff going on and I needed a break.'

'Sweetheart, what is it? You've been there one day.'

As a diversion, as much as anything else, Kate said, 'A lot can happen in one day. Look at Grandad Marsden.'

'Y'what?'

'Grandad Marsden at the Battle of Cable Street.'

'What the bloody hell has he got to do with it?'

'I mean, what if he hadn't been there? Seeing off Mosley's fascists. It could all have been different, couldn't it?'

Bill turned his back and looked out of the window. Kate frowned at her father from the end of the kitchen and persisted. 'I mean, that could have changed the course of history, right? It only takes one person to do something different and . . . well, maybe I'm not meant to be at uni. Maybe I should be here spending time with you and I should . . . I dunno, get a job at Our Price. I mean, not Our Price obviously, because they won't last another five minutes, but—'

Bill turned to face her. 'You're not jacking-in your education!'

'Why are you so angry? Why d'you always get like this when anyone mentions your dad?'

'I wasn't talking about—'

'Is it just a story? Was he not there?'

'Yes, he was there!'

'So why—'

'Because he was there all right, but he was on the wrong bloody side, wasn't he?'

Kate gawped. The only sound in the room was from the washing machine going through a rinse cycle. Bill noted her reaction. 'Oh yeah, that's right. The great hero of Cable Street.' Keeping his voice under control because he didn't want to wake Madeleine, Bill broke into a bizarre on-the-spot dance routine to the tune of 'My Old Man's a Dustman'.

'My old man's a Blackshirt! He wears a Blackshirt's hat! He puts on Nazi trousers, and he goosesteps like a twat!'

Kate gazed at her father as he recovered his breath, recognising the typically English defence against personal humiliation – making a joke of it. She felt a fraction of the pain Bill had been carrying around all this time. Breaking the silence, she said, 'Did you make up some verses too?'

'Several.'

Wordlessly she crossed the room and hugged her dad. 'Why didn't you tell me, you silly old sod?' she said into his shoulder.

'Nobody wants an arsehole for a grandad, do they?'

'I wouldn't have cared.'

'Oh yes, you would've.'

She thought of the white lies she had told Luke about his book in order to protect him; and about the truth she had told him yesterday – memories that had left him not so much rescued as hospitalised. There was no way of

213

knowing if she'd done the right thing. And Madeleine . . .
'Mother's always known, then?'

Bill disengaged and looked sheepishly at his daughter, his hands slipping down to find hers. 'Yeah, 'course she knows. It was part of the reason we got on so well, to be honest. Daddy Theroux was a bit of a shocking bastard an' all.' Kate adapted to this new reality as best she could. She quite liked the idea that her parents' relationship was partly founded as an anti-fascist alliance.

'Anyway,' Bill said, 'they're both gone now. But I won't lie, it was horrible growing up knowing the old man had been one of those people. Yobs on London streets, shouting the odds. Waving their Union Flags, looking for someone to blame. *Daily Mail* egging them on, police not knowing what to do with them. Horrible.'

'Well,' said Kate, almost to herself and with some bitterness, 'those days are gone, aren't they?'

'Maybe,' said Bill, 'but you've always got to keep your eye out.' He went to the kettle and tested its weight. 'They don't come with a calling card any more, not since the war. They don't kick the door down and say, "'Allo, we're the Nazis."' He took the kettle to the sink and filled it. 'But they'll be back – one way or another.'

Kate watched him replace the kettle and reach for a couple of mugs. She said, 'Because people are always going to go through hard times and there's always going to be scared politicians.'

'Yeah,' said Bill. 'That, and the fact that some people are just arseholes.'

She laughed and he joined in. He leaned back on the sink and folded his arms. 'You've always got to be on the lookout. You've always got to do your bit.'

Kate thought of the memory stick she had posted back to Charles Hunt.

'Look, love, I won't go on if you don't want to talk about it. And I'm not exactly in a position to give you a bollocking about keeping secrets.'

'You'd be on a bit of a sticky wicket with that one, Dad.'

He looked down at the floor between them and shook his head at the thought of the 'scene' they had just had. Kate and Bill didn't do drama; not usually. 'Yeah, fair enough. But look, whatever's going on at uni – whatever trouble you're in – if it really is trouble, I'll help if I can. You know I will. But at the end of the day you're eighteen years old. You're a woman. Whatever's going on, you need to face it.'

'I know,' she said quietly.

'All this talk of the past, stories about me and your mum . . . I don't see how it helps you, love. Now, if you want to stay here then nothing would make me happier. But I gotta tell you, Kate – you'd only be dreaming. This will always be your home, love, but it's not where you belong any more. Not really, not you. Don't you think it's time to go back to the real world? Your own life?'

Something inside Kate changed. She felt a clarity blow through her mind like an autumn breeze dispersing the seeds of a dandelion.

She only said, 'Give me another lift to the station?'

Bill nodded in a sad kind of satisfaction. 'Let's have this cup of tea before we say cheerio again.'

'Yeah,' said Kate. 'Let's.'

Chapter 18

Kate jumped off the bus and ran through the amber-lit city towards the hospital. 'Good Yorkshire rain,' Amy would probably call it. Kate, collar up, head down, feeling the downpour batter her scalp, wondered where they got it from, these Yorkshire lads and lasses. What was good about it? Where was the 'good London rain'? And the 'famous London sense of humour'? Why did the Mersey stir more passions than the Thames? Apart from the Kinks, she conceded, dodging into the hospital's main entrance. The Kinks had written the only song about the Thames that most people can whistle. Missing her dirty old river, she slowed to a walk and pushed her fingers back through her hair. She sniffed up the rain-mingled snot and tried to compose herself. The warm fug of antiseptic and controlled defeat was there to greet her: it was Yorkshire rain, but this was a hospital like any other.

At the reception desk she claimed to be a friend of Luke Fairbright. There was the usual benign and slow-moving NHS buggering around with software that didn't properly work. The fact that it still wouldn't properly work in twenty-eight years' time felt oddly reassuring.

Luke was out of intensive care and Kate took the lift to his ward. She had no idea what she was going to say but

216

didn't expect him to be conscious. The point was to be there. That's what friends/wives/widows do. *Also mothers,* Kate remembered, as she rounded a corner and nearly walked into Barbara Fairbright.

Luke's mum had been helping a nurse clear some coffee cups. Barbara stood in the corridor and set down a stack of tessellating porcelain. She was a short, round woman with thick glasses and a knitted cardigan the colours of a subdued rainbow – Kate had to resist a powerful urge to hug her. She approached tentatively. 'Excuse me,' she said. 'Are you Mrs Fairbright?'

Barbara looked up in alarm. There was something prematurely fragile and old lady-ish about her but then, Kate figured, she'd had a hell of a day. 'Yes?' she said.

'My name's Kate. I'm the girl who phoned last night and—'

'Oh, you're Kate!' Barbara interrupted. The laugh-lines around her eyes materialised with warmth. 'Luke's been asking for you.'

'Luke's been . . . how is he?'

'They're saying he's going to make a full recovery, Kate. A full recovery.'

Now Kate really did hug her. Barbara accepted the embrace with a soothing chuckle and rubbed her back. 'Oh, you're soaked through, you poor thing,' she said.

'Sorry. Didn't mean to get you all damp.'

'Gosh, I didn't even know it was raining. Poor Richard – he hates driving in the rain.'

Kate tried to cock her head as if that name needed explanation.

'Luke's dad,' Barbara said in her mild Wiltshire twang. 'Off back home. He's got patients in the morning, and now that Luke's out of danger – come on, you'll want to see him. Me, wittering on. Come on.'

She led Kate into the subdued light and troubled peace of a night-time hospital ward. There were six beds, five of which were occupied by grey men in their fifties variously reading, coughing, snoring or somehow doing all three. The sixth was at the end of the room, enclosed by the wrap-around curtain. Barbara quietly drew it aside for Kate to enter.

Luke never slept on his back and that was the first thing Kate noticed – that, and the clean bandage covering most of his head above the eyes. For some reason he looked more like the Luke she knew in his early thirties – and then she realised: the top of his head was shaved. Barbara replaced the curtain and Kate turned to her. 'He's had an operation?' The other woman nodded and drew up a couple of chairs.

'Yes, dear,' she said as they both sat. 'A craniotomy. The doctor said it was a "depressed fracture", which is very serious. They were worried that there might be bits of broken bone – well, swimming around near his brain and causing a nuisance.' Barbara crossed her legs and took her glasses off to clean them. She looked like she hadn't slept for a week. 'Well, they gave him a scan and they found an "abnormality". Something they said could be a tumour. They said it was probably just a bit of gristle but had the potential to turn nasty. They would normally leave it be and keep an eye on it for the next few years, but since they were "poking around in there anyway" – I mean, it's like the Dark Ages when it comes to brains, if you ask me – the specialist, when he finally turned up, the neuro-oncologist – he said he might as well whip it out.'

Kate boggled. 'They *whipped it out*?'

'They did, yes. Whatever it was, it's gone. Anyway, they've put in a kind of mesh to help his skull heal. Should be right as rain in a few months.'

Kate looked at the young man in the bandage. This was how she remembered Luke – a person who could reasonably expect to live all the way into old age. Except this time it was true. This time there was no lurking menace. Luke had a piece of metal in his head and would need weeks of care; but at the same time, he was healthier than she'd ever known him. She felt relief and euphoria knocking on the door but couldn't quite let them in just yet. She had a question. 'Did the doctors talk to Luke about the tumour? I mean, before the operation, did they tell him about the . . . abnormality?'

'Oh yes,' said Barbara replacing her glasses. 'That was the queer thing. Luke was adamant that they should take it out. I mean, the poor lamb was concussed so we all took it with a pinch of salt. But then he was saying, "She was right, she was right. Tell Kate she was right."' Barbara fixed the younger woman with a look that put Kate in mind of a lioness who didn't care for the way a hyena had just looked at her cub. 'Does that mean anything to you, Kate?'

Kate had her own big-cat tendencies when it came to her husband but she swallowed her indignation. She'd never needed to fight her lovely, canny mother-in-law and this would be a hell of a time to start. She had to think quickly. 'Yes,' she said. 'I told him something about my past and he didn't believe me. I got quite angry and we were arguing when he fell down the stairs.'

'He said that he'd had too much to drink and he just slipped.'

'It's true that it was an accident, but he wasn't drunk. He was arguing with me at the time. I tried to save him, but he was already falling.'

Barbara looked to her sleeping son, her brow crumpling in sympathy as her imagination raced along with the new information.

Kate continued: 'So it was partly my fault. We were so cross with each other and he took a misstep. I'm sorry.'

Barbara reached across and placed a hand on Kate's forearm. 'The doctors said that you'd done well – stopping the bleeding and calling the ambulance so quickly. Thank you, love. Thank you for looking after my boy.'

Kate took Barbara's hand. 'He's going to be okay, Mrs Fairbright.'

'It's going to take time.'

'He's got you.'

'There might be side-effects,' Barbara muttered in a monotone.

'What?'

Barbara straightened up again. 'The doctors said there might be side-effects. Any bang on the head like that . . . they say he might forget things that most people remember. And he might remember things that most people forget. But they're not expecting it to be severe. We'll just have to wait and see.'

'Don't we always.'

Barbara smiled to herself at the teenage wisdom and stood. Smoothing down her skirt, she said, 'They've got a bed for me along the corridor. I might need to take a nap.'

'Oh yes, do get some sleep, Barbara. I'll stay with him till they chuck me out.'

Barbara smiled and offered her hand. 'It was nice to meet you, Kate.'

Kate stood and very nearly curtseyed. 'Nice to meet you too.'

Luke's mum leant over her son and gave him a kiss on the bandage, smoothing one of his eyebrows with a thumb. She left, drawing the curtain behind her.

Kate pulled her chair closer to the bedside and sat gazing at Luke.

'Hello,' she said quietly. 'Stuck with me again, I'm afraid. Y'know – the crazy lady who thinks she's your wife. Trouble is, I am. Or at least I was.' She listened for approaching footsteps but there was just the low-level snoring and farting from Luke's wardmates. She went on. 'Thing is, Lukey . . . I thought I'd let you down. I thought it was all my fault. And that you should have been with someone more sensible. You know, some nice blonde girl who understood about high heels and casseroles. "Anne" maybe. Someone normal called "Anne". I thought Anne would have done a better job looking after you. But I was wrong. It wasn't my fault. None of it was my fault. Anyway . . . there's something I didn't get a chance to say.' She found one of his hands under the bedsheet. 'I love you, Luke. I always will.'

She was about to lean across and kiss his cheek when Luke stirred. She sprang back guiltily and had to concentrate hard to realise she had nothing to be ashamed of. Luke muttered something like 'llollol-stan'.

He opened his eyes and turned his head fractionally towards her. Kate stood so he could see her better. 'What did you say, sweetheart?'

Luke swallowed painfully and said in a hoarse whisper, 'Bollocks to Anne. She pushed me down the stairs.'

Kate rubbed his shoulder tenderly. 'Sorry, that wasn't Anne, that was me. To be fair, I didn't actually—'

'I don't know who you are.' He was only half-conscious and heavily stoned from the anaesthetic.

'My name's Kate.'

'Mmm,' he said. 'The girl from the future.'

'Yes.'

'My wife.'

'That's right. Look, don't worry about it right now—'

'And I was . . . your shit husband.'

'No! No, you were lovely.'

221

He blinked slowly. For a moment she recognised him. 'I'm tired,' he said.

'Go back to sleep, Lukey.'

His eyelids drooped and then opened again with a thought. He slurred, 'I was all right till I met you.'

Kate absorbed this as she watched him drift back to sleep.

She said it for herself, simply and quietly: 'No, you weren't.'

Kate walked back to Benedict, grateful for the rain that hid her tears.

The husband was gone. But the boy was safe.

In her student room, she ditched her contact lenses, took off her wet clothes and climbed into bed.

She thought of what her dad had said.

You've always got to do your bit.

And one other voice – the sweet voice that she'd last heard on a dance floor. What had he said?

I'll be waiting.

Part Three

COME AGAIN

Chapter 19

She woke with her mouth forming a single word. 'Gross.' The bedroom stank of beer.

Woah! What the hell is this? Wrong bed. Double bed. On bed not in bed. Sweaty but dry, dressed not naked, hair unwet, curtains unorange. Not curtains. Window. Light, day, home. HOME! London home, body home, body old. Old body alive! Home and safe.

Safe. Recovered. Back from the dead.

Second chance . . . Charles! Memory stick. Fetch! Dog? Retriever. Fetch stick. Fetch memory stick. Retrieve memory stick from Charles. Stick between teeth. Bit between teeth. Many bits. 16GB's of bits. Do your bit. Do your bit.

Kate sat up in the bedroom of her Clapham home, breathing heavily, her heart thumping in her ribcage like a crazed mouse. *Like Mighty Mouse – the muscle-bound opera-singing cartoon mouse. Not like . . . Wallace! The mouse in the kitchen. The disaster kitchen. The 10,000-day kitchen. Alive. Still alive!* Her scalp was venting an icy sweat. She scrambled to the side-table and found her phone. *Ha! iPhone! Hello, again! Dead. Dead battery.* Siri had missed the do-yourself-in alarm because the battery had died in the night. *Up yours, Siri!*

God bless my disorganised alcoholic self!

She plugged the phone in and waited to check the time. 10.23 a.m. Wednesday. Exactly twenty-four hours since she first shuffled into the kitchen. She jumped off the bed and immediately staggered back onto it. Okay. Heavy again. Not wrong-heavy – normal-heavy. Body acting its age. She stood more carefully, like an old pirate remembering her sea legs. She looked around the room and sank to her knees, weeping with gratitude. Huge, heaving sobs of hope and regret. The dream. It couldn't have been a dream. But there was a second chance. Presently, she blew her nose on the duvet, making a mental promise that this was the last revolting thing she would do to this lovely mess of a room. She stood and rushed downstairs to the bathroom mirror.

Oh . . . mate. There you are. Home.

Forty-five but every line herself, every wrinkle earned. Rings within were keeping count but the tree was in flower. Weathered and renewed.

'Begin afresh, afresh, afresh.'

Where did that come from? Philip Larkin. What made her think of Larkin? She headed to the kitchen.

She'd never been so pleased to see the place. Just look at this shithole! In what previous life had it been a good idea to live like such a tramp? Even Toby's guerrilla clear-up couldn't remove the stench of surrender and fungal Pop Tarts. Kate placed a hand on a hip and leant on the kitchen island for a moment, trying to give herself a break. She had been ill. An illness that's as much a part of life as twisting an ankle or getting the flu. It's just that this particular mental illness had nearly killed her. 'Well, fuck that,' she murmured to herself. There was plenty to live for. There always had been. She saw the plain-papered gift that Toby had left for her.

Oh yes. And now there's even something else. Maybe.

226

She picked at the Sellotape and was immediately exasperated by Toby's meticulous wrapping. 'Only men with no children have the time to get good at this shit,' she muttered. 'There again, that made no difference to Luke.' She scanned the table for a sharp edge and found a pair of nail scissors buried point-down in a derelict brownie. Every Christmas, birthday and wedding anniversary, her husband had faithfully presented her with gifts that looked like they'd been wrapped by elves on crack. She remembered Luke's self-deprecating shrug. She remembered how she had found it endearing and how, as the years went by, that fondness had given way to disappointment, then sadness, then anger. Lazy, shrugging git couldn't even summon the basic respect to competently wrap a bloody prezzie.

But now, as she carefully snipped along the short edge of the book, something miraculous happened in the mind of Kate Marsden. She held the two ideas in balance: her delight in Luke and her anger; her love and her grief. Standing there in the kitchen – and without noticing – she began the long delayed process of integrating the lost past with the new present. Something in her imagination finally began the quiet work of mourning.

She pulled the book free of the brown paper.

It was a slim volume of poetry – *High Windows* by Philip Larkin.

Okay, what voodoo is this, then?

Only just now, upstairs, she'd thought of a line from this very writer. She stood motionless and tried to retrace the steps. What did she know? Well, she had been elated to be back home – geographically, physically, temporally – right place, right body, right time. She knew that she felt renewed. In fact, she felt wonderful. She knew Larkin had a not entirely unfair reputation as a miserable bastard but was also capable of sudden leaps into the sublime. And . . . *ah, there you are* . . . she knew Toby liked Larkin. She associated Toby with Larkin and Larkin with new life. But what did this book mean to Toby?

Caressing the edges, she found a top corner turned down. Even in her elation Kate frowned because she didn't really approve of ear-marking new books. It was a poem called 'Sad Steps'. She frowned again as she saw Toby had made a pencil annotation in the margin of the last verse – she didn't approve of that either. His neat handwriting had pressed lightly with a hard 2H:

I'm lucky to be your friend but to be honest I'm still looking at the moon. Tell me this is absurd and I'll never bring it up again.

She read the poem. She didn't know this one and she forced herself to read carefully before she got to the last two verses – the part Toby had highlighted. He couldn't make it simple, could he?

Kate remembered a favourite phrase of her beloved school English teacher, Miss Benjamin: 'What's going on here, then?'

The poet had got up in the night for a piss, and then noticed through the window the bright moon in all its romantic glamour. Did it inspire in him epic thoughts of all-conquering love? No, he wrote:

. . . No,

One shivers slightly, looking up there.
The hardness and the brightness and the plain
Far-reaching singleness of that wide stare

Is a reminder of the strength and pain
Of being young; that it can't come again,
But is for others undiminished somewhere.

She read and re-read the last verse and tried to see it through Toby's eyes.

Oh boy. Oh, Toby! He was undiminished – he was the 'others'. She was the one whose youth could not come again but Toby was still staring at the moon. Toby was still in love. Her heart raced along with her thoughts. She couldn't organise them – she needed words. She scrambled to her laptop and typed like a maniac into her diary.

Oh, but Toby! It's much better than that! I HAVE come again. I'm here again now. I had a dream of youth but in the dream I wasn't young. I've never been as young as I am in this moment. No one is.

But in my dream – if it was a dream – you were truly young and . . . I shouldn't be feeling romantic, should I? I shouldn't be looking at the bright moon and thinking that it's doing its beautiful thing for me.

He died, you see. My sweet husband died. And I wanted to follow him. That was something of an error.

But let me tell you: right now I'm come again and ready for adventure, my dear Toby. I don't know if that incudes you. I like the way you kiss.

But I've got something to do first. You have to do your bit, right? Give me a couple of hours, you amazing man. I just need to see another old friend. He'll be in a police cell by sundown or my name's not Kate Marsden.

Chapter 20

A fresh, Kate literally went to work.

The journey to BelTech reminded her of what had just happened in 1992: the familiar now crackling with unexpected energy. Who knew that taking the overland from Clapham Junction to West Brompton for the four-thousandth time could feel so invested with purpose?

She had decided to call her recent experience 'The Experience'. She had a powerful intimation that it had affected her but no one else. It was real but it was false. There was no chance that the memory was just a dream and also no chance that anything had actually occurred. It was like a play or a novel or a poem – it was real while it lasted; it would park itself in her memory; it would subtly or deeply inform her view of the world . . . and it hadn't happened.

Nothing in her house had changed. Charles Hunt's profile on LinkedIn was the same pack of lies it had been yesterday. Kate's rescuing him from bullies had made no impact on his future corruption. Kes was still the artistic director of the Duke of York's Theatre in the West End and he was still casting himself in leading roles. Amy was still a French and Spanish interpreter for an NGO. And as far as the rest of the world knew, Kate was still a depressed widow recently sacked from an under-achieving career by a buffoon who was in over his head with gangsters and crypto-fascists.

She exited the tube station and strode for the office. She felt an energy this body didn't deserve. She was forty-five again for sure. But the fit forty-five that hadn't just spent nine months fucking itself.

Belgravia Technologia had, naturally, nothing whatever to do with Belgravia. Charles just thought the posh-sounding name would impress potential clients and, in this, he had been proved depressingly correct. In fact, the business occupied the fourth floor of a taupe seventies office block in a quiet mews in West Brompton.

She rounded the corner of the little cul-de-sac and noticed something out of place. Opposite the entrance to the building, a tall, powerfully-built man in a long black coat was leaning against a white Range Rover and smoking a cigarette. Kate instinctively avoided his eye.

She walked into the building and clocked Ray, one of the two soon-to-retire security guards. As usual, he was picking his nose with his thumb and puzzling through a crossword. He glanced up. 'Ah, Ms Marsden – just the fella.' Ray either hadn't noticed that Kate had been sacked yesterday or didn't care. She had been with BelTech from the start and was an invaluable crossword assistant.

'Bit busy this morning, Ray.'

'Won't take a jiffy.' He read from the clue list. '"Razor cuts clock? Phew! That was close." Four, two, four.'

'Tricky one. Give me a few minutes,' Kate replied as she breezed past.

She liked Ray, but he was never going to be the problem. The problem would be getting in and out of Charles's office before anyone worked out what was going on. Assuming the post office's next-day delivery service had worked its charm, Kate's envelope would have been sorted by now and Charles's secretary Janice would have respected the CONFIDENTIAL note, leaving it unopened in his room. As per the standing instruction, she would have done her best to stuff the mail into the antique toast rack on the windowsill behind his desk. Kate checked the time as she stepped into the lift. 12.34 p.m. She was counting on the fact that Charles was too much of an idle bastard to open his own post before lunch. If she got lucky, maybe he was already out trying to wank off Liam Fox over some grilled asparagus at the Ritz. She would simply wander in, take the memory stick, walk out and hail a cab to the Guardian on York Way.

Breathing as calmly as possible, she stepped out of the lift on the fourth floor and headed for Charles's office. She felt several heads turn in her direction but ignored her former colleagues as she made her way, swiftly but – she hoped – casually, down one side of the open-plan space. Close to Charles's door, Janice was at her desk but thankfully masked by the ample frame of Colin, Kate's IT deputy. He had his back to Kate and seemed to be explaining in some detail the reason why 'Excel can some-times be a very naughty boy'. Kate slipped past them. Charles's door had no window and she walked in without knocking.

Inside were three men, none of whom were Charles. To her right, two tall muscular-looking white guys standing in long black coats. In front of her, sitting across the desk from Charles's empty chair, the back of a thinner man probably in his fifties. Close-cropped grey hair with a straight neckline an inch above the collar of his crisp, dark purple shirt. The man twisted round to look at her and Kate recognised the sleek face of Nestor Petrov.

She froze.

Fight or flight? Neither. Plan A. There's a good chance he doesn't know who I am.

Kate smiled and closed the door behind her.

'Sorry,' she said. 'Janice is busy and she asked me to get something for her. I'm Charles's deputy under-secretary.'

Petrov gave her a frank physical appraisal from head to toe and then turned back to the desk with impatience. He spoke in Russian to one of the attendant heavies. Kate detected a Moscow accent. 'How long can it take for a man to have a piss?'

'You make him nervous, boss.'

Petrov looked at his watch and Kate moved around him, scanning the windowsill behind Charles's chair for the toast rack stuffed with this morning's post.

It wasn't there.

In a daze she walked to where it ought to be and weirdly stroked a gold-plated piggy bank which had been put in its place.

Petrov continued in Russian. 'The problem is that Marsden bitch. The file will be at her house. I don't know what we're waiting for. Some sentimental affection from Hunt, the idiot. Maybe he's fucking her. We should have raided her home last night and put a permanent end to this business.'

This was not the way he tended to talk on *Have I Got News For You.*

Kate's envelope remained stubbornly absent and she realised she was now just a person standing in a room trying not to shake with fear. She stared at the piggy bank, wishing she could climb inside it. Petrov spoke again, this time in English. 'Aren't you a little *old* for a deputy under-secretary?' His English was good: Kate wondered if this was due to or in spite of twenty years of succinct conversations with English football managers and newspaper editors.

Kate turned and began brazenly going through Charles's desk drawers. 'Yes!' she said, winningly. 'Tremendously old. Second career, you see. It's a government scheme for middle-aged women.'

Petrov was watching Kate's search with a frown. 'What is your name?'

Kate trusted her subconscious and came out with the first noises to enter her head. 'Buffindra,' she said. 'But my friends call me Buffy.'

'Buffy?' Petrov's lips curled into something resembling amusement. 'Like the vampire-slayer?'

Kate scanned the cluttered surface of the desk and started moving things around as if to tidy it. 'Yes, that's it. Although, as you say, I'm far too old to be named after the slayer. But I do love her work.' She moved this morning's untouched copy of the *Financial Times* and revealed a bundle of mail held together with an elastic band.

Her envelope!

She tugged it free from the rest and stuffed it in her back pocket. 'I just fucking hate vampires, you see.'

'What was that?'

'Everyone okay for tea and coffee?'

'What did you just put in your pocket?'

Kate was moving swiftly towards the door. 'I'll take that as a yes.'

The door swung open and Charles walked in, wiping his hands on his chinos and saying, 'Sorry to keep you, gentlemen. Bloody hand-dryer keeps – Kate Marsden!'

'Hi, Charles!' Kate walked straight past him and out of the room. Behind her she heard Petrov's raised voice.

'That woman is Kate Marsden? . . . SHE JUST STOLE SOMETHING FROM YOUR DESK, YOU STUPID BASTARD!'

And then Charles: 'Nestor, I can egregiously assure you of the large impossibility that—'

'SHE'S GOT THE MISSING FILE!!'

Kate ran.

Chapter 21

'Ooh Kate, you're in a—'

Kate yelled, 'Klingons on the starboard bow, Colin!' as she raced past her friend and they both heard Petrov repeating his orders at the level of a scream.

He has to tell his men twice. They're not FSB, they're just violent goons. So that's . . . good?

Hurtling towards the fire escape, she instinctively jabbed the lift button on her way past, hoping the sight of an empty lift arriving would baffle the heavies for a couple of valuable seconds. Maybe they would think she was waiting for it – hiding somewhere. *There again*, she thought as she swung round a bannister and clattered down past the third floor, *it's always possible that conveniently summoning the fucking lift for your pursuers is not what you do in situations like this.*

Two, four, six, eight – down the white concrete stairwell she sprang like a demented gazelle. Breathing hard, she strained to hear the sound of heavy shoes above her.

They've both taken the lift.

She barged through the swing door into the ground-floor reception. Ray was still concentrating on his crossword. He glanced up to see Kate racing towards him and heading for the main entrance.

'Nick of time, Ray!'

'What?'

'"Razor cuts clock"?'

Ray looked down and gave an elated, 'Aah!'

Kate glanced at the lift indicator, which seemed to be static on '2'. What the hell was that?

Colin! Colin had the skill and wit to jam the lift software even from Janice's terminal.

Playdate with Carly coming up if I get through this, my friend.

Right, then – get to Old Brompton Road and disappear into a crowd. It's lunchtime. Maybe hide in Elvis Fried Chicken.

Through the door and outside. She turned right towards the main road. But now the third heavy – the suspicious dude with the Range Rover – was running at her and saying something into a mic in his sleeve.

Oh God, they're wired for sound. Like Cliff Richard but even more frightening.

She turned back into the mews but there was only thirty yards of road before a dead end. Helplessly she ran towards a narrow alley at the side of the building that formed the cul-de-sac. There was a metal fire escape to her left but the steps ended one floor up in a bricked-off doorway. Ahead of her was just a deserted junk area littered with urban trash and a builder's skip full of road signs and broken photocopiers. She had run out of space. Panting for breath, she turned.

The big guy slowed to a walk, his eyes scanning Kate's surroundings in an efficient check for exits or witnesses. He spoke into his sleeve again in Russian: 'I've got her.' He was now closing the gap between them with something approaching a swagger.

Kate cleared her mind – save for one quotation from

Star Trek III: The Search for Spock, which insisted on dropping by. It was Scotty complaining to Kirk as usual, this time about the newly-refitted *Enterprise*:

'I hadn't expected to take her into combat, you know!'

Only yesterday she had been a boozed-up disaster zone. She hadn't seen the inside of a gym for nine months, which, by karate champion standards, made her a pitiful slob. On the credit side, she had thirty years of muscle memory and enough adrenaline to stun a baboon. It was just a question of what would happen when the baboon got back up. She brought her breathing under control and imagined the blood in her veins charging with electricity. Habitually, She-Ra sized up her opponent.

Overconfident, 6ft 3ish, about 240 lb, way past optimal BMI but packing muscle, no spring chicken, my age or thereabouts, forget the neck – too fat. Cocky bastard checking his phone, right-handed, tiny hands. Out of shape. This will have to be quick and disproportionate. Like an Elvis Burger. Bit nasty. The others will be coming soon. Poor fucker. He never got a break. Just his shitty job. Don't want to hurt him.

The heavy spoke again into his wrist mic: 'Where d'you think she's hiding it?' He heard something in his earpiece and gave a repulsive snigger. 'Yeah, I'll search her pussy first.'

Okay, maybe do hurt him.

The goon rearranged his plump face into a stony glare and said in English with a thick Georgian accent, 'Give me what you stole and I might not even rape you.'

Kate smiled pleasantly and replied in Russian, 'I'm afraid I can't do that.'

He looked surprised – but not as much as Kate had hoped. He really was a *big* bastard: she needed to push him much further off his balance. She went on, 'Was that your boyfriend whispering in your ear? Is he with you always? That's so sweet! Do you have another earpiece in your ringpiece? Does he press a button and vibrate your tender arsehole? Aah!'

The heavy scoffed, but anger was bringing some colour to his neck. He advanced another step but now appeared indecisive, as if baffled by choice. Exactly what form of violence was he going to inflict on this short, disgusting woman? They were two metres apart.

Just a little closer.

Kate maintained her friendly smile and went on in impeccable Russian: 'Of course, I'm being very stupid. You can't possible retain any device in your anus.' She deepened and slurred her voice, switching to an insulting, durr-brain Georgian: ''Coz Daddy made it too big from all the fucking.'

That did the trick.

The heavy wasted a lungful of power on a weird yell and rushed chaotically at her, his two tiny hands reaching for her throat.

Kate dropped, lunging with as much forward drive as she could and propelling her right fist squarely into the guy's balls. Through his suit trousers and apparently light pants (*silk-effect boxers?*) she actually felt the bellend of his cock against her knuckles, as well as the pinball-machine rebound of his battered nuts. There was a split second of eerie silence as he crumpled over her and she quickly rolled to the left to avoid his huge crashing body. She heard him scream with pain as she came up on her feet. The powerful man was down but not out, scrabbling wildly to get up. A memory of the builder's skip had Kate marching over to retrieve a triangular NO RIGHT TURN sign. Her attacker had made it to his knees as she walked back in three steps, swinging the metal high above her head and bringing it down flat upon the top of his skull.

'Aargh!'

He was on his back and she sprang and dropped, landing her knees into his abdomen. She twatted his face with the road sign while shouting emphatic syllables in the most native of her native South London. 'You DON'T . . . FUCK . . . with TEAM . . . G . . . B!' She got up and tossed the metal aside. Standing over her smashed but still breathing assailant, she added, 'We're perfectly capable of fucking ourselves, thank you very much.'

She got down and levered his unconscious form into the recovery position.

Satisfied that Mr Might-Not-Even-Rape-You would basically live, she felt her back pocket for the memory stick in its envelope. Still there. She turned and ran out of the alley, out of the mews, onto the street.

She looked left and right. To the left, the two heavies from BelTech were finally running out of the door. One of them spotted her and grabbed his colleague, pointing. The other one saw her and said something into his wrist. Kate looked around in panic. *Oh Christ. There!* Across the street, another two heavies had their fingers in their right ears and were looking around.

No, not four of them at once. Two at a push. Not four.

Kate was running again. She ran down Old Brompton Road. It was a convenient thoroughfare for cars and buses but not exactly Notting Hill Market. Or Camden Town. Or Oxford Street.

Damn you, Charles. Why can't you have an office where there are lots and lots of people, you awkward dick?

She looked behind. There were now four big guys in overcoats in pursuit and all of them apparently younger and in better shape than Mr Pussy. There was a junction ahead, Eardley Crescent. She didn't want to run across the junction blind. This whole thing wasn't going to end in her getting run over.

Screw that bathos.

She took a left and immediately saw an opportunity about fifty yards ahead. Halfway around the curve of the crescent was a parked taxi. The driver had set himself up with a little fold-out chair and was having his lunch in the autumn sunshine. Nothing spoke to Kate of home and safety like a black London cab. She speeded up, gasping, 'Help! Mate! Help me!'

The driver was another overweight white guy in his forties. Jesus, they were everywhere. He looked up to see the short woman being pursued by four blokes. He put down his *Sun* newspaper and stood, still holding his large Subway roll.

'What the bloody hell's this, then?'

'They work for Uber!' Kate yelled.

'They WHAT?!'

'They work for Uber and they didn't like my review! They've been using the bus lane during proscribed hours!'

The driver was instantly livid. He fucking knew it. Uber wankers! He put down his sandwich roughly on the seat of his camp chair and started marching towards the oncoming pursuers, his chest puffed out and his Hawaiian shorts and bald head dazzling in the sun.

'Come on then, you Uber scrotes! Leave the lady alone! I'll give you a fackin' review! Once *I* review you, you'll STAY fackin' reviewed!'

Kate had the Knowledge. This wasn't just an impressive recall of hundreds of London roads and landmarks. It was the Knowledge that when it came to bus lanes, London cab drivers could scarcely tolerate the presence of buses. Private cars using this lane were not to be borne. And Uber . . . they were the mortal enemy: the cheapskate, untrained, undercutting plonkers who in the right circumstances would sat-nav a fare into a lake.

241

As she got close to the driver she saw him start to slow and begin to wonder if taking on four athletic-looking guys was quite what he had in mind this lunchtime. It didn't matter. It wasn't the driver she was aiming for.

'Right, then!' he shouted at the heavies as Kate sprinted past him. 'We've all had a pint. Let's calm down.'

Kate glanced behind her and saw what the driver saw: the Russians watching her and working out what was about to happen. They skidded to a halt and started to run in the opposite direction as Kate dived into the front seat of the open cab and started the engine. In the wing mirror she saw the driver turn round in bafflement to see his cab screech out of its parking space with the woman at its wheel.

Kate wrestled her seat belt on and saw in her rear-view mirror that the heavies were crossing the road to a rank of white Range Rovers.

Of course. The white Range Rover – the unforgivable car.

The chase was on.

Chapter 22

She wrenched the cab into a hard left turn. It was a beautiful new TX – an electric cab. For a while before Luke died, Kate had been eyeing them up and thinking *Phwoar* in the same way that another car lover might ogle a Porsche. She felt sorry for the driver whose pride, joy and livelihood she had just stolen; she glanced at the serial number on the dashboard and made a promise to return it to the man fully charged and without a scratch.

She quickly got the feel of it – nippy and responsive; just as fast as the old FX4 Fairway that Bill had let her drive on his days off after she passed her test. But she had no intention of getting into a race on an open road. The cab would be no match for the diesel-chugging shits behind: she needed traffic and tight spots. She desperately fished her phone out of her front pocket and replaced the driver's in the stick-on windscreen holder. Taking a right, she looked behind and counted three Range Rovers.

'Danger in front of you, danger behind you, danger to the sides.'

Why was she trying to do this alone? She was back in the land of the living, wasn't she? Kate stuck her thumb on her phone to wake it. 'Siri, call Toby Harker.'

She was zooming down Finborough Road on a dual

243

carriageway. In her mirror she saw the first of the Range Rovers pull out to overtake the cars between them.

Toby's voice came over the phone speaker. 'Kate?'

'Toby!' She took out a row of traffic cones as she swerved while turning up the volume.

'Kate? Are you okay?'

'Fine, thanks. Well, no, not really.'

'What is it?'

'Erm. Well, the thing is, I found out Charles is . . . look, it's a bit complicated, but the headline is I'm in a stolen black cab being pursued by Nestor Petrov's henchmen because I hacked and copied a file from BelTech implicating him in a massive conspiracy and I've got it on a USB drive in my back pocket and this guy can't be fucking *serious*—'

The Range Rover behind rammed into the cab's back bumper and Kate whiplashed against her seat belt. 'You SHITHEAD!'

'Kate?'

'Hang on.'

She took a wild right turn at speed across the central reservation onto King's Road. Oncoming traffic flashed and beeped like a family of outraged bees. The nearest Range Rover overshot but she saw the other two brake to make the turn. She immediately took another right, which brought her onto a residential road.

Hortensia – it's just going to take me back to the carriageway. No fucking good.

'Kate!'

'Hi. Sorry. So, yeah. Bit stressed, to be honest.' There was the briefest pause as Toby seemed to make a decision.

'You'd better come to the office.'

'What office?'

'My office.'

Kate saw two Range Rovers back on her tail. 'I don't know where your office is, Toby! You've never said!'

'Thames House, Millbank.'

Kate recognised the address as the headquarters of MI5. 'Oh, NOW you fucking tell me!'

'I'd say this is a very good time to tell you.'

The two Range Rovers were gaining on her. 'I'm not sure I'm going to make it all the way to the river in this thing, Tobes.'

'It's okay, I've got you now.'

Kate was baffled for a moment. 'That's a bit forward. I mean, it was a nice present, but—'

'I mean I'm tracking your phone. You're going the wrong way.'

'Oh. Hang on, I'm . . . excuse me, Commander Fucky, I am *not* going the wrong way.' As she spoke, she saw in her mirror that the lead Range Rover was the perfect distance behind for a brief demonstration of the agile turning circle of a London taxi.

Toby said, 'I mean that we can—'

'Shut up for a second.' Kate veered to the edge of the curb, braked hard and swung the cab a hundred and eighty degrees in one movement. She floored the gas and raised her middle finger to the heavy as she powered past him in the opposite direction. 'Three-point-turn THAT, y'shitter!' she yelled as she saw the bulky white car's brake lights illuminate in frustration.

Toby said, 'My God, cabs really do bring out the cabbie in you, don't they?'

The second Range Rover was already braking as Kate flew past, still with her middle finger raised. She got a brief sight of Petrov in the back seat, staring at her in astonishment.

'Fine,' said Toby. 'But I've got CCTV up and you've got another four up ahead.'

'FOUR?'

'What the hell have you got in your pocket, Kate?'

'Never mind that, what the—'

'Take this left.'

'That won't take me towards—'

'Kate, stop arguing and JUST TAKE THE LEFT!'

'All right, all right!'

Kate squealed the taxi left so hard it was momentarily on two wheels. Toby was correct – she had time to see what looked like a whole fleet of wretched Range Rovers ahead on the road she'd just exited.

'The bastards are everywhere!' she said.

'I know. Don't worry. Cavalry's on its way. Stay on this road.'

Kate was merging onto another dual carriageway and could see her pursuers not far behind. 'I can't outrun them, Toby!'

'You won't have to for long. Just open up as much space as you can. I've been in a car with you – don't tell me you can't do it.'

Kate put her foot down and weaved extravagantly between the cars ahead, trying to stay especially alert for bikes and intermittently shouting 'Sorry!' to outraged motorists. All her skill was focused in the moment – she disappeared into the task in hand.

'Did you really like my present?' Toby said.

Kate briefly mounted a pavement to under-take a Deliveroo scooter. 'Yeah, can we talk about this later, darling? Kind of busy.'

'Sure. You're doing great. Not long now.'

'Not long till WHAT? I'm going to cause an accident any fucking—'

At that moment, one of the Range Rovers darted out from a junction on her left. She wrenched the cab right to avoid it and took a glancing blow on the left back wheel. Kate shrieked with pain from the impact and the cab's arse flipped out from under her but she steered into the skid like a rally driver and brought the machine back under control.

'Fucker just tried to RAM me!' she yelled. 'Where's this cavalry, Toby?!'

'It's happening now.'

'What?'

'Check your mirror.'

Kate zoomed past a taxi rank of nine or ten black cabs. And then in her passenger wing mirror: something extraordinary.

Every one of the black cabs squealed out after her. The road had opened up into three lanes and now all three were occupied by black London taxis, separating her from the Range Rovers. Open-mouthed, Kate instinctively moved into the middle lane and allowed cabs to come alongside. She looked left and a young Asian driver gave her a wink and playful salute. She looked right and an older female driver in a tweed cap blew her a kiss. In her rear-view mirror were three cabbies waving at her. She thought of Toby waiting for her.

Friends in front of me, friends behind me, friends to the sides.

Never in her life had she expected to see London's most out-for-themselves, one-person-band, sole-trading loners acting in harmony for something that was surely nothing to do with them. How she wished her dad could see it. She had to compose herself to speak evenly.

'Toby, I don't know how the hell you did that, but it's beautiful.'

'I'll explain later. We're not out of it yet. We're seeing Petrov's guys everywhere – you've flushed out a bloody army.'

'The one I met fought like a child at a brown-belt grading,' Kate said. 'I'm no expert, but I don't think they're Russian intelligence.'

'I should hope not. I'd rather not start World War Three just because you were annoyed with Charles.'

'Oh, screw you, Toby – it's a bit more important than—'

She heard Toby laugh. 'I know, I know – I'm just kidding.'

'Oh, I'm so glad you're enjoying this.'

'Aren't you?'

'Well . . .'

'But listen – I'm watching them and I think they've worked out where you're heading. We'll have to switch to plan B.'

'Okay . . .?'

'Aim for the Duke of York's.'

'Toby, there are at least twenty pubs called the—'

'We're not going for a pint, Kate. The theatre.'

'The theatre? Kes's theatre?'

'The same. We have a small facility there. You'll be safe until we get to you.'

She belatedly processed what she had just heard. 'Sorry, are you telling me you've got a *safe room* inside the Duke of York's?'

'Well, it's always good to have options, d'you not think? Kes was good enough to let us make a few modifications to a dressing room the actors were always complaining about and never got used.'

'Oh, so you can tell Kes you're spy but—'

'Get over it.'

'Ooh, "get over it" he says. Is that an order? Am I your spy bitch now?'

'Kate, please. You're still in considerable trouble.'

Kate had to admit that, despite the danger she was causing to innocent bystanders, it was perfectly possible she was having the time of her life. Her reaction disgusted her. 'Toby, I'm afraid I hurt someone quite badly.'

'I forgive you.'

'No, not you. Although . . . Anyway, there's a man on the ground in Lillie Yard, near BelTech, and—'

'Oh, the guy near the skip. He's on his way to the Royal Brompton. He's going to be fine.'

'Oh . . . that's good.'

'But sadly the driver whose cab you stole had a cardiac arrest and died.'

'Oh my God!'

'Joke.'

'TOBY!'

'Sorry.'

'TOBY!'

'Sorry.'

'That's not funny. My dad died of a heart attack, you prick!'

'I'm really sorry, Kate. High spirits. I've had a tumbler of whisky. Sorry. The cabbie's completely fine. He's in a police station on King's Road doing a lot of shouting. Take the right in four hundred yards.'

'No. I'm going through the park.'

'Don't go through the park. They're waiting for you to go through the park.'

'Toby, if I take the A4 I'll be heading for Hyde Park Corner, which is the second-busiest roundabout in town after Trafalg—'

'It'll be fine.'

'It WON'T be fine. We'll come to a complete stop and thirty beefcake Russians will drag me from this taxi and—'

'I won't allow that.'

'Okay, that sounds very chivalrous, but—'

'I won't allow that.'

Kate paused. It was a fine line between trusting your instincts and being a stubborn bastard in the face of new information. And an equally fine line between feminist principles and refusing to take orders from a man, even if the man happened to be one of the most capable people you'd ever met. She looked to her right and was unsurprised to see that the woman in the tweed cap had moved ahead to give her space for a right turn.

Fuck it. Yesterday she was practically dead anyway. Everything from now on was gravy.

She took the turn. 'I do hope you know what the hell you're doing, dear Toby.'

'I do.'

Kate was alarmed to see that none of the cabs had followed her. They had all carried on up the road or splintered off. The Range Rovers had taken advantage of the gap and were now closing on her at a menacing pace.

That's curtains, then.

She heard Toby say, 'Kate, you've gone quiet. Are you okay?'

She didn't respond.

'Kate, in case you're wondering, the cabs have gone ahead to smooth the way. And there are others waiting at the roundabout.'

This aroused a tiny spark of curiosity, but Kate was sinking back into the 10,000-day kitchen. She said in a monotone, 'It doesn't matter. It doesn't matter who you've got at the roundabout.'

'Kate, I'm sorry you're sounding a bit glum. But . . . You've slowed down there. You need to speed up.'

'I'm a cab driver's daughter. You can't "smooth the way" around Hyde Park Corner.'

'You're not going around it. You're going through it.'

The spark reignited. This time she let it burn for a moment. 'You what?'

'You're going through it. Over it.'

The famous, and famously busy, traffic island was just in view. Wellington Arch, Apsley House, Derwent Wood's naked bronze *The Boy David*.

Nice arse. Like Luke's. Wonder about Toby's. Probably terrific. This is not relevant. Don't be so trivial. Work to do. Bet it's gorgeous, though. Oh, come on! You're not Carrie Bradshaw, you're Boudicca. But didn't Boudicca get horny? Of course she did. You can be Carrie AND Boudicca! AND Buffy AND Barbara Castle AND Mary Shelley AND Valentina Tereshkova AND She-Ra AND Professor Beard AND Frida Kahlo and all the other brilliant fuckers and all of the more normal fuckers too. You're Kate Marsden. You've got this.

Kate's arse-inspired pep-talk allowed a trickle of hope back into her imagination but this became an overwhelming flood when she saw what was happening up ahead. There were black cabs parked neatly in the road on either side of her junction with the roundabout. They had created . . . well . . .

'You've made me an aisle,' she said with the beginnings of a grin.

'Well, I wouldn't quite put it like that, but . . .'

'You're walking me down the aisle again!'

'Erm. I honestly hadn't thought of it like that, but obviously that's very cool of me. Main thing is to step on it. Need a bit of distance.'

Kate started to accelerate but then hesitated. 'Toby, there's a barrier.'

'Don't worry about that.'

'No, seriously, there's a barrier round the monument.'

'Yup. Drive straight for it.'

'I'll get pulverised.'

'No, you won't.'

She was three hundred yards from the roundabout. Beyond the cab-parted sea of traffic was the deserted island of Wellington Arch. But protecting its edge was a security barrier of uncompromising steel.

'They don't make these things out of bamboo, Toby!'

'Kate, you've got to trust me. You've got to speed up.'

'TOBEEEEE!!!'

'Best foot forward, Katie.'

She floored the accelerator. 'You appalling SHIIIIIIIIIITTTT!!!'

She raced at the barrier. She checked the speedometer and clocked 62 mph. This was going to hurt. She gripped the steering wheel with all her strength but refused to close her eyes. She'd done enough sleeping.

At the last moment –

OH, YOU ARE KIDDING ME.

– a central section of the steel barrier casually tipped ninety degrees backwards and disappeared to become perfectly flush with the asphalt. She thought of the way the Tracy palm trees flopped back to allow the launch of *Thunderbird 2*.

Kate screamed like a pirate queen as she powered through the aisle of cabs and sailed over Hyde Park Corner. She'd never seen it from here – it felt like a playground with grown-ups on all sides. The sun was so bright today. She looked up through the glass roof of the TX and the sky was a cornflower blue. In her mirror, the barrier flipped back up again and she saw one – no! three – Range Rovers come to a skidding, chaotic halt. Ahead of her, another taxi-parted sea beckoned her north towards Soho and the theatre rendezvous.

She was elated but a thought bothered her. Her first words to Toby as she made her way towards the West End were: 'Who elected you?'

Toby replied over the phone speaker, 'You see, most people would just say thanks.'

'No one should have this much power.'

'We serve the elected government.'

'What if the elected government are a bunch of arseholes?'

'It's not unknown. We serve them with a certain discretion.'

'Your idea of *discretion* would be someone else's idea of water cannons and arresting George Monbiot.'

'Oh God, I love George! We would never do that to George. Unless he really crossed the line.'

'What line?'

'The law.'

'Toby! You know perfectly well that between us, we've broken about twelve laws in the last hour alone.'

'Yeah. Like I say: discretion.'

'We're going to have a fucking big row about this.'

'Oh good! I'll look forward to that. I'll see you at the theatre. You're going to get there before us. Main entrance, turn right. Door marked "Private". Keypad locked – 1072.'

Kate registered the number. 'Luke's birthday?'

'Aye.'

Kate shook her head. 'You're such a softie. He's fine, you know.'

'What?'

'I mean, obviously he's dead. But he's also going to be fine.'

'Um, right. Anyway. I'm in a car now, but if we can track you it's quite possible Petrov's guys can too. The taxi squad will get you to St Martin's Lane but I can't ask them to do much more.'

Kate snapped out of the enjoyable chat and understood the new risk. 'You're saying . . . I'm going to be there, the shitheads are going to be there, you're *not* going to be there, and the magic cavalry are going to turn back into pumpkins?'

'Um, yup. We won't be far behind. Just get into the safe room.'

'What if something goes wrong?'

'Well . . . you might have to improvise.'

'Oh great! Tell me one thing – are any of them carrying guns?'

'No. No. Absolutely . . . very unlikely. STEP ON IT, LEO! WHAT IS THIS THING, A FUCKING TRACTOR?! No, definitely not, according to the analysts. Erm.'

'Toby . . .'

'Petrov himself is a known killer. Probably best avoid him.'

'Toby!'

'Listen, Kate. You've got everything you need. You always did.'

Kate took some heart from that. It gave her the courage to say something honest. 'Toby, I'm scared. Don't take too long.'

'I'll be there.'

Chapter 23

Kate jammed the taxi diagonally into a small gap across the street from the Duke of York's. She jumped out and was greeted by a huge picture of Kes over the main entrance. He had cast himself as Prospero in some kind of glitzy bums-on-seats production of *The Tempest* called *Tempest!* He looked like Gandalf after a satisfying Christmas.

Kate glanced at the board of performance times and saw that he was cramming in an outrageous three shows today. She shook her head as she realised Kes and his unfortunate, slave-driven company would just be nearing the end of the morning matinée. She was suddenly alerted by a cacophony of beeping and yelling from the south end of St Martin's Lane. Three Range Rovers were causing a commotion.

Arrogant bastards are actually driving the wrong way up a one-way street. I really am starting to hate these guys.

Heavies were already getting out of the cars and looking straight at her. She ran across the road and into the theatre.

For a second she was disarmed by the cosy normality of a West End foyer: the gold leaf wallpaper and tattered red velvet everywhere, the warm enveloping mood of dusty civilisation with the promise of chocolate raisins and over-priced ice-cream. Surely the men pursuing her couldn't get in? Surely guys like them would burst into flames if they tried to enter a place like this? But maybe, Kate thought, maybe she was being a cultural snob. Maybe some of those men grew up loving Chekhov and under different circumstances Kate could form a book group with them where they all took it in turns to read out the funny bits from Dostoyevsky. Well – maybe.

She strode towards the door to her right, marked 'Private'.

At the last moment her way was blocked by a heavy woman in her late twenties with a severe ponytail and an usher's waistcoat. 'I'm sorry, madam,' she said in a deafening sing-song as if to an elderly relative, 'but you can't go in there. It's private.'

Kate read the name badge and spoke quickly. 'Hi, Tassy. I'm a friend of Keven Lloyd's and he said it was okay.'

Tassy maintained her front-of-house smile and volume. 'With the greatest respect, madam, I find that hard to believe.'

'What?'

'I know Keven *extremely well* and, as head usher, I would have been informed if he'd pre-sanctioned a member of the public to just *wander around* backstage during a performance.'

Kate shot a glance at the main door. 'I haven't got time for this.' She tried to dodge round Tassy's impressive frame but the younger woman placed a large hand on one of Kate's breasts and shoved her away.

'Ow!'

'I have to warn you, madam, that I'm trained in the martial arts.'

'So am I! You can't just poke a customer in the boob like that!'

'As far as I can see, madam, you're not a customer. Unless you'd like to show me your ticket.'

Confounded, Kate checked behind her again. The leading

Russian was at the window and heading for the entrance. She was out of time.

'Oh, for fuck's sake.' Exasperated that today of all days she had run into the most psychotically jobsworth usher on the London theatre scene, she turned and bounded across the foyer towards the stairs to the dress circle.

'Madam!' Tassy barked.

On instinct, Kate grabbed a show programme from a concession stand. Halfway up the red-carpeted stairs she realised that the heavies were going to demand to know from Tassy which way she had gone. And if Tassy continued with what was apparently her trademark attitude, she was going to get hurt. Kate turned and ducked down to see three of them advance into the foyer. She produced the envelope from her back pocket and waved it in front of her. 'Oi, dickheads! Looking for this?'

The three men started after her. She turned and leapt up the rest of the stairs, hearing Tassy's voice behind her. 'Madam! Gentlemen! Mr Lloyd is *extremely* particular about latecomers!'

She swept aside a black curtain and pushed through a heavy swing door, finding herself at the top-left of the dress circle. It was about a quarter full: mainly older people and tourists. She moved swiftly down the aisle but years of theatre conditioning had her performing the same apologetic hop that people do when briefly passing between a wedding photographer and a large cake. Adjacent to the front row was another door, also marked 'Private' but with no code-lock. She pushed through this second door, just as her pursuers emerged from the first.

It was a dingy backstage stairwell, filthy and lit with flickering naked bulbs. She rattled down three flights of narrow spiral steps. Two more doors: to her right, presumably the stalls of the auditorium. Ahead – she guessed this one would lead to a wing of the stage. She heaved open the soundproof door and let it swing closed behind her. Now she entered the relative gloom of the stage-right wing, subtly illuminated with blue working-lights. She could hear Kes proclaiming a soliloquy from near the end of the play. Most of the cast were onstage but a young woman in black clothes stared at Kate in astonishment. She was holding some kind of fairy costume by the shoulders, ready to help an actor with a quick change. Kate gave the costume assistant an excited smile and a thumbs-up as she darted past. 'Break a leg!' she randomly whispered and quickly started to climb up a metal ladder bolted to the side of the wall. She'd never been backstage at a proper theatre before and, despite the imminent potential for getting her own legs broken, had to admit to being a little thrilled. Or maybe that was just terror.

As she climbed she saw the three heavies bundle into the wing below. Endearingly, they were keeping their voices down, although Kate considered that maybe that was because they were listening for her as well as frantically scouring the dark. Then they looked up and spotted her.

Kate was now in the fly-tower of the theatre and scrambled onto a steel lighting gantry that stretched across the roof to the other side. It was narrow, with a low handrail on the side nearest the audience and nothing but a twenty-metre drop on the other. It was the natural habitat of lighting technicians wearing safety harnesses. She took a few steps across but spotted one of the heavies already halfway up the ladder of the opposite wall. She turned back and another was already at the top.

This one first, then.

The heavy walked towards her with an intimidating calm, the gantry wobbling slightly on its framework. Kate took the theatre programme from her back pocket and rolled it into a tube. The big dude chuckled at her pathetic weapon and was a metre away when Kate grabbed one of the powerful lights pointing down at the stage and swung it straight in his eyes. The lamp was red-hot and Kate muffled a scream of pain but leapt at the blinded heavy and jabbed him in the eye with the end of the rolled-up programme. He fell back and flailed uselessly at the end of the gantry, blocking her escape.

She turned to see the other heavy clattering carelessly towards her, vibrating the steel bridge and almost losing his balance. Shorter, this one – but fast and sturdy. Kate panicked at the thought of how easy it would be to trip the idiot and see him fall to his probable death below. She dropped the programme and raised her arms. 'I surrender!' she said. He stopped in surprise. She continued truthfully in a slowly enunciated Russian whisper: 'The strange thing is – I love Russia! And I'm sorry you've got wankers in charge! So have we! Let's go downstairs and talk about Colonel Gagarin. I used to have a poster of Yuri and thought he was magnificent!'

The heavy blinked momentarily and then swung a vicious left hook at Kate's head. Disappointed, she flipped away from the swing, taking her weight on her strong right leg, calf, core – down, she coiled, then sprang! Jack-knifed herself forward into the air, whipping her head back and now down with horrible power into the face of her opponent. The heavy's nose exploded with blood as the headbutt smashed into it. Kate recoiled with a lightning pain to her forehead but landed drunkenly on her feet. The man staggered back, his hands clutching his broken nose. Instantly moving, she swiped the blood from her dizzied sight and took three running strides to follow up with an airborne kick to the man's chest. Her heel crashed into his solar plexus and she bounced heavily back onto the steel gantry as the Russian toppled like a modest fir tree and landed flat on his back.

Kate climbed to her feet and stepped carefully over the groaning heavy, taking a breath and sprinting to the ladder at the opposite end.

She jumped down the last few rungs and landed on the deck of the stage-left wing. She spotted the third heavy looking deeply unhappy. He was engaged in a muted, pushing-pulling argument with an outraged gaggle of actors and technicians. The performance was ongoing and Kate could see Kes still at work under the lights in a massive grey beard, throwing irritated glances at the noises off. The heavy spotted her, roughly shoved the skimpily-clad young man playing Ariel to the ground and rushed at Kate. She grabbed a sword from the props table and wielded it with two hands above her head. It was metal but blunted. Perfect.

Actually, not perfect. Possibly a mistake. I don't know what the hell I'm doing with this thing.

The heavy didn't care about the sword and barrelled into her before she could bring it down. Her nostrils were accosted by his vinegary aftershave as the two of them collapsed into a balsa-wood throne, smashing it to fragments. Kate was under the man and felt his hands reaching for her throat.

She twisted to the side with all her might and managed to jab the heavy in the temple with an elbow. He yelled with pain and she struggled from under him, staggering to her feet. She ran onto the stage but the heavy rugby-tackled her to the floor again. She felt the warmth of the stage lights and wished she could have made a more dignified entrance.

'Stop wrestling me!' she yelled, face-down on the deck. 'I don't know anything about wrestling. Stand up nice and straight so I can hit you, you awkward bastard.'

The man now had his arms around her waist and was trying to squeeze the life out of her. Feeling the blood swelling in her face, she looked up to see Kes in some kind of see-through wizard's gown over gold pants. He was staring at them in a state of apoplexy. But he was also a true pro and would surely incorporate the stage invasion into the performance.

'Marsden! What the LIVING FUCK are you doing?!!'

'Sorry!'

She reached back and grabbed the heavy's ears in two fists and pulled as hard as her triceps would allow. He gave a low roar and his grip loosened enough for her to wriggle free. The heavy was first to his feet: as Kate turned, his fist ploughed squarely into her left cheekbone.

She felt the wooden stage rush to meet her, the pain of the blow only registering as her head bounced against the polished floorboards. Her vision was blurring but she caught sight of Kes's veiny bare feet.

Why don't they ever wear shoes any more?

She gave her training a micro-moment to translate the pain into mere information.

Always the bare feet. People in real life don't go around in bare feet the whole time. Absolutely weird.

Flat on her back, she aimed her trainers at the gantry high above and summoned what was left of her power. Her knees halfway to her chin, she exploded up onto her feet in a single jump and turned, whipping round with a punch aimed at where she hoped the guy's stomach would be. She wasn't far off but he blocked with his right hand and now caught her in the face with the back of his left.

Okay, element of surprise gone. This one knows he's fighting a fighter.

She spun from the blow and went down again. In her dazed world she realised that a large portion of the audience were laughing and applauding. The Wednesday matinée tourists and pensioners were flabbergasted but impressed by this daring take on *The Tempest*. The reviews had said that it was avant-garde but until now they'd assumed that was just to do with the reggae music.

Now the heavy was advancing but Kate got a good view of Kes's impressive gold-laméd arse as he stepped between them.

'How DARE you strike my friend, you ATROCIOUS CUNT!'

Kes squared up to the Russian and delivered an excellent stage punch – which is to say that he missed by a perfect two inches. Astonished that the Russian hadn't obligingly gone down in a feigned knockout, Kes stood frowning as the man delivered a hefty upper-cut that sent Kes sprawling backwards onto the ground and out cold. Kate was getting to her feet as she heard a scream: Ariel in a chiffon leotard had jumped on the heavy's back, getting a skinny, muscular arm around his neck and punching him in the ear with the other fist. The heavy wheeled around in confusion and now Miranda, Caliban and Antonio (the usurping Duke of Milan) all dragged him to the ground and piled on top.

In the same moment, two more heavies invaded the stage from the other wing. Kate was given an extra second of recovery when the men stopped dead, bamboozled by the spectacle of their colleague drowning under a sea of torn Lycra and naked legs.

Kate looked to the lip of the stage. She needed to get the memory stick to safety. She imagined jumping the metre down and making a dash for the exit.

But now, a voice. A deep one with a Russian accent.

'Wonderful!'

She turned and was astonished to see Nestor Petrov advancing onto the stage. He was giving the kind of slow clap that made her think he ought to be wearing gloves and blowing a whistle to summon the von Trapp children.

'Wonderful,' he repeated. Middle-aged and handsome, with his short grey hair and his dark suit, carrying himself with the perfect posture of a bad actor, Petrov walked past his motionless and freaked-out henchmen to take centre-stage.

Nestor locked his green eyes with Kate for the briefest moment before turning to the audience. 'Is anyone filming this? You should! Get out your phones! Don't be shy, this is part of the show! The theatre is too elitist. It belongs to us all!'

Kate peered into the dark of the auditorium. The stage lights meant that she could only see the first two rows of the stalls: a look of delighted recognition on most of the faces. But nobody reached for their phone.

Petrov went on: 'Nice to see you – to see you nice! I am Nestor Petrov. You probably don't recognise me but I sometimes appear on beautiful shows like *Have I Got News For You* and *The National Lottery Live.* You may also know me from a less successful show called *My Football Team Win the Premier League!*'

A ripple of amusement from the audience. Petrov put his hands in his pockets and gave a self-deprecating shrug. 'Well . . . maybe one day, yeah?'

The visible fame and wealth of the actual Nestor Petrov was not what the audience had been expecting this Wednesday lunchtime. But given recent events in this exciting production, anything was possible.

Petrov wagged a knowing finger at the audience and continued. 'I know what you're thinking. What has this to do with our wonderful Shakespeare's famous *The Tempest*? Haha! I will tell you.'

Kate stood with her black eye; her bleeding hands by her sides.

Petrov took a modest little stroll, a few feet left and then right, marking out a patch of territory at the front of the stage, always keeping his eyes on the audience. 'I identify with Prospero,' he said with an abrupt sincerity. 'He is my brother.'

Erm.

'Like me, he comes from nothing and had to work hard to become king of his island.'

Double erm.

'It's not something you'll hear from the mainstream media, sadly. The elites don't like it. A humble man like me needs to be brought down by the Establishment . . .'

Kate tried to judge how this was going down with the audience. But then she experienced a moment of clarity.

Fuck the audience. The audience have no idea what a galaxy-class shit they're dealing with.

'Excuse me, Mr Petrov,' Kate said, raising her hand like a schoolgirl. 'Can I say something?'

'Of course. I am a free-speech advocate. People should be free to say what they think.'

'That's good of you.'

'Including women.'

'Thanks.'

'In Russia, I was considered something of a feminist.'

'Fancy.'

'Of course you can go too far with this.'

'Right. What I'd like to—'

'Ultimately, a man is a man and a woman is a woman.'

'Uh-huh. I was going to ask—'

'You, for example are not really a woman.'

Kate had been slowly approaching the showboating paedophile. But her curiosity was piqued. She had absolutely no intention of entering a debate with this unpardonable man. The hearts and minds of this audience would be best won by reading about his criminality tomorrow in a respectable newspaper. But she couldn't help being interested in how his awful brain worked. 'Am I not a woman?' she asked with her most reasonable smile.

'No. You are part of this show, are you not?'

'As much as you are.'

'And you have given a splendid performance. The way you pretended to attack these men. Impressive. But Shakespeare was right. The stage is no place for a woman. Maybe I am old-fashioned.'

'Shakespeare said no such fucking thing. He was working within the context of—'

'You see, your dirty language is not fit for the public space. Indeed, the plays you say were written by Shakespeare were more probably written by your Earl of Oxford—'

'There's no evidence that—'

Petrov extended an open hand towards Kate and slowly closed it as if closing a puppet's mouth, saying rapidly: 'A-shoo-shoo-shoo-shoo-shoo-shoo-shoosh.'

I mean, sorry, but fuck this.

She broke his arm.

Or, to go back a little, in the blurred space of a second she: grabbed his wrist, twisted it over herself, transferred her grip as she swiped his legs from under him, levered the arm straight and then punched down on the back of his elbow with all her remaining strength, snapping it backwards.

'Earl of Oxford, MY HAIRY TWAT!'

Petrov screamed and passed out.

It was at that point that the matinée audience began to wonder if this performance of *Tempest!* was going entirely as rehearsed.

Three astonished heavies looked at each other in a frenzy of indecision. The one nearest to Kate regarded her with a face of pure murder. He began to move towards her. So did the others. Kate had nothing left and wondered at what point during what was about to happen to her anyone in the audience would understand that this was real.

'Security service! Nobody move!'

Toby Harker strode down the left aisle with six armed MI5 officers behind him. Another three were marching down the parallel aisle. 'Thank you for your patience, ladies and gentlemen. Please keep your seats. This won't take long.' Toby leapt up the treads to the stage and Kate saw him containing his anguish as he registered her cut and bruised face. He pointed at the heavies in turn. 'Right, then. You, you, and you – you're under arrest under the Prevention of Dickheads Act, 2008.'

'That's not a real law,' protested one of the heavies.

'That's okay, we're not real policemen.'

One of Toby's agents moved ahead of him, aiming his pistol at the Russian. 'On your knees, hands behind your head. Right now, you silly man.'

Toby nodded towards his agent. 'See?'

Leaderless and drastically outnumbered, the newcomer's unanswerable authority had the men glumly doing as they were told. Toby's agents holstered their weapons and hand-cuffed the hired muscle.

Toby approached Kate and muttered, 'Really sorry I couldn't get here sooner.'

Kate smiled painfully. 'You were worth the wait.'

A partially recovered Kes joined them and said woozily. 'Nice to see you, Tobias. Marsden, why didn't you use the facility?'

'Tassy wouldn't let me.'

This made complete sense to Kes. 'Oh God, yes. We're all scared of Tassy.'

Suddenly, a voice from the back of the stalls: 'He's got a gun!'

Kate spun round to see a recovered Petrov standing right next to her. In the hand of his non-broken arm he was pointing a pistol at her head.

'These people want to tell you lies about me!' he yelled hoarsely into the dark. 'But it's all fake news, my friends. Whatever you read in their Jewish newspapers—'

He didn't get any further.

Without a moment's thought, Kate dropped backwards and delivered a kick at Petrov's wrist that sent the gun spinning high into the fly-tower. She sprang straight back up and delivered a powerful chop to the side of his throat. In one fluid movement, Toby caught the gun and dropped its magazine on the deck. Petrov crumpled to the ground. Toby tucked the safetied weapon in the back of his belt and knelt by the unconscious Russian.

'This prick needs an ambulance,' he murmured to one of his agents.

Kes was aware of the excellent acoustic qualities of his theatre and that Toby's comment would have been audible from the back of the stalls. Still half-concussed, and with his grey beard hanging off one side of his chin, he decided to incorporate the line into some kind of conclusion.

'This prick needs an ambulance,' he intoned with a solemn inflection while swaying slightly. 'And yea . . .

Our revels now are ended. These our actors,
As I foretold you, were all spirits and
Are melted into air, into thin air:
And, like the baseless fabric of this vision,
The cloud-capp'd towers, the gorgeous palaces,
The solemn temples, the great globe itself,
Yea, all which it inherit, shall dissolve

And, like this insubstantial pageant faded,
Leave not a rack behind. We are such stuff
As dreams are made on, and our little life
Is rounded with a sleep.

Kes caught the eye of his colleague up in the lighting box, who obligingly delivered a blackout.

The audience seized the formal invitation to bring this extraordinary spectacle to a close and burst into wild applause.

When the lights came back up, the volume of the applause doubled as they saw the short, kick-ass woman playing the Karate Expert and the dashing Scot playing the Security Services Officer in a passionate embrace. Kes took the hand of Ariel, his husband, and gathered the rest of the cast on the forestage in a ragged line-up. Miranda and Ferdinand broke up Kate and Toby's hug, leading them to the middle of the line. Kate and Toby held hands and laughed at each other's obvious embarrassment.

But there was nothing else for it: they took a bow.

Chapter 24

Kate put the ice-pack down and sipped her tea. 'What's going to happen to Petrov?'

'Better if you keep that on your eye.'

'I'm fine.'

Toby looked at her for a second and poured a splash of milk into his own cup. He spoke quietly even though this was his office. His tone had something of the 'bedside manner' about it. Kate appreciated his softness after all the violence and couldn't help thinking of the path Luke had nearly taken.

Another frustrated doctor.

They sat on opposite sofas across a low glass table at the comfortable end of the room.

He said, 'Petrov's toast. The CPS will go berserk about the concealed weapon. We'll let the rest of the truth come out when it's convenient.'

'And what about Charles?'

'I liked your two-million-to-charity idea. I stuck another million on for what he said about Luke. In exchange, I'm going to keep Charles where he is. I've a feeling he's going to be terribly helpful.'

She was slightly chilled by Toby in spook mode, despite his gentle manner. There again, Kate was content that

Charles being blackmailed but protected by MI5 for the rest of his life was a frankly excellent result for such a dangerous fool.

They had been driven from the theatre by Toby's young assistant, Leo. Toby had given orders over the phone, holding Kate's hand all the way. She had appreciated his steady warmth as she encountered some post-traumatic shakes.

A small medical team from St Thomas's over the river had been waiting as the dark-windowed people-carrier had swung through the electronic gate at the back of Thames House. She now had a couple of stitches in her forehead and a generous dose of co-dydramol doing its pleasantly dopey work in her system. But the day wasn't over and she strained to focus.

She said, 'What about the file?'

'Kate, we don't have to do this now.'

'I'm okay. Go on.'

Toby regarded her with a particular seriousness. Kate wasn't sure if he was thinking how much he admired her or just assessing her for PTSD. Either way, he replaced his cup in its saucer. 'Our friends in Moscow know we've got the Moncrief tape and who made it – that'll calm them down for a while. We can't stop them assassinating everyone they don't like but they won't be doing it around here again any time soon.'

Kate nodded and took another sip of tea. She looked to the far end of the room: his desk and his magnificent view of the Thames. 'Haven't you been busy all this time?' she said quietly.

Toby eased himself forward and sheepishly looked down at his palms, slowly rubbing them together. 'I couldn't tell you, Kate.'

'I know.'

'They let you tell your parents. A spouse, if you've got one. But you sign up to this thing in the knowledge that you're going to spend the rest of your life lying to your friends.'

'It must be hard.'

Toby looked up to check if he was being teased and saw that he wasn't. Disarmed, he said, 'It's kind of you to say that. Sir Steve would have been less forgiving. To put it mildly, we're really not supposed to march into public spaces waving guns around.'

Kate had been reaching for her teacup but her hand stopped as her fingers met the warm handle. 'Sir Steve?' she said faintly.

Toby was alarmed by her reaction. 'Oh God, I'm doing this all backwards. Sorry, Kate.' He got to his feet and strode towards his computer, muttering crossly to himself, 'Just the vague semblance of competence would be nice.'

'Sir Steve,' Kate repeated, almost to herself.

'Yep. I should have told you this first.' Toby was suddenly energised and leaning into his desktop as a laser printer beside him whirred into life. 'My bad!' he yelled to her. 'Don't get to come out, as it were, very often. Last time was when I was living with Kes in 1998 and he got quite good at following me to work.' He snatched a page of A4 from the printer and walked back. 'Unemployed actor with nothing better to do. Got him to sign the Official Secrets Act. People tend to take that quite seriously, even Kes.'

For a second it looked like he was going to sit next to her on the sofa but then he seemed to think better of it and retook his seat opposite. He placed the page face-down on the glass table. 'Right, then,' he said. 'Tell me what you know about Sir Steve.'

Kate was distinctly vexed. Toby was treating this like some kind of mildly dysfunctional Radio 4 panel game. She just stared at him for five seconds, waiting for the puppyish enthusiasm to die on his face. It did. 'Sir Steve,' she said at length, 'is a name I know from my childhood.'

'Right,' Toby replied sheepishly, calming down and apparently remembering that the person opposite had recently hospitalised four men. He started to pour himself more tea but his cup was full so he put the teapot down again.

'He was someone that my dad used to go fishing with,' Kate said deliberately.

'Yes, indeed. The ponds on Clapham Common.'

'So I suppose my question would be . . . WHAT THE ACTUAL FUCK?'

'Sorry, yes. Let me try and put this in a sensible order. Sir Stephen Bellingham was my immediate superior here. He's no longer with us, sadly. He became friends with Bill in the early nineteen-eighties – through, as you say, fishing. Most Sunday mornings, I believe.'

'Every Sunday morning.'

'Right.'

'But we never met him. Mother was beside herself that Dad never invited him back – imagine Madeleine entertaining an actual Knight of the Realm. We started to think he wasn't real.'

'No, he was very real. And he was my predecessor in this job.' Toby produced a pair of reading glasses and began to polish them.

Kate considered this. 'It says on your door, "Director".'

'There are several directors – we're in charge of different things.'

'What are you in charge of?'

Toby put his glasses on and looked at Kate. 'Recruitment.'

Kate began to shake her head slowly, not sure whether to burst out laughing or just upend this table into Toby's face.

Hastily, Toby said, 'Your dad wasn't one of us, Kate. He didn't lead a double life and I doubt he ever needed to lie to you.'

Kate made a slow beckoning gesture with her bruised hand. 'But . . .?'

'But . . . as he and Stephen became friends, he was allowed to know what Stephen did for a living. And they began to talk about London taxi drivers.'

The first curl of a smile appeared on Kate's lips. Something was falling into place. And instead of feeling ambushed or cheated, she experienced the beginnings of this new understanding of Bill as a wave of pride. There was something inevitable about this. 'The early eighties,' she said. 'National Front on the streets. Militant tendency eating Labour alive. Danger to the right, danger to the left.'

'That's how they both saw it, from their own respective sides of the fence. Stephen was what used to be called a "wet" Tory. Bill, as you know, was a socialist but with zero patience for the Bolshevik headbangers. No offence.'

Kate reflexively touched the stitches in her forehead. 'None taken.'

'Between them they hatched what I gather a lot of people around here at the time saw as a rather outlandish project. But it's been useful. A small group of heavily vetted London cab drivers – publicly-minded but no extremists – were put on a small retainer to keep their eyes and ears open around, for example, the Chinese and Russian embassies. Where those people go for a drink to let their hair down. What they might be chatting about at the end of the night. They're modestly trained in what to look for and what might be useful. Supplied with certain bits of kit for co-ordinated action. It's officially known as HPS-156.' He turned over the piece of paper in front of him and slid it towards Kate. 'But they call themselves Bill's Brigade.'

273

Kate cautiously took the printout. The first thing she saw was the image that Toby had copied with his phone in the 10,000-day kitchen: the snap of the nine-year-old Kate with her dad in his taxi, giving a big thumbs-up. Second, she recognised her stolen cab's number plate and a code that would allow the recipients to track its location. And last, a message: 'BILL MARSDEN'S DAUGHTER PURSUED BY UNFRIENDLIES – HELP HER FIND HER WAY HOME – RENDEZVOUS 19'.

Kate looked up at Toby. 'You sent them this?'

'Yes.'

'The taxi rank on Bracewell Street?'

'Yes.'

'There *is* no taxi rank on Bracewell Street.'

'I was surprised you didn't notice that at the time.'

'I was a bit busy.'

'Fair enough. No, usually there's no taxi rank there.'

'You got your ten cabs to assemble in one location in a matter of about five minutes?'

'No, I got the ten *nearest* cabs to do that.'

'How many have you got working for you?'

'These days? Just over nine hundred.'

Kate sprang to her feet and clapped her hands together in a near-hysterical mixture of delight and outrage. 'Are you fucking KIDDING me!?'

'Noop.'

She began to pace around the room, occasionally glancing back at Toby. He kept his seat and reached for his tea.

Kate turned and said, 'You're telling me that you've got – no, hang on – my DAD and your boss started a scheme that now means you've got NINE HUNDRED London cabbies spying on private citizens?!!'

'Foreign nationals. Diplomats and the like.'

'British politicians you don't like the look of?'

'No.'

'Lefties? Greensters?'

'Absolutely not.'

'Extinction Rebellion?

'Kate, if I didn't work here I'd probably join them.'

Despite her recent encounter with the braided and pony-tailed young Toby, Kate raised an eyebrow at this. 'But you *do* work here.'

He shrugged. 'They can do what they like as long as no one gets hurt.'

Kate remembered she was essentially talking to a posh policeman. She gave herself a moment to collect herself and slowly crossed to the window. A tourist pleasure-boat was making its way slowly upstream. She thought of the picture of herself and her dad and how warmly Toby had spoken of him; as well as her dad's obvious admiration for Toby. She sensed him joining her at the window.

'He recruited you, didn't he?' she said. 'My dad. He's the reason you're here.'

Toby followed her gaze and watched the same boat. 'Yes.'

Kate chuckled to herself and said, 'There was some conversation where Dad will have been "casting off", or whatever anglers do, and he'd have said' – and here, Kate did a fair impression of her father – '"By the way, Steve. As you know, my Kate's just finishing at York and she's pally with this young bloke called Toby. He fancies the civil service and I reckon he's got his head screwed on. What d'you think? Shall I send him your way?"'

Toby replied in a spirited English RP. '"Good God, Bill! Why didn't you tell me before? Let him complete his civil service exams and I'll take a look at him. Assuming he's no duffer, then we might—"'

Kate interrupted. '"Oh, he's no duffer, Steve. Very bright lad."'

'"Is this a *romantic* relationship with your daughter, Bill? This Toby sounds wonderful as well as very good-looking."'

Kate loved the cheek of this. She replied, '"Well, I'm no judge, Sir Steve. But yes, I'd say he's a comely lad."'

'"She should bonk him immediately. That's what young people call it? Bonking?"'

Kate sniggered. '"Young Kate has very firm views about who she might or might not bonk. Toby may be out of the picture, despite his many qualities."'

'"What a pity."'

Kate sensed Toby introducing a serious note to the playfulness. She met him there. '"The thing is,"' she said, '"she loves this other lad. Luke, his name is."'

Another pause. Toby's voice softened. '"Tell me about this Luke."'

'"You seem very interested in my daughter's love-life, Sir Steve."'

'"I'm a student of human nature."'

Kate kept her eyes on the boat as it followed the bend in the river and disappeared from sight. Her own voice was merging with Bill's. 'His heart's in the right place, our Luke. But a bit of a dreamer if you ask me. Anyway . . . they look set.'

A pause opened up and then Toby said, also in his own voice, 'I'm sure they'll be happy.'

'They were,' she said simply. She turned to him. 'But things change. And life goes on. You can only fall in love for the first time once. That doesn't mean it can't happen again.'

Toby searched her eyes helplessly. 'But this conversation didn't happen.'

'Yes, it did. Just now.'

She reached up and kissed him. He placed a tender hand on the non-bruised side of her face, the same side as when they were standing in the middle of the Blossom dance floor. She was only one kiss ahead of him: and this one was as good as new.

She had no idea what would happen next. Even better, she didn't know what *ought* to happen next. She let the moments fall before her, each with their own potential. She broke off and glanced at Toby's computer screen. 'Just one thing,' she whispered.

'What's that?'

'When I came in downstairs and walked through that grey archway thing in reception . . .'

'The metal detector?'

'Is that . . .? Oh right. It's not one of those x-ray scanners where you can see people naked?'

'No. You're thinking of Heathrow Airport. We're spies, not perverts.'

'Oh good.'

'Anyway, I wouldn't have looked.'

Kate smiled at the thought of his awkward chivalry in Amy's room when she was putting on her jeans. 'I know you wouldn't.' She adopted a very solemn expression as if she was about to say something deeply significant. 'I just wouldn't want your first sight of my bare boobs to be with them all squished up in this bra. I imagine that looks weird.'

This remark delighted Toby on about sixteen levels but he just about kept his cool. 'Is there then . . . some likelihood of my seeing your unsquished boobs in the near future?'

Kate jabbed him in the ribs. 'Ooh, Mr Darcy! Now you're asking!' He laughed as she put her hands behind her and took a few paces backwards. 'Well, you would certainly have to ask me out on a proper date.'

'Gladly. Coffee? Lunch? Dinner and a movie?'

Kate's mind was in blossom. 'Take me dancing,' she said.

Epilogue – Nine Months Later

'Marsden! You've eaten all the Kettle Chips!'

'You're sitting on them.'

Kes shifted his weight on the battered old sofa and retrieved a half-full bag of crisps. 'Oh yes. Nice and warm now. Perfect.'

A small afternoon gathering in the basement of Danielle's bookshop was breaking up. Danielle and her partner Betty would be holding a proper retirement party that night upstairs. It would feature as many regular customers as could be safely squeezed into the shop, as well as a couple of local authors. Celebrity attendance never did the shop any harm and Danielle had asked them to give a reading from their latest work in the hope that they would have the tact to say no. They had all done so, with the exception of a YouTube star turned children's writer.

'The poor dear will be reading some of it for the first time,' Danielle said. 'Let's hope her ghost-writer hasn't suddenly branched out into words of more than two syllables.'

'Some people might call you an appalling snob,' said Kate.

'But you wouldn't.'

'No. I think you're exactly the right kind of snob.'

'Then the shop is in safe hands.'

Danielle had given the bookshop to Kate.

It was a family business but Danielle had run out of family. Over the last nine months, Kate had spent more and more time helping out as Betty's arthritis had begun to make a serious impact on all the lugging and humping involved with the technology of very large amounts of glued-together paper. Here in the basement, the pre-party was as much for Kate as for the retiring booksellers. The bequest in Danielle's will was already in motion: Kate was the new manager of Northcote Books.

Toby had sold his flat and moved into her house. They were in the midst of a long domestic honeymoon of fantastic sex and semi-hysterical bickering over the best way to scramble eggs. As she had predicted, Toby was almost infuriatingly easy to live with. He was self-sufficient but still *just* young enough to rediscover cohabitation as a pleasure. A few more years of living alone and Toby might easily have gone Full Bachelor, with all the usual neurotic schedules and nudist ironing. Kate knew she had risked slotting into similar tramlines, despite the return of her health and the fact that she could now miss Luke without reliving his absence as a presence. Most days, at least. Sometimes he was still there in a song or a peach or a weather forecast – but this was another welcomed cohabitation: she was making her peace with the present.

In the basement stockroom, Kes finished the crisps in a couple of huge mouthfuls while his husband Josh plonked his trilby on his head and said, 'Come on, dear heart, we don't want to be the last to leave again.'

Kes mildly belched and stood. 'Darling, you know perfectly well that when you leave a room, the party dies anyway.' Josh had the young-actor vibe of studied diffidence and now rolled his eyes without particularly arguing.

Kes said, 'Very well, then. Mocktails at the Ritz! Who's coming? Toby?'

Toby kept his seat on an upturned wooden crate and gave an apologetic shrug. 'That sounds reassuringly expensive, but I'm staying for the main event.'

Danielle began tidying paper cups. 'You really don't have to stay, Toby darling. Bad enough Kate has to hang around to watch the old fossils being interred by Dame Lip Gloss of ArseTube – you should go and have fun.'

Toby had drained his Prosecco and gave a complaisant smile. 'I stand with my shipmates.'

Kate leaned over and cradled his shoulders from behind, whispering, 'In that case, Mr Spock, go upstairs and help Betty with the chairs.'

'Surely.' Toby stood and turned to her, wrapping his arms round her waist. 'But I think you should know,' he said, 'that if you thought I was quoting Spock in *The Voyage Home* then it was "Captain" Spock by then. Not "Mr" Spock.'

'Oh my God,' Kes announced. 'It's a match made in Geek-O-Vision.'

Kate kissed her spy-geek lover.

'Come, Josh!' Kes continued. 'Not five minutes ago we were surrounded by lesbians!' He put an arm around Danielle, who pursed her lips and reached up to straighten his hat. 'But now Toby and Kate are violently reasserting the orthodoxy. I am totes triggered by that and we must no-platform ourselves in the direction of—'

'Stop talking shit, babe. Let's go.'

'Quite right, Joshua. Just trying to keep up.'

Josh gave an all-purpose goodbye smile to the others and led the way upstairs. Kes followed him, walking backwards and tipping his hat. 'Since I am literally at the foot of the stairs, I will leave no hostage to *l'esprit de l'escalier* and merely say: see you soon, you lovely bastards.'

Toby waited until they were out of earshot and then said, 'Another six months or thirty years?'

Kate elbowed him. 'You're such a gossipy old lady! But yeah . . . with them it's obviously one or the other. I'd say thirty years as long as Kes stays off the sauce and is able to maintain a viable erection.'

Danielle was leafing innocently through a stock delivery list. 'A thirty-year erection,' she said. 'There you are, Toby. You can't say you haven't been told what's expected.'

Toby genuinely blushed and murmured, 'Right, well, I'm not sure there's much I can add to this conversation so I'll go and help upstairs.'

'See ya later, boyfriend!'

Toby gave a courteous nod to Danielle and went upstairs, on the way giving Kate a firm slap on the backside.

Kate and Danielle exchanged a frowning smile. Danielle returned her eyes to the manifest but said quietly, 'You two are wonderful.'

Kate couldn't help asking: 'More wonderful than last time?'

Danielle unfocused her eyes as if looking through the list to the floor. This was the first time Kate had even obliquely referred to Luke since her awful rant all those months ago. She said carefully, 'Differently wonderful.'

Kate approached and touched the older woman on the arm, a gesture which immediately turned into a warm hug.

Danielle held her tight and then disengaged, keeping her hands on her friend's shoulders and beaming at her. 'Look at you,' she said. After a moment she added, 'Thank you for looking after this old place.'

'It's an honour.'

'But you didn't always want to run a bookshop.'

'No, I wanted to beat up Skeletor. But you didn't always want to run a bookshop either and you seem to have done a pretty good job.'

'Pretty good! I'll take that as high praise.' Danielle dusted a non-existent speck from Kate's shoulder. 'I remember you saying that I had ended up in retail by accident and was actually a born teacher. I rather liked that.'

'All booksellers are teachers.'

'HA! Idealism!' Danielle gleefully broke away and picked up her clipboard. 'The public will soon beat that out of you.'

'Oh dear.'

'Just try to love them. It's not hard – they're you.'

'What if I don't especially love me?'

'When it comes to self-respect – fake it till you make it!'

Kate blinked and looked down at her trainers.

Danielle sighed. 'Right. Upstairs for chairs and vol-au-vents. Make sure the delivery checks out, would you?' She thrust the clipboard at Kate. 'It's such a bloody boring part of the job, I can't believe I didn't make you do it in the first place.'

'Yes, ma'am.'

'Ooh, I could get used to that.' Danielle began trudging up the stairs. 'Betty! Kate just called me "ma'am"! I strongly suggest you should follow her example.'

A croaky Canadian voice carried from the shop upstairs. 'You can dream, honey! You can dream.'

Kate smiled and glanced at the delivery list. She decided it would be more fun to start with the stock and then tick off the list, imagining it was like opening presents and then making a note of thank-you letters. She took a case-knife and pulled out the nearest cardboard box.

This was how Kate had decided she would 'do her bit'. She would try to help people understand each other in the form of lies. When it came to fiction, the contract was complicated but stable. The novelist said: 'None of this happened, but this is what I think is true.' And the reader said: 'Okay, buster – you tell me what you think is true. But I want to believe it *did* happen, at least for a while. So, y'know . . . good luck.' The success of the enterprise varied but author and reader were in good faith. That was the only way it could possibly work – with an agreed innocence.

She slit the two ends of the box and ran the blade lightly down the centre. The opening cardboard flaps revealed the top layer of books: six copies of –

Kate dropped the knife and staggered back, bumping into the opposite shelves and causing an avalanche of greetings cards to fall on her head. Stepping gingerly forward, she stared at the covers of the books before warily taking a copy from the box.

It was a standard hardback with a colourful dustjacket featuring an unidentified young woman – an unknown actress or model in her early twenties. She was looking off at an angle with a distracted expression, a breeze blowing her dark brown hair to the side, partly obscuring her haunted blue eyes. But it wasn't the image of the girl that made Kate's heart beat so loud it could be heard from the moon. It was the book's title and the name of its author.

The Girl From the Future
by Dr Luke Fairbright

She flipped the book over and read the blurb.

It's a strange thing to have lived an impossible story . . .

In this startling and original memoir, Dr Luke Fairbright tells of his invention of Photon Imaging Therapy and how it was inspired by a mysterious woman he met as a student at an English university.

I lose my balance at the top of the stairs. She reaches to save me but I'm already falling, falling . . .

Fairbright shares for the first time the story of how the unaccountable disappearance of the Girl from the Future led him to a career in medical research in the United States and a revolutionary cancer treatment that would save the lives of millions . . .

Kate quickly opened the back cover to reveal the inside of the dust-jacket. Here was a picture of Luke with what appeared to be his family. Luke was in his forties but with all the signs of American middle-class grooming: blue-white teeth illuminating his confident smile; deep tan and fully grey hair in a prosperous bouffant. He had his arm around a neat-looking woman of nearly the same age, the sensible bob of her blonde hair tossed into disarray as she laughed at something apparently hilarious. Between them they wrangled three absurdly photogenic children – two boys and a younger girl – also captured in near-hysterical mirth. It must have been an exhausting photo-shoot. Kate

284

read the caption: 'Dr Luke relaxing at the ranch with his wife, Anne, and their children – Richard, Rodney, and Katherine.'

Kate stared at the photograph.

Oh my God. You really did find an Anne, didn't you? Not just a blonde but someone who let you name your kids after your dad, your goldfish and me.

Kate dropped the book and reached for her phone. She thumbed Luke's name into Safari and there he was – three preview images and another six links on the first page. She tapped the Wikipedia link.

Dr Luke Fairbright <u>FRS MD PhD</u> (born October 20, 1972) is a noted <u>neuro-oncologist</u>. He is chair of the Neuro-Radiation Dept. at <u>Barrow Neurological Institute, Phoenix AZ</u> . . .

Kate scrolled down to 'Early life':

Fairbright was born in <u>Salisbury, England</u>. He is the son of Barbara Jane Fairbright (née Walters; 1946–) and Richard Maddox Fairbright (1943), a <u>general practitioner</u> of medicine in <u>Salisbury, England</u> . . .

The photographs didn't leave much room for doubt that this was the same Luke but the details of his background confirmed it beyond question. Kate clicked impatiently on 'Recent work':

In Spring 2020 Fairbright published <u>The Girl From the Future,</u> a memoir of his early life and an account of the development of his pioneering work in <u>Photon Imaging Therapy</u>. The book has been critically well-received and entered the *New York Times* Non-Fiction Best Seller list at number 4. The book is notable for the way Fairbright structures his story around the encounter with, and the sudden disappearance of, a young woman to whom he gives the pseudonym 'Jess Larsden'.

Despite her state of shock, Kate snorted. Jessica Zed was alive and well but Luke couldn't help making her second name rhyme with the real thing.

He describes a meeting on the first night of his Freshman term at the University of York, England, in 1992. Fairbright recounts conversations on that night with Jess Larsden and how she claimed to be not only from the future, but from a future where she was Fairbright's grieving widow. Her insistence that Fairbright's brain was harbouring a meningioma (see: brain tumour) led the two into an altercation resulting in Fairbright falling down a flight of stairs at a student discotheque.

Kate sighed through the inevitability that one of the most important documents she had ever read had to be written by a stuffed-shirt Wiki-geek with his 'altercation' and his 'discotheque'. She scanned down.

A subsequent MRI scan confirmed the existence of the tumour. Fairbright ascribes his memory of Jess Larsden to a retro-active fugue state, caused by the injury to his brain in the staircase fall.

Kate put her phone away and picked up the book. She sat down on the upturned crate recently vacated by Toby and turned to the beginning.

Introduction

It's a strange thing to have lived an impossible story. But then, I like stories. Believe it or not, I used to want to be a writer. I'd gotten used to the idea by the time I hit college. Looking back, I guess a lot of it was pretty painful stuff – youthful scribblings with a big bag of I.O.U.'s to my teenage "influences". That's where I was headed when I signed up for a course in English Literature. I'm from England, by the way. You don't hear it so much when I do talk shows. Sometimes the host gets me to do my home accent and the audience indulges me. It's kind of them but I'll level with you – these days it's only an impression. Phoenix, Arizona has been my home for twenty-eight years and I've been an American citizen for twenty-five. I like the sunshine. You ever been to Salisbury? It's beautiful but it rains. A lot.

So I'm going to tell you a story. I've been aware while I was at home writing this book, when Anne would bring me a coffee or little Kate would wander in and demand that Daddy tie the bow in her hair, that my story is literally unbelievable. Unless you believe in God, which I'm afraid I don't. Or unless you understand Quantum Theory, which nobody does.

Reader, you might know the easier parts – the stuff that is public knowledge already. I worked for a long time with colleagues at Barrow to develop a new treatment for cancer. The best way I can describe it is that it's a way of getting photons to . . . take a photograph. But an active one. You know that old idea that we have about Native Americans? That they used to believe that taking someone's picture removed a part of their soul? Well, Photon Imaging Therapy is kind of like that but benign. In recording the image, the image is changed. Specifically, a cancerous tumor, say, is exposed to light in places the tumor doesn't want to get lit. And that causes problems for the tumor. Big problems. Since the technique started rolling out in 2012 there are varying estimates about its impact on the treatment of brain malignancies and its potential for other parts of human anatomy. But allow me to be an Englishman again for a second and pick the most modest assessment (I'm not really modest! I'm crazy about what we've achieved!). The 2019 UN Report on Global Medical Advances estimated that P.I.T. had saved at least three million lives. And there's so much farther to go . . .

Kate paused. The account of the science was all very well but the re-existence of Luke was another matter entirely. Her gifted but essentially primate brain was doing its best to keep up with the 4D possibilities. She was suddenly irritated that she'd never taken an interest in quantum physics and privately blamed 1990s playwrights for constantly going on about it and putting her off.

But okay. Here was a parallel Luke – making at least two Lukes in total. There was the one she met the first time and loved and married. He died. Fine. Not fine, but – there it was. She was taking care of that.

But now there was another Luke who was around because her involuntary freak-ride to 1992 had caused a split. Nobody else remembered this – her second appearance in 1992 – not Toby, not Kes, not Amy, or for that matter the rest of the world. As far as they were concerned, she might as well have dreamt the whole thing. She had begun to believe it too – it was easier that way.

But Luke had remembered. *This* Luke remembered his encounter with her so well it had changed his life. And he in turn had changed the lives of many, many others. From his point of view, *she* was the dream. Kate read on: American Luke had a folksy charm but he was taking his time – she skimmed to the end of the introduction.

. . . This, ultimately, is the harder part – the part you'd be crazy to believe. I know one or two things about the way a human brain works and I have colleagues who know a whole lot more. The best any of us can come up with is that the person I call Jess was a figment of my imagination. After my accident, falling down a bunch of stairs, Jess was a necessary invention that my recovering mind improvised in order to stay on the right side of sanity. What she knew about me was so impossibly accurate that my head did a somersault and the only way I could explain her was to invent her. It sounds a little *out there* but just about possible, right?

Well, I don't believe it. I know she was real. I know I met a time-traveler. But that's not the kind of thing you say out loud when you've just moved to a new country. It's not what you say when you're applying to medical school and it's *definitely* not what you say when you're trying to get tenure as a scientific research fellow.

But now? Sure, let's go. Let me tell you. Some people will call me a crank. At this point, that's fine by me – one way or another, I think I've earned it.

Let's believe in the Girl from the Future. I don't mind if it didn't really happen – it sure happened to me. Jess came back to save me and the consequences were real. You've heard wilder stories, I'll bet. The fact that this was real for me is almost incidental. It's what we believe about each other that counts.

We are social creatures, we humans. We live in each other's imaginations. We save each other.

Kate scrabbled back to the beginning: '. . . had saved at least three million lives . . .'

She tried to sit back on her chair but realised just in time that she wasn't sitting on a chair. She splayed her legs and flailed her arms, keeping her seat on the box. The slapstick movement made her snort out a laugh as she recovered herself and then slowly closed the book.

Luke had changed her name and he hadn't come looking for her. 'Kate Marsden' wasn't exactly exotic but he could have found her by now if he was really looking. She smiled as she thought of him on his ranch with his three kids and his Anne.

Quite right, Lukey. Why would you look? When your present has meaning, there's no value in buggering around in the past.

Kate's friends knew no more about cutting-edge medical advances than she did. But the new-found celebrity of Dr Luke Fairbright was about to change that. Toby, for example. The second love of her life was about to notice that his girlfriend's dead husband had just published a bestseller.

Life, then . . . let it come.

Kate sat and listened to the mumble of conversation and laughter drifting down to her from another room. She looked around the walls of the basement, amazed by gratefulness.

Tenderly, she replaced the book in its box and rose.

Acknowledgements

Thanks go to my wise and patient editor Francis Bickmore as well as the luminous Jamie Byng and the whole lovely team at Canongate, including superstars Anna Frame, Jenny Fry, Megan Reid and Neal Price.

Thanks to my literary agent, Ivan Mulcahy for his continuing guidance and friendship. I am also indebted to others among Ivan's excellent team – Sallyanne Sweeney and Samar Hamman.

Thanks in advance to my theatrical, TV and everything else agent of twenty-three years, Michele Milburn for all the help she is about to give with co-ordinating the book's extra-curricular activities. Also for her forbearance in carving out enough time for me to get it written. And let us not forget the general splendour of Tara Lynch and everyone else at MMB Creative.

Come Again is an adventure story and while I doubt that it will be accused of burdening the reader with a superabundance of detailed research, I do have some people to thank. In advising me that certain events in the story are unlikely but not impossible: thanks go to Sarah Logan, Niraj and Shama Goyal, Tom Hilton, James Bachman and Ellis Sareen. All howling implausibilities in the fields of medicine, Karate, computer science and national security are entirely my own but I thank them for the advice offered.

Thank you, fellow writers. I ruined what could have been a nice lunch with the brilliant Robert Thorogood by pitching the entire book at him while whining about having to write it. Absurdly under-exploited given their copious talents, Mark Evans was consulted on a crossword clue and Jason Hazeley advised on the funniest musical note. The idea of performing a musical on a single note was one which I thought I had stolen from Robert Popper but turned out I had actually stolen from Peter Serafinowicz. Thanks Peter.

God knows what I've stolen from David Mitchell. Every so often I came across an idea or a turn of phrase and thought, 'Was that me just now or was that David in 1996?' David had no influence on this particular book and every imaginable influence on the writer who wrote it. I'm going to have to thank him forever, aren't I? Yes! Thank you, David.

Speaking of long marriages between writer/performers, let me begin to thank my wife, Abigail Burdess. I thought that the character of Madeleine Theroux was an admiring but comic characterisation of Abbie's mother, Marion. It has been pointed out to me over several calm and sophisticated marital conversations that I am mistaken. Madeleine is not my version of Marion. Madeleine is my version of Abbie's version of Marion, which Abbie has been writing and performing for a good twenty years: notably in Abbie's beautiful play, *All The Single Ladies* but in many other forms. I would also like to say to Marion – we love you. You only keep turning up in this stuff because you're magnificent.

More generally I'd like to thank Abbie for her advice on the structure of the story which considerably improved it. And more than anything for the love and support she has offered over these years.

She is, of course, the original Girl From the Future.